In Good Company

Volume six

In Good Company

volume six

A Short Story Collection

Edited
by

Alexandria Tirgan

Cover photo © 2007 Istockphoto

For information call:
Live Wire Press
toll free: 866-579-3850
fax: 636-773-3784
padler@cstone.net
www.livewirepress.net

If you are unable to order this book from your local bookseller,
you may order directly from the publisher.

lccn: 99-067352

ISBN: 978-0-9727531-5-9
10 9 8 7 6 5 4 3 2 1

Printed in the United States

ZERO CIRCLE

Rumi
—Coleman Barks version

Be helpless, dumbfounded,
Unable to say yes or no.
Then a stretcher will come from grace
to gather us up.

We are too dull-eyed to see that beauty.
If we say we can, we're lying.
If we say No, we don't see it,
That No will behead us
And shut tight our window onto spirit.

So let us rather not be sure of anything,
Beside ourselves, and only that, so
Miraculous beings come running to help.
Crazed, lying in a zero circle, mute,
We shall be saying finally,
With tremendous eloquence, Lead us.
When we have totally surrendered to that beauty,
We shall be a mighty kindness.

Table of Contents

Part I: Passages

Part II: Choices

Passages

The Algebra of Snow

Virginia Moran

You should be brought up to date, the way I would have told it to anyone.

The day after the first snow I stand in the canned fruit and vegetable aisle, looking at the cans of mandarin oranges in the cart. I look at the grocery list. It does say "mandarin oranges," right under "t.p.," third on the list. But I am pretty sure I meant one or two cans when I wrote it. I count them again. There is no excuse. I think about putting eight back but go down the aisle and put eight cans of green beans in with them. Abandoning myself to the pleasure of a decision finally made, I load up on succotash, tomatoes, and beets. I head for canned meat.

At the checkout counter the man scans all the beets and then wises up: he scans one can of deviled ham and multiplies by ten. Everyone is loading up on food, but I can tell he is a little surprised by the amount I am putting on my end of the conveyor. It is more than even an orphanage would need to get through the next snow

"My dog disappeared yesterday," I say to him.

I have an acquaintanceship with this checker, having passed through his line often enough since last summer to recognize him. Still, he wouldn't see my dog's disappearance as explanation for the food. No wonder. Neither do I.

"Paper or plastic?" he says.

He flaps open a bag. Someone comes to help.

"A border collie," I say. "Black and white. Her name is Galen."

"Oh," the man says. He looks at me.

I will him to ask the right questions. But his own concerns lap across his face.

"Do you want to drive up?"

At least we have the satisfaction that we both understood that as a stupid question. In silence, I take the register tape with my three cart numbers on the back.

At the cabin, it takes two hours to clear all the books off the shelves on the wall outside the kitchen, put them in other rooms and stack the cans alphabetically. I am satisfied enough with the order to try calling my father, the judge. No answer. I call my lawyer.

"Roger," I say, "Galen disappeared yesterday."

"Oh, sweetie," he says. "I'm sorry."

"There was a snow storm, the first. She wanted to go out. It didn't look very bad. She didn't come back. It was simple."

"Well, Amelia," he says, "maybe she's roughing it in a cave somewhere, enjoying her freedom. Maybe dogs go off to winter camp there."

"What do you know about dogs in the Adirondacks?"

Roger is the son of a colleague of my father's and as children we had spent summers together on Lake Saranac. If I can rely on him for that kind of answer, anything is possible. I have been away long enough that either I have forgotten about irony or it has taken over my life.

"Look, Amelia, I was in a conference," Roger says. "Do you want me to tell Ian about the dog?"

"No," I say. "Don't tell Ian anything. Don't tell him I just bought $200 worth of cans. I don't think he'd be interested."

"Amelia, are you okay?"

"Yes, fine. How are the divorce papers?"

I meant to invoke a business tone as a means of letting Roger know I wasn't losing it, but the question comes out sounding to me like an inquiry into the health of the papers. I put my hand over the mouthpiece to keep Roger from hearing me laugh. He has known me as mostly level headed, even as a child, and he might not appreciate the form my humor is taking.

He misses both the implications and the laugh. He tells me everything is moving ahead smoothly. With the house sold and the profit divided with Ian as agreed, there is no reason the divorce won't be final in a couple of weeks.

"Dear Mom," I write, "My divorce will be final in a couple of weeks."

I read the sentence, then reread it aloud, but the idea doesn't attain reality. I write "Sold," bumping my pen across the embossed address under my name at the top of the page, but that doesn't do it either.

My mother died of cancer when I was six. Before she died, we played games together while my father was at work, imagining we lived in a castle with endless rooms she furnished with surprise. Whenever I asked, she got out the iron and ironed the remnant of my baby blanket so that it was warm when I held it against my face.

After she died, with a murmur of encouragement from my father, I started writing letters to her. I stopped when I went away to college. Through graduate school, marrying Ian, and teaching mathematics at NYU for two years, I didn't think of writing her again. I had never considered the letters aberrant and didn't when I started one at the cabin. I just wondered whether it was more telling that I had started writing again or that I had been silent for ten years.

"You never knew Ian, but you would have liked him. He has a sense of humor. He was the husband."

Mom would have laughed over "the husband." The definite article would have tickled her. She would have appreciated the humor in the health of the divorce papers too.

"About as well as can be expected—they got such a bad start in life," she would have said. Or, "They're doing a little poorly, if you must know."

She would be concerned over my stockpile of groceries, though. And she would have gone completely silent when I told her about Galen. Then she would say she was sure Galen would come back, and, for a while, I would believe her.

"Galen's gone," I write. "I don't believe she'll come back."

I fold up the letter and stick it in the woodstove. However true, it seems cruel to say that, even to a mother I haven't seen in twenty-two years.

Now that I know where I am heading I can trace my steps and see the intentionality. Although I had always thought of myself as sociable before, even afraid of being alone, when I view my life from the vantage point of the cabin this early winter, I think of it as solitary.

I had had a satisfactory number of friends at the schools my father sent me to and, although my purpose seemed to have more to do with solving as many problems as possible,(the more abstract the better), I remembered laughter, too. My father hired good, gray women as housekeepers to cluck over me when I was home at breaks. I had had the required number of dates in high school and the right amount of unhappy love affairs in college. But I remember myself as the only constant, a spotlit character in a crowd scene where everyone else is dressed in gray suits. Even my mother's and my relationship had been very private, a club that admitted only us two, and was, like any good country club, much more compelling for its exclusivity.

I met Ian when he appeared in one of the classes I t.a.'d at Columbia, although he was older than I. He was very smart and added another dimension to my class and then to my life. He was mercurial, moving faster and having more brilliance than anyone I could remember. He came up with theorems and probabilities that had no basis in reality, no practical application, but were the sort of conundrums that are to a mathematician what truffles are to an epicure.

He was also the most obviously neurotic, exploding with insecurities. Considering the even-handedness of my life, I felt I'd been let back into the magic kingdom. We knew each other for one phosphorescent month before we suddenly got married. When I called Father in Vermont he congratulated us, although he didn't know Ian's last name. I imagined his white face and bald head in the darkness of his study, the face that all my life had been pouched with dispassion.

(One letter I write to my mother as the winter comes on recounts every detail of the courtship. What Ian said, what I said, where we were. Mom would have approved of good sex, so I tell her how my heart had been stupefied with pleasure, how like puppies Ian and I had been dancing home from a movie we had talked all the way through, how our hands rose up from our books and our papers and went to each other's bodies. It was impossible to have him in my class anymore, I tell her. Passion makes straw of pedagogical distance.)

I got a job at NYU; Ian finished a degree in English and took up freelancing. With Father's help, we got a small house in Long Beach. I picked up my dogs, whom Father had kept for me in Vermont.

For a while Ian and I commuted into the city together, met for lunch in Washington Square.

For a while, we maintained a freewheeling, if delicate, symbiosis of interchangeable adult and child.

Then Ian began staying home more, trying to write a novel. It may have been set at Jones Beach: he spent most of the day there. He began having phantom pains and nightmares that no applications of my body or mind could lessen. The fourth, last, year of our marriage came. Our equation no longer had balance. Although I knew with my mind that Ian had his locus of grief, I did not understand that, in conjunction with my own, our pasts would form a parabola that swept the two of us out of its path. Banter turned into sniping; there were near-infidelities, fights, accusations of emotional crimes. He slept more; I slept less. Then there was the dense month at the end of which was the recognition that the worst had happened: for no discernible reason, we had fallen out of love.

After he moved out, it took a few months to shed the memory of all that laughter. Sometime in that period it all began to seem familiar to me. I knew what to do—baths, women's magazines, the right amount of alcohol. We filed for divorce and put the house on the market. When I met him for dinner just before I left for the mountains we sat on opposite sides of the booth, slumped over on our haunches, hapless.

I thought I was coming to the Adirondacks for a summer vacation. Despite the anxiety of the woman who repeatedly showed me houses closer to the village, I took the farthest cabin out. I hadn't known then what I was up to and had accepted invitations to lakeside parties. I met two sorts of people there: ones who confessed charmingly that they couldn't add (neither can I) and ones who thought mathematics professors were economists. I kept having phantom conversations with Ian about everything under the sun while I was at these parties and finally stopped going.

Roger came up a couple of times in the summer, to visit and to discuss divorce details. I was glad to see him and enjoyed sailing around the lake, touching places we'd picnicked at as children. But I always pretended I didn't notice the tentative invitations he extended at bedtime and went into my bedroom alone.

I had pleasure there, lying in my narrow bed alone, listening without distraction to the night noises and going down the cool steps of sleep. First there were a lot of immediate thoughts—the distance covered that day in the boat around the perimeter of the lake, what there was for breakfast. Then there were more removed ones—the way Ian holds a tiller, negligently; the sight of my dogs running through a field in the sun somewhere. Then the field is full of a carnival and I buy a ticket to the ferris wheel from a dwarf in a Navy uniform. Sometimes my heart had a galvanic contraction and I woke up enough to know that I'd been falling asleep. Then I dropped myself into the dream with an absolute satisfaction. These were subtler self-abandonments.

Then the summer inhabitants began to thin out, taking with them the bright colors and shouting children and parties, leaving behind the more muted natives and me, glittering water withdrawing from creviced rocks. The nights quickly became cool enough for coats. One morning I remembered to call and arrange a semester's leave.

Ian's and my divorce is uncontested (We aren't having a contest, I tell my mother. Who could win? What kind of a jackpot was it when all you got was the relief that comes from knowing that the worst had already happened? Could they tie a big pink ribbon around that?), so Roger didn't have any excuse to come up by the end of August.

I hope Roger doesn't feel rejected and, thus, imagine himself more in sympathy with Ian. Ian and I haven't rejected each other, if volition is necessarily implied in the definition. By the end of October, I am very calm on the subject. I think of me and Ian as the black-and-white Scottie dog magnets I played with as a child which, turned one way, rush together and, turned the other, bounce apart. I keep moving from the inertia of the initial repulsion.

Now I sleep the dark, unpopulated sleep of the dead.

With a stock of cans on the shelves and a sense of anticipation for the much deeper snow the weatherman promised, I have to acknowledge that I mean to go all the way in this new extreme of solitude; I am going into it like going home.

"Dear Mom," I write in December, "Galen has been gone a month today. George doesn't seem to miss her. I took her rug up from the floor near the woodstove yesterday."

I put down the pen. I've written a letter a day for the past month, telling my mother every detail of the ten years we'd been out of touch. The letters gave me what I thought of as surcease. But, for the last few days, they have been getting shorter until I have trouble filling up even half a page. Today I can only think of those three sentences. I leave off "Love, Amelia." I fold the paper and sail it across the room. It lands delicately just outside the cylinder of the trash can.

I go to look outside. Standing in the doorway, I reject the idea of snapping on the narrow skis for my dawn walk. Ordinarily, I am up before the sun. I write letters while I wait for the sky's lightening, then come out and ski for an hour or so. But there was a thaw yesterday and overnight the snow has gotten an ice covering. The skis would twist out from under me. I go back inside and come out in hiking boots. I push my foot through the glaze and begin my walk, the aimlessness of which is its ritual. I find that most of the time I can step through the ice with my heavy, man's boot, but in places I skate, sometimes fall.

My golden retriever, despite his size, almost always skates. George, who before this winter has never been vicious or a hunter, catches a scent and slips and runs after it. He disappears into the forest to my left, his high, excited new hunting bark receding until the only sound left is my boot making muffled, regulated thunder as it goes through the ice.

I go a different way each time I walk. So far I never stay lost for long, but the relentlessness with which I choose the unfamiliar direction at every chance to choose indicates a desire either to find something new or to lose my way.

I am losing other things. I've lost Galen and I am losing weight. Sometime back I unplugged the telephone and put it in the extra bedroom. I had paid a large deposit for the electricity when I extended the lease and it is still on. I wonder if that large a deposit is customary for all winter inhabitants who might get separated from their mail by snow or if I looked unreliable. When I check my face in the corroded bathroom mirror, I don't appear crazed, only mute as the Hunter's moon. For the first time in my life, I have lost the need to be endlessly chattering in my mind.

I don't have a television and I put the radio next to the telephone in the empty room. I suppose the divorce papers are in my post office box, but I don't go get them. After one more trip to the grocery store to complete what I think is an adequate supply of food, I've lost touch with humans altogether.

George, though, never loses touch with me. He comes sliding back over the glaze, the animal he pursued having joined the conspiracy that makes all living things around us phantoms. He skitters comically for a moment, trying to stop himself, and bumps against my knee. I almost lose the balance I've found on the ice just inside the forest.

I am watching a house.

The summer vacationers, perched in warm Manhattan apartments, know nothing of the lives their houses live in winter. I don't mind at all that my sense of reality has loosened up enough to allow a belief that the house looks back at me over the drifts under its windows, hunched in snow-protected relief until it is violated again by clumsy children, racketing adults, and summertime.

But I have made a mistake about this house. As I watch, a square, gray-haired man in a plaid jacket comes out and begins covering the woodpile against the promised snow. He is too far away to hear George's snarl, but he looks around anyway before going back inside. There are, after all, wolves in the woods.

I stand absolutely still, hand on George's head, until I am sure he won't come out again. I think he must be a city slicker, a stockbroker who, underestimating the difficulties of winter here, had come up to relax for Christmas in a house that wouldn't provide relaxation for another six months.

I lift my arms, palms outward, toward the house, pushing the man away. For the entire summer I had mistaken every man I saw for Ian. It is a measure of the grief already passed that I do not believe, even for a second, that this man is my lost husband.

Back at my cabin I shake off my coat, stamp my boots, rub George down with a towel. I put wood in the stove and fill the kettle on top of it. When I straighten up, I begin humming the song about Lucille and dance a forward sliding two-step, arms lifted to include an absent partner, toward the pantry.

You picked a fine time to leave me, Lucille.
With four little children and corn in the field,
You picked a fine time to leave me, Lucille.

I twirl under an upheld arm on the woman's name, end up facing the shelves, and consider whether to have corned beef hash or beef stew for breakfast.

I decide on stew, open the can and dump it in an unwashed pan on a trivet on the stove. George is asleep on his rug beside the stove. I observe his oblivion to the empty space beside him. He and Galen had always slept haunch-to-haunch. I squat down to rub his gold head and then stand up to stir the stew. I don't talk to him, although I had before the winter set in. He doesn't seem to miss the conversation any more than he misses Galen.

I fill the time between breakfast and the next time I will be so restless I have to walk again with a review of the letters to my mother.

The first ones, telling about college and graduate school and teaching and Ian had brought the same sort of satisfaction I'd had recounting my life to her as a child. But the last ones irritate my hands. All that past—the deeds, the feelings, begin to seem puny compared to the high white silence I am coming in to. The letters begin to look like a senseless attempt to hang unconnected entities together in a dark web of significance; the words themselves look like arbitrary black scratches on a pure white field which, although undisturbed by the presence of language, would, if left alone, plump up, become more satisfied like a pasture put to rest by snow.

I put the mass of paper in the stove without hesitation.

On a torn piece of paper I write:

Two things that belong in the kitchen which we aren't sure what is in:
—Angustura Bitters
—Kitchen Bouquet

I drop the paper on the floor.

I am surprised, when I look up, that night has fallen. So this, then, is the next step. If I am x and the day's passing y, then the coordinates no longer have a point of intersection I can recognize. Within the next month I stop walking. The snow never stops. I find that I cannot move through the drifts and no longer try to. The electrical wires to my house hum, compressed by the cold, and sometimes fail.

I have closed off rooms in the cabin and ended by living in one room. I sleep on the couch beneath the uselessly large, summertime window. I notice without horror that I have not planned my food stock carefully enough. I've eaten most of the vegetables and all the fruit. And I am not even halfway through the winter.

I don't need much food. My body has become honed, as a wild animal's will, by the discipline of winter. I think it possible that a body might be taught to desire only what is available. I imagine that, if I walked on all fours, my belly, taut and empty, would curve upwards, like a female wolf's, between my pelvic bones.

I keep on the same long underwear, gray rag socks, jeans, flannel shirt, and two sweaters. When my body's heat is inadequate to the task of keeping me upright, I curl into the pile of blankets, Galen's old rug, and clothes on the couch. I don't have enough fat on my body to keep a menstrual cycle going.

The diminished food supply and the dwindling of my body do not impress me. What impresses me is the silence. At some point, it has changed from the soft-edged, billowing spirit that fills the room to a starker presence: an absence of sound. It cuts the dust balls out of the corners of the room. It makes my eyes so dry they sting when I blink. When I notice it, it makes me sit bolt upright.

Sitting up, I write in pencil the words that my mother would have appreciated ("contumely"; is it ever anything but heaped?). The scraps of paper accumulate on the floor, drifting, my own drunken boats, when the door lets in the wind. They curl from heat near the woodstove, from cold near the walls. My or George's passage through the room causes them to sail in different patterns, a regatta without a goal.

Sometime after I stop walking, George begins to prowl on his own. He must hunt because, though thinner, he does not have the collapsed belly I have. He goes out for what might be days, as far as I can tell. I sometimes go to the door if I notice the gray turn to black, but I never call for him. When he comes back, he scratches at the door; I open it; we go to our separate places in the room.

Indoors, he growls at any noise—wood falling in the stove, a piece of mortar coming down from between the logs in the wall, mice and squirrels scrabbling in the uninhabited rooms. Once when the snow falls in a series of soft bumps from the roof, George charges the door, teeth bared, hair on his back up. After a few minutes he comes back to me on the couch, sniffs the part of my head not buried and drops with a grunt to the floor. His head comes up, ears forward, when the next roof avalanche slides, but he stays down. His growls die out in time.

One day, mid-February I wake up in what is clearly the morning. I try to sleep again, but my eyes insist on flying open. Behind my back through the absurd window, the sun is rising. I push aside the covers and sit up on the couch. George whines, sensing some change in pattern.

"I don't like it either," I say, "but not even I, your resident goddess, can make it go back down."

George thumps his tail where it is confined between the couch and floor.

I open the door. I don't need to dress; I've been sleeping in my coat and even my ski shoes. I snap on the skis that lean just outside the door. I move through the forest at first cautiously and then with more and more speed. George goes at a full run beside me.

We cover miles of forest, skimming past empty houses and gliding back into the forest whenever we get near civilization. I don't pay attention when the sun rises into the higher haze and the snow begins again.

George stays beside me the whole time and, when we get back to the cabin, we are both panting and I am euphoric. I stop by the ancient maple tree at the edge of the clearing and lean against it on an outstretched arm to catch my breath. The texture of the bark feels good through my glove, moving with life but in a very solid, dependable way. I take off my gloves and hold the bark on either side of the tree, pushing to make an impression in my palms. I take my Swiss army knife out of my pocket and lightly carve "Amelia + Ian" across the tree's crevices.

I carve it not because I really think we could have stayed together or even want us to but out of some more general hope that pleasure endures, does not alter or disappear so arbitrarily or so absolutely. Just at that moment, on some other plane, Ian and I have never fallen out of love.

I ski up to the house, swinging my hips side to side, dancing in the snow, leaving a zigzagging track. I almost don't see the carton of milk nearly covered by the new snow beside the door. It has been left recently enough that it isn't frozen but not so recently that the tracks of whoever brought it haven't been covered. After I ski around the house looking for signs, I take the carton inside. I put it on the table and leave it but come back and look all over its waxed surface.

"Field's Dairy Homogenized Vit D" is its only—contentless— clue. I try to open it, but my strength is down. I cut the slit with my knife. I take a sip and run my tongue along my upper lip. I put the carton down again and walk away but come instantly back and drink as much of it as I can hold. I pour some in a bowl for George and then drink the rest.

Afterwards we sleep the rest of the day and all of the night.

For the next few weeks, food appears at my door: unexpected, incongruous foods like a red plastic net of grapefruit planted next to a block of Tobler chocolate. It doesn't come every day, or with any pattern I can detect. Although I sometimes sit facing the big window with only a candle lit inside, I never see whoever is bringing it. It is as if whoever it is understands a system to what I think of as an arbitrary schedule and can predict when I am going to be aware and when not. I gain strength against my will; I take a resented interest in the mystery.

But, in late February or early March, the food stops. There has been a thaw. One evening through my dreaming I hear a crack which resounds through the dark. It might have been a huge, high, tired limb which broke finally under the unbearable weight of wet snow. The next morning I am out for a short ski and run across the cabin where I had seen the man covering the wood earlier in the winter.

His house is closer to mine than I'd realized. George and I back away from it quickly. There are two snowmobiles outside and men carrying blankets in on a stretcher.

I back and back. However awkward, I can't turn around and ski away. For one horrible second I hear the branch breaking again, see blood and parts of the inside of a body on the wall, like a slide flashed on the empty scene. With the flash, I am released and can turn and ski very economically away. As I fall asleep that afternoon, I am catapulted awake by a voice that is unmistakably my mother's calling my name.

Although my brain, trained in theorem in proof, can't comprehend it, I come to the conclusion anyway that the man in the other cabin has been the one who brought the food and that he, living in a more recognizable despair than mine is, had tried to help me but was overwhelmed by the need to put a shotgun to his head.

There is no evidence for this, any of it. And I do not recognize at first the real meaning of it; at the time I don't see the first lesson the snow is teaching me: although he had offered me tids and bits of love, my father had always been dead to me.

And it takes an even longer time to realize that that unconscious lesson is an explosion of sense that leaves me free to confront the real ghost, my mother. At the time, I only understand that the coordinates of time and self have taken on a manic energy that sends me more and more quickly on a trajectory off the page, turned into one of those incomprehensible diagonal lines with an arrowhead that says it all and says nothing.

The next afternoon I go out into the monochromatic landscape, where all color and sound are hushed by the hiss of snow. I put on the skis, clear out the snow that had collected in my tree carving with one finger, and ski through the forest again.

This time I come out above the village. Instead of turning back into the forest, I go down the hill and begin to circle the town, skiing around the bowl that holds it, keeping my distance. It is dusk by then and lights go on in the houses.

I see the post office on the far side of the town. I ski cautiously toward it. No one is in the street. I go up to the building, also deserted, and bend to release my skis. The part of the post office where mailboxes are is unlocked.

I can remember my combination but not the number of my box. I try ones that are full of letters and ones that are empty. None I try is right.

Coming outside, I am caught in the cross fire of a snowball

fight. The children are yelling and don't see me. I back against the door, flattening with my palms on the glass. The children move farther down the street. I fumble with my skis, positioning the toe of one shoe wrong and then missing the other one altogether as I snap the bindings. Finally I ski up to the forest in a hurry.

When I get to the woods I call for George. I recollect that he had disappeared as I went into the town. I don't remember which direction my house is in, but I begin pushing through the snow toward where I think it is. I can't find the right rhythm for my stride.

The snow has stopped at some point and the sky has cleared. A nearly full moon rises. I stand in thick woods. I turn around, moving my skis by inches so they won't cross either in front or back and trip me into the snow. Stopping the awkward revolution arbitrarily, I ski off between the trees again.

I lift a gloved hand, interrupting my stride, to wipe my cheek with the back of it. The leather pole strap scrapes my skin.

In another clearing I stop again and call for George. He doesn't come. Then, my voice rebounding from the trees and echoing up through them to the moon, I call for Galen. My voice is round with hope. As I turn around I trip over my skis and fall. I get up, jabbing my poles into the snow harder than is necessary to pull up on.

Not knowing for a minute that I am home, I try to figure out what is significant about the particular maple I am looking at. When I figure it out I am more angry. I call for George: "Come here, God damn it."

Wind sends snow across itself.

Curtly, I ski to the door. When I reach it, though, I hesitate. The austere cabin can in no way contain what I feel. It would explode, burn with no apparent cause.

I take off my gloves and skis. I lean the skis against the house and use the poles to get back to the tree. I look at it. With some consideration—false, the kind one uses when drunk—I drop one pole in the snow and lift the other. With a two-handed swing, I hit the tree with the pole, its clang eaten up by the old wood.

As the frail metal bends I call for Ian, my voice at first ironic and then invoking. When one pole is twisted into uselessness, I use the other. I call for them all, a catalog of the dead and missing.

Ian. Galen. The man in the cabin. Father. George.

Mother Mother Mother.

Unappeased when both poles are destroyed, I hit the tree

with my bare hands. By the time I feel the pain I am calling my own name, with the confused and half-laughing thought that I am the other Amelia, who, once an expert pilot, had dropped her plane into the sea.

When I wake up, deep in the pile on the couch, my knuckles are swollen and covered in blood. George, present by some miracle I don't remember, is watching me. I get up, put wood on the fire and heat a can of soup. I feed some to George and clean my hands. After I eat, I sleep through the day and night.

And today I got up with the sun, ate, dressed my hands, and watched George through the window as he patrolled the perimeter of our territory. I found a pack of notebook paper in the bedroom.

By the afternoon, the sun is strong enough that it warms me through the window. I pull the couch out and bring a table and chair to sit on in front of the window I take off the sweaters.

I can feel the raw skin under the bandages. I feel that my whole body is raw. I won't see people for some time; I am flayed. I don't mean to starve, though, and I believe that I will grow new skin, maybe something with fur on it this time.

A smell burns up my nose, rising from my body, from between my breasts. For a minute I believe that it is the smell of sex, of Ian, the smell that is almost stink but is desire. But then I know, with no need of conscious memory that it is really the stink of birth—under all these skins: this child. I thought it was Ian I wanted. But it's not Ian, not Daddy. I know now, like knowing the value of *n*, it's you I wanted, Mama. You. And now, here, alone in the great white silence of your absence, I am creating myself, the same way I made you.

Quicksand

Don Amburgey

My first meeting with Cooley and Blinker went well enough.

Burning with eagerness, I took my first teaching job far from a county seat in East Kentucky. Roads were not so modern and the superintendent had said, "Teachers have to room and board locally." With college training I could cope with anything.

Ten days before Poplar Fork School started, I rented a room from an Army veteran and his extended family; and I decided to park my old '49, two-tone Dodge at my dad's house during the week.

A sinking feeling crept over me as if walking into bog lands. I had to earn money to pay college debts and to help with mortgage payments on the family farm. But, I had my teaching certificate.

One Sunday afternoon in August, with grip in hand, I walked a timber trail over the mountain and down to the veteran's home, a vine-laced, battened house set at the far side of a wide grassy yard. A pebble-stone well box stood near the house.

A man, coming across the yard, wiped sweat from his face with a red bandana.

"You the new teacher?" he asked. "I'm Hollis Blackmun. Come on in. Anna and Baby's out visitin'. They'll be back by supper time."

Anna was his wife. She had rented the room to me earlier.

"Glad to meet you," I said, and introduced myself, setting my valise in a shady place. "It's my first job."

Hollis wore Army fatigues with shirtsleeves rolled up; green cabaret girls were tattooed on his forearms.

"This sun's mighty near a killer," he said. "It's hell."

The weather was scalding.

Hollis had been using a push mower and his right thumb bled where the nail had been stripped back. We shook hands anyway.

"Hope you can stand us here. I'm a retired Army vet. I saw action in northern Germany." His short sandy hair dripped sweat.

"My uncle was lost in combat in Germany," I said, and thought of the gut-ripping ferocity there and felt a numbing fear.

I smelled the crushed dog fennel, the fresh cut grass, and the catnip. "Bet you have cats here," I thought. Hummingbirds hovered and supped at the crimson-eye hollyhocks growing along the paling fence.

Suddenly, like quarter horses dashing, two dogs shot from under a jeep, ripping through the grass and sliding on forepaws to a stop, growling in deep throaty vibrations with hackles rising.

I ignored them. I did not even see them. I could never be sure how to take dogs, unlike cats or people. I had been allergic to dogs earlier in life, my mother had said. But, they would be at a distance, out in such a large yard.

"That's Cooly, my bird dog, and Blinker, best squirrel dog between here and Possum Trot. Blinker rushed a skunk when he was a pup and got his eyes burnt," Hollis said, as he pointed to each dog. He wrapped his bleeding thumb with a handkerchief cursing, "That damn mower!"

One of Blinker's eyes squinted and looked snake-mean.

"They won't bite. They're friendly mutts."

Like hell, I thought, then volunteered, "Bet they're practically members of the family?"

Hollis looked at me, then away, and said, "They sleep wherever. Even under my jeep out here."

Cooly sat calmly on haunches just looking. He was a mixed cur and pointer with dark brown spots and soft orange eyes. Blinker was coal-black except for a white brisket and tail tip. His injured eye blinked faster than the other. His hackles kept rising and falling.

"Come on in. We don't have so much, but . . . Anna's a good cook. And this orchard and garden," he said, sweeping his arm over an acre of land to finish his statement.

"I'm sure I'll like it here." I felt Blinker's mean eye glinting at me.

Coming up to the well, Hollis bailed a cooling drink; water beads fell hissing from the metal chain. I stole a look inside the yellow gourd dipper and drank refreshing waters from the deeps. How astonishing to find it so good here! *Do the dogs go inside the house?* I thought. Cooly and Blinker heeled beside Hollis and near the door.

The old house roof sagged; its gray-green shingles had feathered at the edges. A window was cracked like a fanlight, the sections flaming like fire in the hot afternoon sun. I felt a chill even in the August heat.

Hollis took me to my room. I settled in. It had a view over the orchard and garden. Coal oil lamps were still in use here since electricity had not yet come to all the local houses. The lamps gave a shadowy, soft light. It reminded me of living as a child in grandpa's log cabin.

While unpacking, I glanced through the screen window and there sat Blinker squinting at me from under a sweet apple tree, his hackles rising. God, that gimlet eye!

"You're an eavesdropping mutt," I said low, and gave him my meanest stare, directly into his evil eyes. I was sure mine had fire in them. Blinker growled showing his sharp teeth and crinkly nose, and slid around behind the house. Cooly followed lifting his leg at the apple tree to mark it, then did a slow lope around the corner.

I slept well enough but had intermittent dreams about crossing the mountains in the night. Fox fire gleamed and glinted licking flames out of rotting, hollow trees.

We all gathered early around the kitchen table next morning; school was starting that day. Cooly and Blinker sat under the table glaring at me, no doubt hoping for a morsel of food, at my third myopic meeting with them. Bright sun shone through the kitchen windows.

"Mommie, it's Teacher," Baby said. She was a little girl with sparkling eyes, in pigtails, and slowly revolving a triple-decker lazy susan, set in the middle of a large table.

"Good morning, Teacher. Did you git any sleep? Sit right here," chatty little Anna Blackmun said. She had set a steaming cup of coffee before me. "Cream and sugar?" she asked.

Bowls of sugar and fresh cream like liquid gold had already been placed higher on the Lazy Susan.

"Sit, Blinker! That dog snitched a piece of bacon," Anna said to Hollis, who was standing by the washbasin.

Hollis washed his hands with a red soap cake and placed it back in the abalone shell.

"You say it's your first school?" he asked me. "Lay down the rules and regs now, like I did in the Army. They'll learn. It's tough learnin' life's lessons. They begin right here."

"I only earned my Certificate for teaching this August. There'll only be eighteen pupils enrolled," I said. "But I will have all eight grades." It was a one-room school.

"So many people move north of here to git work," he said. "We're glad to have you; hope you will be satisfied. Listen, Ol Man Moser up here just bought a new TV set. You could go watch it some nights."

"Young people go sparkin' there," Anna said, and beamed a smile. "Ain't these dog days a caution?"

"I'll think so, walking to school, Mrs. Blackmun."

"You know what me and Mommie saw?" Baby went off in an explosion of giggles.

"El! Hush now, Baby, hush. Be purty for Teacher," Anna said, and kicked at Blinker.

I started to speak but Cooly took advantage and grabbed my biscuit, then scuttled under the table. I thought, *He'll need caning later. Now, I'll just kick him under the table.*

Murder was intended. Anybody could get bronchitis . . . smelling dogs at breakfast. I wanted to protest.

"Never mind these mutts. Git under that table, Cooly. Good sportin' dogs and members of the family," Hollis said, then it seemed he laughed to himself. I could not be sure of the expression in his dancing brown eyes.

I did not acknowledge the dogs. But, once during breakfast as I laid my hand in my lap, Cooly, begging, touched it with a tongue like the smoothest grain of sandpaper. *A lesson may be learned on why not to keep dogs in the house*, I thought, *Not all lessons are taught in the classroom.*

"Have some ham for starters, Teacher. Teaching is a hungry job. My wife's a good cook. Eat hearty now," Hollis urged settling at the table, giving the Lazy Susan a whirl.

I was like a starving wolf.

Fresh eggs sunny and smiling were heaped on a platter. There were scratch biscuits, thick cuts of fried country ham and hickory-smoked bacon sizzling hot; brown gravy and young fryer chicken a crispy honey brown; wine saps cooked fresh from the orchard, not to mention fresh yellow butter from igloo molds and honey to go with it.

Anna stood over the table, serving; her soft dark hair put up in a bun. She kept turning and turning the Lazy Susan like a merry-go-round. Baby helped and kept her rich brown eyes on me.

I kept thinking of all the good things we had to eat and the blending of aromas like paradise, except for the smell of dog.

Intruders always get in gardens, somehow. Dogs in the house? Bet they sleep in as well, I kept thinking.

"I'll pack ham and biscuits for your lunch, Teacher," said Anna, "And some peanut butter with new-made apple jelly.

"Sounds like Heaven to me, Mrs. Blackmun."

"This fall I want you to taste-test my sulfur-smoked apples and lime pickles. Mother left me the recipes."

"Say no more. This November I will bring you some fresh-killed deer from Buckhorn." I had to offer something in return; I knew all the local wild game hunters. Anna was a jewel. I hoped breakfast would stretch to eternity.

"Time to go. I only worry about how to teach," I announced, and prepared to leave for school. "I hope I'm worth my salt."

I did a slow walk toward Poplar Fork, gripping my new wallet and record books with sweaty hands and swearing vengeance on those intruders, Cooly and Blinker.

Grasshoppers crackled in the brown grass as the morning sun radiated intense heat to my face from the dusty road. A woodhen spotted me and screamed high-pitched warnings.

I set the school routine and grew to love my eighteen pupils; but, uneasiness kept at me growing like a mushroom in a dark coal mine. Did the dogs cause it? Would the school officials be pleased with my method of teaching?

By Halloween I was yet unsure of my footing with the dogs. I had not yet touched them, spoken their names, or withdrawn the death threats. Why had I not developed an allergy? Breakfast was the worst time to attempt ignoring a wet-dog stench. They growled their greetings.

One night before Halloween, I stayed in the Blackmun's bedroom; they had banked a fire in the open grate, "to knock out the chill." Hollis drove his family in their jeep to the county seat to buy groceries, treats, and a masquerade suit for Baby. The trip would be a long one over rough roads and would keep them out late.

Quietness settled in the warm room. I kicked off my shoes to lie and read awhile on the bed. Being tired from teaching duties, I fell asleep even before dark.

Suddenly, I awoke. The room danced in Jack-O-Lantern shadows from the banked fire. Some noise had awakened me. And nature was calling; I would need to reach the outside convenience. The room was too warm. I had had coffee at supper, that being the local custom.

I set my bare feet on the hard puncheon floor. Instantly, Cooly and Blinker lunged from the hearth shadows howling convulsively as if they had been run through with a sharp kitchen knife! Their claws ripped splinters off the floor, sharp fangs snapped, vicious snarls choked off in slobbery throats.

They struck directly at my feet; I wheeled onto the bed. They crashed to a stop and snuffled circling the bed. They howled and whined like wolves. I could see Blinker's white chest glowing like fox fire. Finally, their anger calmed as if they saw no threat from me. Had I submitted? They returned to the hearthstone.

My heart raced like a wild rabbit thumping the earth; blood pumped in my ears like a train pounding the rails. My groin pulled and wrenched in an aching knot!

The dogs had entered as I slept. I had no shoes on; they were down on the floor somewhere. The room heated up more and more; and I would have to get outside.

When Cooley and Blinker snored again, I touched one foot to the floor, hoping to escape. They struck again at my heels, slashing wildly sliding over the wood floor trying to sink their needle teeth into my feet. I escaped gripping jaws by an inch and dived under the covers!

Cooly stood guard at the bedside while Blinker circled round baying in high-pitched howling, in extreme excitement. His teeth clashed, he snarled and snuffled, like a bear ripping apart a rotten log; then, he started biting the quilts.

My skin tightened until it hurt and the hairs on my arms felt like screen wires sticking me. Would the dogs come onto the bed? I had no defense. After an eternity, Cooly and Blinker returned to peaceable sleep at the grate.

The fire blazed up, the room got burning hot, and I suffered agonies of hell under a WWII Army blanket! My tee shirt scalding, I itched as with blistering poison ivy. I was in quicksand with floating kidneys! Then, the owls started a raucous calling from the enclosing mountain walls, as if laughing at me. "If ever I get out . . . I'll get in my green Dodge . . . but I'll have to see Cooly and Blinker on their own turf."

The Blackmuns returned at eleven o'clock.

Cooly and Blinker offered no protest when I left the room. But I would have to soften their rough edges. I had to live with them.

Right away I started greeting them by their names, feeding them bits of bacon and biscuit under the table, and stroking their soft muzzles. Our relations gradually warmed. Could I believe in miracles? Getting friendly they would even lay their heads on my knees and I would smile at them. I looked into their eyes.

They ran to greet me on Sunday afternoons and followed me to the yard's edge on Fridays, as if genuinely sorry to see me go home on weekends.

I saw and better understood canine nature.

Sweet relief! Jesus! A real truce? What a flashing insight on that November day as I left for the holidays: *Dogs have sensitivities, too. And people may scale upward from bottomless depths of ignorance, using wits as weapons!*

I took light steps up the mountain trail being careful not to tread on the sharp edges of rocks. I stopped. I turned, and looked down on the old vine-laced house that seemed to snicker in warm afternoon sunlight.

The Blackmuns must never know I got treed in their bed!

One True Day

Jason Atkins

I am Motke. I am the last of my village left standing. I will tell you a story so true you will have to venture past the radius of words to believe.

I survived the Chelmo death camp! At the age of forty-seven years I returned to this Rzuszow Forest in Poland to tell you this story of one true day. The ghosts of memory still haunt the margins of my words. I tell you voices from unlived lives. Voices will speak in a mingling of past and present. I returned to this peaceful tree-covered spot to kneel and kiss a holy ground. Returned to hear the humming beat of a thousand human hearts. By pressing my ear to spirit earth, I hear the beat of Mama's pulse. I hear the sound of brother Itzhak's scream and Papa's moaning curse at murder's gun. Time's memory causes the rocks themselves to chant. Pine wind songs enter my senses as I stand in this green-carpeted camouflage. Planted to conceal their murder scene from all generations of a future world.

The memories float out of my soaking mind like visions. Visions I pushed back for thirty years.

We lived as family in Grabow village, a short twelve miles from this killing field. At first, they came for only a few of us as product pieces for the gas. Then, the day before *Hanúkkáh* they came for all the rest of us. The German S.S. troops and Polish police prodded us with clubs into Grabow square. In huge trucks, before daylight, they transported us to Chelmo village. We rode together as frightened children in dark swaying vans. Adults held their babies. Old grandmothers were pushed screaming to the floor. We could not see or know each other. The

Polish police unloaded us with clubbing and constant shouting. There was always noise and cursing. It took only four uniformed German soldiers to guard us. The Polish police did all the work.

We unloaded like cattle, driven with clubs into a huge Catholic church in Chelmo. Its thick stone walls provided a convenient prison. Our Rabbi prayed we trade our hidden gold for mercy and release. Some held high their silver candelabrum in a pleading tradition set for a past thousand years. Some, fearing our path ahead, prayed to the cross and Mother Mary painted on the ceiling over our heads. Our large hysterical eyes sought hope from any icon, from any faith, for any comfort, and deliverance. Dawn lighted up our last winter's day beaming down through rose-tinted windows: beaming down on hungry Hebrew mothers waiting, with a plate of devils at their door.

The church's double front worship doors were opened to three transport trucks. Our human sorting has begun. Women and children were pushed into first two loads. Our men were herded by Polish police into a third truck. My papa and Uncle Franz were brave. They struck a guard screaming, "Why?" The guard, a Polish neighbor they had known, curses a luger shot, point blank into the open foreheads of them both. I watched a *Capo* throw their lifeless bodies into our truck of men and boys. We took the short, swaying ride to the open doors of Chelmo Castle.

The shouting, shoving guards unloaded us into the two large front halls of this cold, half-ruined ancient fort. We strip and stand and wait. Soon, I watched naked, freezing white-bodied women driven down a ramp into waiting vans of death. Marched by are mama and her sister Mista for their slowly-measured rides to forest graves. Slower rides were timed to force the killing carbon monoxide gas into the dark, closed vans of screaming souls. The gas soon muffled all screams to moans and silence. The tall green pine trees sang wind songs, as the final *Kaddish*, for ditch-side deaths beside waiting, open graves.

As I stand here on their grave spot, telling you this story of one true day, brother Itzhak calls to me. His voice is as clear as on our childhood playground. He calls in a scream that has haunted my sleep for thirty years. We were brother twins. They separated us from the unloading truck at the castle door. Separated us from the boys without pubic hair. Being blessed with strong young working backs and looking older than our thirteen years. We were chosen in the lucky lot. Chosen with six other muscled men to buy some life days by working to bury the dead and sorting their shirts and shoes. We were marched with rifle guard to an outside barrack, built beside a white wooden fence. Watching our freezing line of naked men with cold, shrunk scrotums was the handsome Commander SS Major Rudolph Link. He stood, soldier erect, dressed in long coat of black and green with warm fur collar. He was holding the leash and harness of a huge, black shepherd dog straining and snarling toward our line. As we marched by, brother Itzhak, our high school running star, broke ranks and ran toward the wooden fence. SS Oberscharfüher Link waved down the aiming rifle guard, to bend and unleash his great beast, Bruno. The dog's huge jaws pulled brother down biting into Itzhak's open throat. Huge white teeth crushed his carotid, causing dark red blood to spurt over Bruno's lips and ears. Brother's shrieking death scream ended in a gurgle. Proud Major Link rehooked the beast and petted proud "Congratulations, good dog," for a job well done. Some of brother's blood dripped from Bruno's jaws on the Commander's shining black uniform boots.

I stood shaking in line watching the Capos take brother away. My feet turned to follow them when two strong hands grabbed my naked shoulder from behind. A voice said, "stay-stay-swim. You must stay and swim on top as long as possible. Float on it! Ride each new wave at all cost. Think of nothing else. Survive, survive to tell, tell the world." The fingers squeezed so hard I became conscious of pain. I recognized the voice of our soccer coach, a neighbor who knew us from our village.

I survived the Chelmo death camp. I worked as part of the mess detail separated from the other prisoners. I lived in the rabbit shed with shackled feet. My work was to raise, feed, and butcher rabbits for the soldiers' mess. I swam on top watching other villages of innocents from all over Poland and Lithuania die in Chelmo. Two hours before the Russian army liberation, all prisoners were shot. I survived a glancing bullet to my head. A Russian surgeon saved my life. I survived to tell you of this one true day. I lived to return at age forty-seven to this Rzuszow Forest. My telling is a kind of prayer! I did not tell my wife. I did not tell my son. To live I must forget again. I deed my story to you. I am the last of my village left standing. I am reunited by *The Book*. I am Motke.

Life's Photograph

John Atkinson

Bobby, Henry, and I were close as brothers and our friendship made even tighter by one adult, Mr. Crow. He was a special man. WWII was raging when we were born six months apart. I was four when I first met Mr. Crow and our conversation started out something like this:

"Mr. Crow, are you kin to a bird?"

"No, Johnnyboy. Why do you ask?"

"Because,"

"All right then." Mr. Crow stopped what he was doing. Somehow I got his attention. It was plain Mr. Crow was a nice man. He smiled at me and that made the day brighter. "Okay Johnnyboy, because why?"

This was my chance to speak to a grown-up. I'd been waiting for this moment as long as I could remember. Mama said children should be seen and not heard. But she had given me permission to speak to Mr. Crow. "Because a crow is a bird, and your name is Mr. Crow, and Mama said they are spelled the same way, and I know you don't fly and a crow does, and you don't do anything a crow likes to do, and I like crows because they call and flap their wings and tease me a little, and Mama said you wouldn't do that, and . . ."

"Hold on there, young Johnnyboy," Mr. Crow said with a chuckle. "I'll have to talk to you while I do my work."

I looked at Mama to see if she was good as her word. Will her promise still hold true? Could I speak with Mr. Crow? She stood firmly with arms folded. She nodded down at me and off I went again. "Mr. Crow, Mama said you'll have to if you want to get anything done around me." Mama and Mr. Crow laughed at that one.

Mr. Crow's hair was as white as Mama's stationary. His dark, brown eyes, behind wire-rimmed glasses, stayed focused on his task as he fastened a handle to an old coffee pot that needed fixing. He talked to Mama and me while he worked, but once he gave me a wink. That made me laugh. Mr. Crow's hands shook while he tightened the screws.

I liked him because he gave me time that first day. When I became a teenager, I learned he helped not just my mother, but everybody in our rural neighborhood. Mr. Crow could mend a broken heart, the ladies said. All the boys wanted to be like him, especially Bobby, Henry, and me. Mama said he had qualities of a real gentleman. He was kind, patient, and willing to take part in any task, no matter what. Mama said, "That's the markings of a strong man, Johnnyboy."

His shop was a simple, A-roofed carriage house with two swinging doors, which were only closed Sunday morning when Mr. Crow went to church. Although the carriage-shed had a dirt floor, every tool, nut and bolt were neatly stashed away or hung where he could find them readily. Without Mr. Crow, my close friends, Bobby and Henry, would have been left out getting our bikes fixed.

As the years went by I couldn't see much of a change in Mr. Crow. We got taller and Mr. Crow seemed shorter, but his glasses got thicker and heavier on his nose. They wanted to slide down like sleds on a snow bank. He was forever pushing them back in place with his middle finger.

At his shop one day, Henry told Mr. Crow his mom's washing machine wouldn't start even though it had a full tank of gasoline. "You'd better come before Mother stomps her foot off cranking the engine."

It took Mr. Crow awhile to gather his tools but he never stopped moving. He seemed to know beforehand what was wrong because he went straight to the problem, and with good cheer, fixed it.

"Just a little trash in the carburetor," Mr. Crow said to Henry's mom. "I'm glad I could help."

The women loved Mr. Crow. They made over him because he was left behind during WWII. I'd heard he was too old to join the fight. Mama said Mr. Crow proudly showed a picture of his company of soldiers who had marched into France during WWI. Mama said there were two things in this old world Mr. Crow loved, that picture and my friend, Bobby. I knew well that Bobby adored Mr. Crow because his dad had died in the war and Bobby took to Mr. Crow like a baby duck to its mama. And Mr. Crow took in Bobby like he was his own.

I loved Mr. Crow too, but no one loved him more than Bobby. I followed in Bobby's footsteps, and he talked about the old man constantly. Bobby was forever saying, "Let's go to Mr. Crow's shop. Maybe he's working on a new gadget."

"Yeah," said Henry. "He could fix an airplane if someone asked him to."

"Don't be stupid," I said. "He's good but not that good."

Bobby butted in like a foul had been made on the ball field. "I don't know. I believe Henry is right."

Bobby and Henry were always playing some foolish trick on me, but I was wise to them. I was riding double with Bobby on his bike when I grabbed the handle bar and shook it wildly as though we were out of control.

"Stop, we'll crash," Bobby yelled, and we did. We were near Mr. Crow who was sitting on a stool outside. That was a good spot to break down.

"Look what you did, Johnnyboy. You bent my wheel."

"I didn't mean to, Bobby. I'll ask Mr. Crow to fix it. He'll understand."

We were only a football field away from Mr. Crow.

"Mr. Crow," I yelled, "will you help me?" But the old man never moved. He sat staring into the summer sun without answering. A folded newspaper lay scattered on the ground beside him.

Bobby said, "Something's wrong."

We ran to the old man and Bobby screamed. "Mr. Crow!"

"He ain't moving," said Henry. "I bet he's dead."

"Shut up," I said, punching Henry with my elbow. "He might hear you."

We moved closer. I looked into Mr. Crow's eyes and realized Henry was right. Mr. Crow was dead. Bobby acted crazy. He talked to Mr. Crow as though nothing was wrong, and that the old man would get up and fix his bike. While that was going on I recalled my first conversation with Mr. Crow but couldn't remember what I had said to him the day before. Perhaps it was the stress of the moment. But soon my thoughts turned to Bobby. Bobby adored the old man, and Mr. Crow had passed on without saying goodbye.

The frail Mr. Crow didn't weigh hardly anything because

Bobby easily moved him into his shop. The WWI picture fell from Mr. Crow's hand and I picked it up and hid it in my shirt pocket. Bobby was crying like I'd never heard before. It was more like he was howling. I could only imagine the heartbreak Bobby felt because I'd had enough of my own. With him moaning I imagined a far off wolf would answer Bobby's pain.

"What have you got there?" Henry asked me, pointing to the picture in my top shirt pocket. "Let me see it."

Henry snatched the picture from my pocket. I'd taken a quick glance and knew it was the photograph of Mr. Crow and his soldier friends . . . the picture that everyone in our community knew so well.

"You know what?" said Henry. "I bet Mr. Crow's soul went inside this picture when he died."

"Don't let Bobby hear you say that," I said, astounded by Henry's remark. We stared at each other awhile and listened to Bobby's sobs flying from the inside of Mr. Crow's shop like bats from a cave. I spoke in a whisper, "But that's a good thought, Henry. Look how happy the soldiers are." I pointed to the picture where I thought Mr. Crow stood. They all looked sharp in their uniforms. Following my whisper, Henry said "That's Mr. Crow . . . the third man on the right. I want to look like him when I get older. Mr. Crow showed me this picture a thousand times, Johnnyboy. We'd better tell someone what's happened here."

We went inside and I told Bobby we were going to get help, but he didn't listen or make a reply. Without looking up, he waved us away. Bobby had removed Mr. Crow's shoes and placed him on a cot . . . the one the old man used every day for naps. Bobby's knees were on the dirt floor and his arms and head rested over Mr. Crow's shins. It was a humble sight, one I'll never forget. I felt bad for Bobby. I had to say something to help my hurting friend. "Bobby, Henry believes Mr. Crow's soul went inside the old picture." I rested one hand on Bobby's shoulder and Henry placed the picture on the cot near him.

Not knowing how to deal with the situation, Henry fumbled with his thoughts. "At least he's with his buddies now."

Bobby raised his head. His eyes were red from crying but they were as wide open as a dump truck's exhaust pipe. "You think so?" said Bobby. He held the picture close to his face. We three were close like brothers and could say what we felt without worry. "Yeah, Bobby," said Henry. "That's where his soul went."

I spoke, backing up Henry's genius idea, "Yeah, I believe that's what happened too."

The good news held Bobby for a long moment. Ten minutes later, between whimpers, Bobby came out of his sadness. Henry and I knew Bobby couldn't make it if he thought Mr. Crow had truly passed. As boys that's how close we were. "That's a happy looking gang of men, especially Mr. Crow," said Bobby.

We jumped on that thought like the afternoon school bus. Bobby stayed with Mr. Crow while Henry and I left for help. Hardly anyone could believe Mr. Crow was gone to his reward. Who would fix things in the neighborhood? All the ladies would miss him greatly.

Mr. Crow's family from out of town gave Bobby the old photograph. Although I haven't seen the picture in nearly fifty years, I still recall there were happy faces on each soldier, especially Mr. Crow, the third man on the right. I remember well because that day it was a snapshot of joy contrasted by Bobby's tears.

After they took Mr. Crow from his shop and latched the two swinging doors, Henry echoed to comfort Bobby. He touched the picture Bobby held like he knew not to damage it. "Yeah, that's where Mr. Crow is right now. Hey, lets get our picture took. Maybe someday we can go there too."

It wasn't a bad idea, the three of us. And that helped Bobby move on with his sorrow. We were tough kids, but had kind hearts because we had learned a lot from our single parent moms. We learned a lot from Mr. Crow too. He seemed to know the secret of life . . . that it's much more joy in the giving than in the taking. That Mr. Crow was quite a man in our eyes. Because Bobby was my friend, I would never tell him I believed Mr. Crow flew away with the birds, that his soul soars the heaven. Mama said I was wise to keep that to myself. I knew the first time Mr. Crow winked one eye at me where he was going. That was sixty years ago.

Bobby died and left me the old picture. But something strange was now in the photograph I didn't notice before. A man with great resemblance of someone I knew well. It was oh, so macabre. I held the picture and looked into the mirror. Holy Mary, Mother of Jesus. I saw Mr. Crow's likeness in my reflection. All was needed was the wire rimmed glasses. Mr. Crow was a lady's man during the war and did his part. He was the father of Bobby, Henry, and me.

Miss Liberty

Laura J. Bobrow

"Jim?" Mother said softly into the phone. "Marilyn's here. Just now. Why would you check the hospitals? She'd never! She's scared is what she is. Hysterical." She kicked the door shut with her foot. I had to get really close to hear the rest of the conversation.

"Jim? What in the world does Lionel Barrymore have to do with Marilyn being pregnant? Look. I can't talk now. Come get her. Give us until tomorrow night. You can come and stay over. And Jim? Marilyn is my best friend. But she's your wife, and I'm not getting involved in this one."

I was the one who saw Aunt Marilyn coming up the path to the beach house after the taxicab dropped her. She was walking lopsided, dragging her suitcase. Her mascara was dribbling. I ran to meet her.

"Yo! Miss Liberty!" I said.

"Don't ever call me Miss Liberty again," said Aunt Marilyn, pushing past me. Her jaw was poked out so far I thought it would dislocate.

Ever since Aunt Marilyn married Jim Liberty last year I've called her that. She's not my real aunt, either, but Mother and Aunt Marilyn have been practically sisters, since college.

By the time Aunt Marilyn reached the door she was out of breath and hiccupping. Mother hurried her to the deck.

I could hear Aunt Marilyn telling mother about babies, and Doctor Gillespie. The pitch of her voice got higher and higher. Then she ran to the bathroom to cry, and that's when Mother made for the phone.

"All right, Miss Big-Ears," Mother said to me when she had hung up. "Why don't you go down to the beach? Go see what

Kevin's doing." Kevin is the only one around here this summer to talk to even though he is younger than I am.

By supper time Aunt Marilyn was better. She had put on more mascara and eye shadow to cover the dark circles, but you could still see them. Every time she started to say, "Jim . . ." Mother would stop her and glance at me. "Uh-uh. Tomorrow. We'll talk tomorrow."

Aunt Marilyn and I shared my room. It's the rule when single guests come. We save the guest room for two people together. It was awful! She kept asking me questions like, did I mind being an only child. "How would I know?" I told her. "I've never been anything else." And when she finally fell asleep she ground her teeth so hard I thought she would break them. I couldn't sleep.

In the morning, after I complained, Mother said to Aunt Marilyn, "Come to think of it, Marilyn, why don't you use the guest room? We can break a rule. No sense your being disturbed. Miss Big Ears, here, gets up early."

That much was true. Every morning there is something Kevin and I have to do before breakfast. We go down to the edge of the water and draw fish on the smooth part of the sand. We are making up for all the fish that have been caught. The waves crash on them and wash them into the ocean. You have to be quick and give them fins and eyes and mouths before the water takes them. We must have given a million fish to the ocean already this summer.

"But," I said as soon as I could get Mother alone, "I was not the one doing the disturbing. Why did you have to blame it on me?"

Mother said she knew but it was not really about disturbing. She just made that up. It was because Aunt Marilyn didn't know that Jim Liberty was coming and would I please keep it a secret and she loved me and Aunt Marilyn was her best friend.

"I am your best daughter," I thought, but didn't say.

So that was all right. If the two of them were going to use the guest room they could stay as long as they wanted.

Aunt Marilyn got hysterical again after lunch. I was trying to read. Mother and Aunt Marilyn were talking about what they needed for the cookout for Kevin and his folks. Aunt Marilyn said she would take Mother's car and go and do the shopping. Mother said OK but to go early before the stores got crowded. As soon as Mother said "crowded" Aunt Marilyn stiffened, and then she stopped talking. Altogether. She just clamped her jaws shut and held out her hand for the car keys.

"Oh, Lord," said Mother. "What did I say? All right, Marilyn, let's have it."

The silence was exactly like waiting for the tea kettle to whistle. It must have lasted three minutes. And then there it came, high pitched and tinny. "The ba-a-a-a-a-a-stard!"

It started at the breakfast table, Aunt Marilyn said. She told Jim Liberty how scared she was and did he think they should have the baby or not have the baby. And he said he didn't want to discuss it at breakfast because they had already discussed it at dinner and to drop it because he was reading the *Times*. So she got mad and spilled coffee on the newspaper. She said she told him she swore, on her grandfather's coffin, that if he didn't stop reading that instant and talk to her she was going to leave him. But she really wasn't thinking of leaving him, not then. She said she screamed at him, "Look at me! Help me! I'm too old to be pregnant. I could die! Women die having babies."

I hadn't ever thought about that. I thought having babies was just something you did.

"People don't die these days," said Mother. "Besides, you're only six weeks. There's time."

"That's exactly what he said, the crumb!" said Aunt Marilyn. "I wanted him to tell me he loved me and he wouldn't let anything bad happen to me. And what he said was to get a grip on myself. And that after breakfast there was something he wanted me to see." Only it came out "se-e-e-e-e," when Aunt Marilyn said it, like the tea kettle again. Then she cried so hard it took a while to hear the rest.

Jim Liberty said for Marilyn to go into the living room. He had a movie cued up on the VCR, one of the Dr. Kildare movies they use on the *Old Time Movie Classics Show*. There is this scene where Lionel Barrymore, who plays Dr. Gillespie in a wheel chair, has a patient who is afraid to have a baby. He wheels himself over to the window. "Look out there, my dear," he wheezes. It is rush hour so the street is really crowded. "Every one of those people had a mother."

Aunt Marilyn said she couldn't understand how Jim Liberty expected her to look at that scene. He knows how afraid she is of heights. The camera pans over to the window and looks down, way down. Doctor Gillespie's office is on the top floor of Blair Hospital. Then Aunt Marilyn got dizzy and threw up. In the living room.

"That's why she ran away," I told Kevin later while we were collecting driftwood for the cookout. "Do you think he did it on purpose? She says he did. She says she'll never have the baby now."

I make babies, too, but it's a secret thing I do when I am by myself. I go to the rocky place, the cove way down the beach where almost no one ever goes because you can't swim there. I make babies out of the loose stones by piling them up, however I want. Not people, exactly. Not animals, either. They are just my babies, but they are real. And the waves don't come here so I think they will live forever.

The cookout was swell. It must have done Aunt Marilyn a lot of good to talk because she was fine. She had her hair up in a pony tail with a bandanna hanging off of it. She wore a pinafore and leather sandals. She leaned against the deck railing, arms straight back, chin lifted high so everyone could see her long neck. I heard her say to Kevin's father, "It's heaven here. But what do you do for culture?" I didn't have to listen. I knew the rest. She would tell him how she was a dancer but she gave it up when she met Jim Liberty at the television studio . . . the same old stuff.

By the time Jim Liberty came it was late and I was ready for bed, seeing as I hadn't gotten any sleep the night before. Aunt Marilyn screamed a little and then the house got quiet.

When I got back from fish rescue in the morning, everyone was at the breakfast table. Mother and Aunt Marilyn were watching Jim Liberty peel an orange. He sat right across from Aunt Marilyn and he stared at her the whole time. First he pierced the skin of the orange with a big kitchen knife. You could see the acid mist which should have made his eyes smart, but he didn't even blink. He turned the orange around and around. The peel spiraled onto his plate without breaking. He touched the corners of his lips with his tongue. Suddenly he plunged his two thumbs into the fruit and tore it apart. Juice ran down to his wrists. "Get your things, Marilyn," he said. "I'll be in the car."

We stood on the front porch until Aunt Marilyn came out dragging her suitcase. Jim Liberty already had the motor running. Mother kissed Aunt Marilyn on the cheek and sort of punched her on the arm, but not hard.

"Listen, Marilyn," she said. "Are you sure? Do you think you're making the right decision?" She turned her back to Jim Liberty in the car. "You can stay here and think it over."

What was that I was hearing? Who called Jim Liberty and told him to come out here and get Aunt Marilyn in the first place?

"I mean," said Mother, "this is major. It's your whole life! It won't hurt you to take a few more days to think about it."

But Jim Liberty was definitely leaving. And from the sound of things, Mother was trying to persuade Aunt Marilyn to stay. In my room!

I picked up the suitcase. "Yo! Miss Liberty!" I said. "Can I carry this to the car for you?"

Ocean's Rose

Richard Corwin

The tropic night air was heavy with humidity that hung like thick motor oil in every breath. When combined with the stillness and eerie darkness, it gave the river a mood as if it were the end of the world. With sails furled, we had been motoring without running lights for hours through an endless blackness; horizon, stars, or moon gave the illusion there was no up or down; forward or backward. One of the two Chinese crewmen on the bow was sweeping the water ahead with a flashlight looking for obstructions but the darkness absorbed the light as if shining into an empty, bottomless well. The atmosphere was very tense despite assurances from Terry and Grif that everything was fine. Then in the distance flickering lights, shimmering in long streaks over the ebony, calm waters split the gloom and a welcomed sense of balance between feelings of uncertainty and confidence came over me. Although some uncertainty remained, much of it disappeared with the sight of the far-away lights.

We had been at sea for almost three weeks and, as if trying to make a deadline, stopped only on some small Island in the Philippines for provisions. My work was standing limited watches when the weather was fair; giving everyone else a break. Finally after reaching some nameless river on the Southern coast of China, in the late afternoon, we were making our way slowly into one of the many obscure branches that seemed to crisscross the river. It was easy to understand why Terry and Grif had only Chinese crewmen for this trip. The two apparently knew where we were; taking control of the Black Rose once we got into the rivers.

When we neared the flickering lights it became clear they were from torches in the water meant to light the way, along the river's channel, into a very small and otherwise unlit port. The first light was a small, crudely made, candle-lit, bright red lantern of paper and bamboo, hanging from a pole. As we passed Terry snagged it with a boat hook and quickly extinguished it.

"The red lantern lets us know the torches need to be on the port or left side as we go into the narrow channel so we don't run aground," Terry explained with a whisper. "If it was green we'd have to keep them on our right side."

Not knowing how to respond or what to say, except to shake my head as though I understood, there were no further explanations for the secrecy and no reason for me to ask. It was completely unexpected there would be this much mystery when leaving Honolulu. Now it was too late to do anything except for me to remain intensely on guard while being cautiously excited.

Grif went below and returned quickly with a couple of well-oiled shotguns he said were for self-defense, just in case there was trouble. Terry stopped the engine as a narrow dock emerged from the dark. Looking at the whole scene in the oppressive darkness seemed almost bizarre: the silhouettes of our Chinese crewmen holding dock lines ready to throw to several motionless figures standing on the low, wooden pier as we drifted slowly and silently up to the dock. The stillness underscored everything. The lines were thrown to the silent men who quickly tied them, fore and aft, to pilings; securing us tightly against the fragile structure. Two figures dressed in white suddenly appeared, like ghosts from the shadows; jumped aboard without a word, quickly descending through the open hatch with Grif close behind.

"Stay up here and keep watch," Terry told me tossing me one of the shotguns, "this shouldn't take too long then we'll be on our way. See anybody you haven't seen before, stop them." Then he, too, went below decks shutting the hatch-way behind him.

I was in the middle of some really strange, unexpected business, filled with mystery. Not knowing this before leaving would probably have made no difference in my decision to make the trip. It would have just let me be better prepared. It was my first long sailing trip and my enthusiasm wasn't spoiled by these curious events. It was an intriguing adventure with the potential for real trouble.

Alone on the deck, and a long way from home, with a shotgun cradled in my arms with nothing to do but pace back and forth in the dark, gave me time to think aimlessly. As a teenager, I had an uncontrollable urge for changes, guarded anticipations, subdued fear, and a thirst for worldly knowledge; the result of being raised in a military family. This gave me many challenging experiences but this one on the Black Rose was proving to be way beyond any of my expectations.

Looking at the sails, now loosely furled between the main boom and gaff now resting in the gallows where they were cradled, made me openly laugh when thinking back to my first taste of sailing in the backwaters of the Chesapeake Bay. Finding a small, sodden rowboat in the swamp grass, awash in a shallow creek near where fishing for crabs was my pastime, I salvaged a waterlogged, mud-filled boat, dried it out, and patched the holes. A make-shift sail was then made from a boat cover, and a mast from a piece of a two by four from which hung the clumsy sail. Proudly launched, it became my first sail boat and the boat's cover performed remarkably well. However, sailing a row boat was not without its drawbacks.

Once reaching the windward end of the cove it was necessary to turn the boat around, drop the sail, and row back. Some days the wind would shift making for a longer voyage but it also made for a longer row back to shore. Looking up at the tall masts of the Black Rose and remembering that primitive sail boat and the smell of its moldy wood and swamp mud, brought back fond memories that seemed like yesterday. Standing watch on the Black Rose during the trip and seeing her full sails and feeling her roll and pitch in the sometimes stormy Pacific, caused me to also remember my favorite high school art project—a painting of a Spanish treasure ship.

I had devoted almost an entire semester to carefully working on the fine details of the ship's complex rigging; applying mixtures of various shades of blue to create an angry, boiling ocean, topped with wind-swept white caps; all suggesting an approaching squall. Towers of sails were carefully highlighted to give the billowing canvas distinction against a background of rain filled, ominous dark clouds. It seemed as if the sails would split at any moment as the ship sailed full force into the storm driven seas. While applying more paint, I was swept away into a daydream of a sailor's life; almost tasting the salt air, feeling its sting on my face and hearing men loudly yell orders above the high pitch of wind and sea.

Then, during a semester break, my painting disappeared. It was an insult that someone would take it without knowing the painting; of treasures and secrets hidden deep in her hold or see the sailors who were rushing aloft and on deck preparing for the approaching storm. Nor would they ever explore the exotic islands or make new, exhilarating discoveries I painted into that ship. My painting was gone but not my imagination or enthusiasm for sailing.

When the Black Rose came into my life so would more paintings of ships. My first sail-boat and treasure-ship painting, however, was never far from memory.

Suddenly a strange clatter from the dock startled me. Jumping with quick reflexes, my heart pounding with fear, the shotgun was shaking in my hand ready to nervously shoot anything or anyone unrecognized that moved on deck. Everything had little more than formless, unrecognizable shapes in the darkness. I cautiously approached the place where the noise came from, then made out the dim outlines of some men in the shadows along the shoreline. The noise had come from unloading their truck. It took a while for me to calm down enough to relax again. Being alone in the darkness with only a dim glow on the deck from the covered port holes, that guided me back to the deck house, made the gloom seem more perilous. The men unloading the truck were softly chattering and laughing. It made me nervous not able to understand what they were saying.

Finally, after what seemed like hours, they finished unloading what looked like heavy rope and diving gear. My first thought was how strange that we would sail all this way to go diving at night. The puzzle was put as far away in my mind as possible; it was far too tiring to mull over or try to figure out the night's strange events. It was exciting to be here despite my nervousness and all the secrecy. My heart finally normalized to a dull beat and relaxed. We'd be gone soon.

Terry and Grif, although older, were not particularly good friends but they were two guys who taught me a lot about sailing while in Honolulu. It was a great birthday gift when they allowed me to accompany them on this trip. To be finally called a sailor made me begin to feel a real fraternal spark of achievement. In the dark, the familiar aroma of varnish and new paint, of new and musty wood, brought back a flood of memories of time spent visiting marinas along the Chesapeake, looking for ideas on how my simply rigged row boat could be improved. Then it sank one day when its two by four mast plunged, like a spear, through a rotten board in its bottom.

In Hawaii, my spare time from school was spent exploring some of the many marinas that spot the island. It was at the Keehi Harbor where one particular yacht became the focus of my attention and curiosity. The Black Rose was an impressive eighty-five foot, two masted, gaff rigged schooner from California. She was tied up with her port side against a concrete and wood dock. Her black painted hull, tall varnished masts, neatly furled sails, and many belayed lines created an indefinable excitement that reached deep within me, stirring memories of my stolen painting.

After discovering the Black Rose, my free time was spent at the marina to stand and stare at her as time allowed. Her decks were always clean and uncluttered with curtains drawn over the deck house port holes. Always taking a pad and pencil to sketch her from several angles, I would later spend many hours improving my drawings. While standing on the dock sketching, it seemed odd not to see anyone leave or go aboard. The ship and marina seemed unusually quiet, lonely, and at times, deserted.

Then one day, daring to cautiously approach the seemingly empty schooner until near enough to step onto her decks, there was conversation coming from below that caught my attention. Pacing back and forth on the dock, scraping my feet loudly against the concrete hoping to be noticed, I was disappointed when no one appeared. Oh well, maybe next time.

For several weeks the trips to the marina were ignored because of school commitments. Final exams were over and summer vacation would give me free time to spend at the marina. My fears the Black Rose would be gone, never to be seen again, haunted me during school and the bus service couldn't get me to the marina fast enough. There were the tell-tale masts rising above all the other boats. She was there and this time several men were on her deck. Opening my sketch book without wanting to seem too curious, while wandering nonchalantly over to where they were standing and casually pencil in another drawing, seemed to be the best approach. They stopped talking and unsmilingly watched me. They seemed mannequin-like except their eyes moved. Both men were dark brown from what may have been years of sun exposure; dressed in blue jean cut-offs, sun-bleached flowered Hawaiian shirts and wearing well-worn canvas deck shoes. Several other men, apparently crew, were working in the rigging above deck.

"How you guys doin'," I blurted out. "That's really a beautiful ship. Lotsa' work I bet."

They stared, then gave me a half nod while I fumbled with my sketch pad; dropping it. Standing, after recovering the wayward book, they were gone and the bus ride home was filled with disappointment.

Returning another day to the marina, the Black Rose was gone. For several weeks, languishing in despair and searching for a diversion that would take my mind away from this deeply personal loss, time after school and week-ends was spent on a summer league bowling team and working on my sketches and paintings.

It was a month of boring, mediocre, uninspiring summer bowling league games, before venturing beyond the base again and to the marina where the Black Rose was berthed. There she was. Just as beautiful as before she left and on deck one of the men in cut-offs. This time, though, he unexpectedly smiled and waved.

"Come aboard," he said in a friendly way, "I've seen you hanging around before. You some kind of artist, or what?"

"No, not really. I just like sail boats and hope to own one some day."

"Well come on and I'll show you around. We just got back from a business trip to China and we're trying to get the Rose cleaned up before our next trip. She's a real mess."

Looking around it seemed to me that nothing was out of place; she was a beautiful, neat and tidy schooner with a few odd lines lying around. Two Chinese crewmen were busy coiling lines and hanging them neatly from the pin rails.

"I'm Richard," I said. "My dad's stationed at Schofield."

"And I'm Terry. Glad to meet you, Richard. Let me see your sketch pad, if you don't mind."

Handing him my sketch pad filled with pencil drawings of the Black Rose; some traced with ink lines to give some dimension to the drawings, Terry slowly leafed through the pages making approving nods.

"You're pretty good," he said handing back my book. "Do you sell them?"

"No I do it for fun and never thought about selling them."

"Tell you what," he said as he reached in his front pocket and pulled out several twenty dollar bills, "I'll give you twenty bucks for the one on the fourth page."

That was one of my favorites because it depicted the Black Rose under sail at sea. Agreeing to the twenty bucks we exchanged money and drawing. Lost in my excitement and trailing behind Terry from stateroom to galley to engine room we went below, all the time talking about sailing. The focs'l—quarters in the front of the ship where the two crewmen had their bunks—were tidy as on deck where they were working.

Following him back up on deck, he pointed out the lines; halyards for raising the sails; shrouds that supported the masts;

lines to trim the sails; and he pointed to the pin rails where all the ship's lines were fastened to belaying pins. My joy was hard to conceal. My welcome had run its course though when his partner showed up and Terry saw me off the ship.

"Glad you could come aboard," he said as he patted me on the shoulder while gently urging me to the gangway. "Come down and see me again."

"Thanks," I said, "for letting me look around." He and the other man went below out of sight.

Those first meetings made me feel there was an air of mystery surrounding Terry and the Black Rose. More so when seeing the Black Rose hauled out at a nearby ship yard. It was discovering her total shape and bulk; her construction that she could provoke a profound sense of nervous adventure and how important it was for me to have more than a dreamer's attachment to this bold fraternity of sailors.

Her Douglas fir masts were unmistakable and easily seen above the other boats. Hoping to see Terry again to talk more about life aboard a sail boat and deep-water sailing; this trip to the yard was disappointing when he was no where to be seen.

Surprisingly it was how much larger than her eighty-five feet the Rose looked once hauled out of the water. After walking around the large whale like hull for several minutes, staring up at the recently scraped bottom, the view gave me a new appreciation of a ship's design. Very noticeable on the keel was an unusual place where it appeared as though a piece several feet long had been damaged and repaired. Seemed peculiar to me that such a repair would be made with what looked like lead. While bending down to inspect a small unusual spot of bright yellow, which caught my attention under the reddish paint, a strange voice startled me.

"Hey, you." It was the other guy with the faded Hawaiian shirt and cut-offs. "What're you doin?" he bellowed.

"Just looking at your boat," I turned and replied nervously. "Terry invited me down to visit again and I was . . ."

"So you're the kid that was here a few weeks ago?" he interrupted sounding almost apologetic. "Well Terry aint' on board so you better get away from here before somethin' happens and you get hurt. You're some artist," he said as he grabbed me by the arm and steered me away from the boat. "Terry got your picture framed and hung in the galley. It's really nice."

"Hey Grif, what's goin' on? Terry's voice was loud but firm. "That's Richard. Remember I asked him to come down to visit?"

Grif let go of my arm and apologized. The three of us climbed a ladder and went below. Sitting motionless and listening in awe for hours, as they described some of their trips to the Orient and around the islands, made the world seem a lot smaller.

A few days later the Black Rose's hull and bottom were painted and she returned to the dock. For the time being the odd repair and paint on the keel was forgotten. She left shortly afterward and was gone for more than a month. This time, though, forgetting ten pins, concentrating on school and my paintings with confidence she would return soon, time passed quickly.

As weeks turned into months, visiting Grif and Terry when they were in town, my ship-board sailing lessons continued and developed. As time passed, deep water was the missing factor for me to become a real sailor. One day, following a trip to California, the Rose was hauled out again to be readied for another trip. The three of us were sitting at the outdoor marina bar celebrating my eighteenth birthday; me with a coke, when they suggested they would take me on their upcoming trip to China. Parental permission was granted and my first-ever ocean voyage became a certainty. My excitement was unparalleled.

Again a loud noise came from somewhere on shore as more equipment was unloaded and dragged to the dock. Standing up with a little less fright than before, all my thoughts about the past quickly evaporated, when the activity around the ship became frantic as the two men with Terry and Grif reappeared on deck. Several men on the dock, who were dressed in diving gear, slipped like fat shiny eels into the water as others dropped block and tackle into the water behind them followed by loud banging on the outside of the ship's hull. It wasn't long until the banging ceased; divers returned to the dock, removed their gear and assisted the other men heave on ropes attached to something quite heavy submerged in the river.

Before seeing what it was they were hauling up, Terry started the engines, the crewmen untied the ship's lines, the Black Rose was turned around and headed back to the river. Watching off the stern of the ship, as the men continued their struggle, they seemed to be fastening the lines to what looked like the silhouettes of horses. Then all was consumed in darkness; only a few remaining torches guided us out of the channel and into the main river not far from the ocean.

Knowing not to ask questions, enjoying the long sail home though, the events were being silently tossed over in my mind about what had just happened. My thoughts raced way beyond the boundaries of reason or rationale. That was my state of mind for the trip back to Honolulu. Even with a number of storms plaguing us for several days, thoughts never ceased to poll my imagination for answers. Despite all my snooping there was not a clue of what happened that night on the river. There were no explanations given therefore no reason to be dissatisfied with an answer. Surviving the experience, the trip home was shortened by my occupation with the mystery.

Everyone, including me, was happy to see me safely home. Not mentioning the mysterious trip seemed best. Telling them of the wonderful time stopping at several small islands in the Philippines and the great trip home kept them entertained. Terry and Grif hauled the Black Rose out again for what they called routine maintenance and repairs. Stopping at the yard, where the ship was out of the water, and seeing the empty hole in her keel gave her an odd appearance making the bottom look incomplete. Lying on the ground was a large, rusty iron ingot that seemed to be about the same size as the missing piece with two large holes in both ends. Terry and Grif were arguing inside the ship, giving me time to study the strange shaped piece. It had holes large enough for two huge bolts lying nearby. The iron bar seemed to be made to fit into the opening. When bolted into the keel it would look like the earlier repairs. The iron block was, by my quick estimation, to be almost six-feet-long, twelve-inches-high and as thick. It was then I decided to leave quickly before they saw me there. My affair with the Black Rose had to end before it became too complicated and dangerous. One day, while standing on the beach, not long after getting my courage to end the friendship, the Black Rose appeared under sail on the horizon and slowly faded away in the distance as the weather clouded over and a cool wind rose out of the west.

Time quickly passed and my life traveled many roads; most full of audacious adventures; many at a high personal cost, none with regrets. It was after living in St. Thomas for a number of years, that realizing my life's dream of owning a sail boat had become a reality. It was a fine, sleek, Oregon-built fifty-foot yawl.

One day, in the marina at Yacht Haven, everyone's attention was drawn to a black hulled ketch being towed into the harbor. Her hull shape looked vaguely familiar. The similarity to another ship in my past made me look more closely. Looking her over, once she was docked, revealed it was, in fact, the remains of the schooner Black Rose hidden under years of neglect and alterations, now named the Black Swan. The hull was a faded, dull black with rust stains covering her like spider webs; old sails hung limply and lay in dirty laundry-like heaps of stained canvas. Faded decks badly needing caulking looked like bleached bones of some large skeleton. The schooner that had sailed from Honolulu was no longer the mysterious, sleek, beautiful ship that sailed to China. The Black Rose was reminiscent of my first painting in high school; both disappeared and like that painting, the owners would never feel her passion, feel the same wind, or taste the same salt air of adventure with Terry and Grif. The Black Rose was now a battered ghost of her former glory.

Benny, the new owner of the schooner's remains, talked proudly about her over a cold beer with me sharing my exciting and youthful experiences with the Black Rose. Then he revealed more of her recent history. He was told by a Coast Guard friend the Rose was captured off the West coast of Panama under suspicion of smuggling gold from California to China. The authorities were unable to find any gold, after a thorough search of the schooner, or prove their suspicions, so the two men, assumed to be Terry and Grif, were released. The two men reportedly returned to Honolulu and sold the ship to a new group of smugglers who were captured by the Mexican navy near the coastal town of Manzanillo with a cargo of heroin hidden in the ship's secret compartments. The Black Rose was given to the U.S. Coastal Geological Survey agency and was promptly renovated into its present unfamiliar ketch rig and renamed the Black Swan.

She was replaced a few years later with a newer ship, put in a Miami government dock and put up for auction along with many other, newer, confiscated boats. That's when Benny saw her. With a few, low, disinterested bids, he succeeded in purchasing what seemed to everyone else as a dying ship. Like a true sailor, he did see beyond the neglect and into her strengths.

Benny towed the Black Swan to St. Thomas and hired a crew of workers to make her ready for charter. Although he could not afford to return her to the glorious schooner she once was, he did manage to restore her dignity, beauty, and sleek lines despite the government's faulty make over. The Black Swan and Benny became a charter success story. Unlike my personal losses of ships over the years, the Black Rose returned, with many changes and a new owner. If a ship could ever seem grateful, the Black Swan responded to Benny as only a ship with gratitude for a new life and dignity could: dependable and seaworthy.

With his chartering successes Benny took a year off and

sailed on a trans-Atlantic crossing producing a slightly profitable movie of that experience before returning to St. Thomas. We became pretty good friends after he returned, tirelessly talking for hours about the ship and our experiences with her.

I sailed back to the States, aboard another schooner, and never returned to the islands. A few years' later friends in Fort Lauderdale told me that Benny had sailed to Martinique to pick up a charter party and for some reason decided to anchor in the harbor instead of the yacht basin. When the charter party and the ship's crew showed up at the docks, the Black Swan was gone; nowhere to be seen in the harbor. The crew expressed concern over the yacht's disappearance and in spite of days and hundreds of square miles of Coast Guard searching; Benny and the Black Swan were never found. Her whereabouts had remained a mystery for almost two decades—some claimed to have seen her sailing around the Bahamas Islands and as far away as Hawaii.

While searching in a yacht harbor in Titusville, Florida for friends who sailed their boat Westwake up from Fort Lauderdale, I spotted in a dry-dock cradle behind the maintenance building, the weed-covered remains of a familiar graceful schooner. Now bare of masts and rigging the Black Rose had finally reached an irreversible, humble, and humiliating end. In shock and disbelief I walked through the weeds to stand under her whale-like rust-colored hull, now pocked with dead barnacles, and found the tell-tale scab in her keel. Whatever had been bolted there had been removed.

The dock master didn't know Benny or who owned the now-derelict boat although each month a check was received to pay her dockage. A note had been sent that stated instructions would be forthcoming as to when she was to be burned; and that her ashes and fittings were to be sent to a Honolulu address that would be provided along with instructions and funds for shipping.

A Promise Kept

Sharon Dorsey

The stooped figure pulled her coat more tightly around her and bent her head into the wind. Her gloved hands dug into the dumpster and pulled more things onto the ground. She worked steadily, pulling, tugging, tossing, her breath creating small puffs of white mist in the frosty night air.

Occasionally, she would stop and look more closely at the item in her hand, holding it up high to catch more light from the street lamp. Sometimes, a smile tugged at the corners of her wrinkled mouth. She fished out a piece of white embroidered linen, edged in tattered lace. Erika remembered the day she completed the embroidery and placed it, starched and pristine, on the small table in their first tiny apartment.

It was their first anniversary and Karl had spent a few precious pennies on a bouquet of lilacs for her. He was in his last year at the university and money was scarce, but he knew how she loved the lavender blossoms with their rich, sweet fragrance. They meant summer was really coming, along with graduation, and, she hoped, more time to spend together—time to find a small house of their own, time to start the family they both wanted.

She touched the wrinkled fabric to her nose. But instead of lilacs, she sniffed only the mustiness of mold and age. She dropped the tablecloth to the ground, returning to her task. She mustn't daydream. She had to find it, soon, before the first sliver of dawn broke through the night sky.

Erika continued to search, tossing more and more things on the ground around her feet. There was clothing, lots of it, dresses and blouses and shoes. Impatiently, she tossed them aside. But a dusty suit bag caught her eye. Inside was a green woolen Army

46

uniform, embellished with tarnished gold buttons and ribbons. She took it out of the crumpling plastic and held it close to her body, feeling it through her thin coat.

When she closed her eyes, she could feel Karl's warmth and strength as he had held her in his arms at the train station the day he left to go to war. They hadn't expected that, so soon after graduation and what was supposed to be the beginning of their new life. How lost she had felt as the train sped away, leaving her there with all the other women and children, waving and wondering if their men would return. She had been one of the lucky ones. He had returned, wounded, but alive. She had nursed him back to health and their life together had gone on, their love for each other deeper and stronger for the testing.

A faint hint of pipe tobacco clung to the uniform and Erika breathed deeply, feeling Karl's presence. When he had died and she went through that wrenching process of disposing of his clothing, she had kept the uniform. On the long, dark nights when she missed him the most, she would sleep with her arms around the old woolen uniform, finding comfort in that scent, and feeling like a young bride of twenty, instead of an old lady of eighty-two. She placed the uniform back in its plastic bag and laid it carefully beside her, trying not to think about the ten long, empty years since then, without Karl by her side.

She resumed her digging. The next layer was all books. They were heavy and harder for her to pull out. Karl had loved books, all kinds of books, but especially poetry. It was his favorite subject to teach in his literature classes at the university. A small, thin volume fell onto the ground and she picked it up, smoothing its wrinkled cover. Robert Browning! How many times Karl had read the love poems aloud to her on their many lazy picnic days in the country.

He had read them to her on that day in August when she had told him the news she had just received from the doctor. She wouldn't be able to give him another son, to fill the empty place in their hearts left by the tiny, sickly infant who had left them on his third day of life. She had been so hopeful. But it was not to be. She had wept into his shoulder that day and he had held her, soothing her, telling her it didn't matter, as long as he had her. He had read the poems to her that day for the first time, and again and again in the years that followed.

Erika shook her head to dislodge the ghosts. She mustn't be distracted. Time was passing and she still hadn't found it. Beneath the piles of clothing and books, she found all sorts of other things—more linens, dishes, glasses, even kitchen appliances. She tossed them all aside. There were boxes of letters; from friends, from relatives, all long dead, and from Karl when he was overseas. She resisted the urge to open them and relive the stories they contained.

There were other things, personal things, cosmetics—powder and lipsticks, even hair curlers. Erika had always taken pride in her appearance. She loved looking pretty for Karl, even when he had his nose in his books and didn't notice.

He always told her how proud he was to have her on his arm at college functions. She was the best-looking woman there, he always said. And the best helper, he would add. She entertained his students and colleagues and in his early days on the faculty, even typed his papers and books. Everyone said they were a great team. Even after Karl was gone, Erika still liked to think he was somewhere watching, smiling at her. So she tried to look her best, for him. Even in the hospital, when she was so ill and later in the nursing home, she made sure her hair was combed and her lipstick on straight. She had no patience for those women who wandered around all day in their nightclothes. She always insisted on being dressed, thinking of Karl.

So much junk, she thought as she continued to search. There were souvenirs of vacation trips to England and France, seashells from their many beach week-ends, magazines she'd saved, planning to read sometime. Why had she kept all this stuff?

And then she found the photograph albums, dozens of them. She had become an amateur photographer in her middle years and had sent many happy hours assembling chronicles of their trips. When Karl was ill and confined to his bed so much of the time, they had pored over them, reliving the fun. Toward the end, it was the only thing that distracted him and still made him smile. She hesitated, tempted to look through them again, but the time was growing short. It would be daylight soon and the workers would return to finish clearing out her house. She must find the box before then.

She was growing quite weary when she finally spotted it, a large white cardboard box in the bottom of the dumpster. The top was squashed and the box was falling apart but she managed to summon enough strength to hang over the side, and pull it to the top of the dumpster. She dropped it on the ground beside the green uniform in the plastic bag. The contents spilled onto the uniform.

There was a pair of ivory slippers spoiled with green stains. Erika smiled, remembering. Their wedding had been in her parents' rose garden early on a Sunday morning when the dew was still on the grass. Carefully, she lifted from the box a chantilly lace veil and a yellowed ivory satin wedding gown, with long, pointed lace sleeves and a lace bodice that fastened up the back with dozens of tiny pearl buttons. In the bottom of the carton was a black velvet box. Inside was a choker, made of delicate white satin ribbon and pearls, a bracelet to match and a pair of tiny pearl earrings. Erika laid them aside, along with a stained lace handkerchief and a small white beaded purse with a tarnished gold clasp. She barely looked at them. It wasn't here!

She had been so sure it would be in the box. She turned the empty carton upside down, looked under it, and shook out the wedding dress. A cracked and wrinkled photograph fluttered to the ground. It showed a slender, smiling young woman in a white satin wedding gown, holding a bouquet of lilacs, her hand cradled in the arm of a tall, curly- haired young man, who gazed down at her tenderly.

Tears began to well up in Erika's eyes. She had to find it. She had promised. It was almost daylight. One more time, Erika peered over the side of the dumpster. It was so dark at the bottom, so hard to see. She leaned over the side and reached down as far as she could, running her fingertips over the bottom. Her fingers brushed something small and soft. She pulled out a black velvet bag and ripped it open. Gleaming in the lamplight was a gold ring, small and thin from years of wear. Erika closed her fingers around it protectively, wondering for the umpteenth time how she could ever have allowed the doctors to remove it from her finger when she was taken from the nursing home back to the hospital. She had promised Karl on their wedding day that she would always wear it. And she had always kept her promises to him.

The sound of a car engine startled her, and Erika looked up to see headlights approaching down the deserted street. She glanced around at the piles of things at her feet, the effects of her life. How unimportant they were, she thought. They were just things, that had served their purpose and outlived their usefulness, like her. Sliding the scrap of gold back onto her finger where it had been for seventy-two years, she slipped away into the dim light of morning.

Two heavy-set women emerged from the beat-up truck and stared in dismay at the pillaged dumpster. The older one picked up the photograph of the smiling bride and groom. "I wonder if this is her, the lady who died. So sad, no family, nobody to even take care of her things."

"Don't be so sentimental," the younger woman scoffed. "At least it gave us some work, cleaning out the place. And the old lady's dead. What does she care about anything?"

Grumbling, they set about the task of refilling the dumpster.

The Chicken Chronicles

J. S. Gill

It was the year we paved the driveway, after ten years of a quarter mile of gravel to the old farmhouse. For the benefit of my bicycle tires and my youngest daughter—Anna's—basketball game. Jenny Lakin was Anna's best friend, and for some strange reason Jenny felt compelled to give her mother chickens for Mother's day that year.

The Lang's had kept chickens before (they had all been eaten by wild creatures and neighbor's dogs), and when they ended up with twice the number ordered we ended up with half. Without, I might add, my own concurrence in the decision. "After all," my wife explained, "You just have to build a chicken coop. We'll take care of the rest."

This is where I'm reminded of Anna's phrase: 'as if.'

I built the coop, and, prophetically, they did come. I learned to feed, water, and round up at night time. As if. You couldn't really chase them, I learned; chickens are like daughters, they have to be coaxed, even for their own good. Especially for their own good.

If that's the message, I've brought it out awfully early and without any digging. The *Chicken Chronicles* was not the year of great subtlety.

Anyway, I became the chicken caretaker: it was too early in the mornings (after the dogs had a run) for children on (summer) break, and, besides, it only took a few minutes, right? Or so. Cathy worked out of town, the girls usually had afternoon and evening plans, I got home by 5:30, so the evening ritual was mine also. I would have been resentful, but I got to kind of like them: Napoleon, the large red, white and black rooster (I let him present as the ostensible alpha male), the two white roosters

50

who'd do the staring match thing, the Guinea hen, the two Rhode Island Reds, a few with fluffy feet, etc . . .

They really weren't much trouble, a little feed, some water, and when I talked to them they didn't give me much shit. Or if so, literally.

It was also the summer Molly finished at G'town, having partied, drank, and occasionally studied her way to a degree she had no idea what to do with. Having fled home myself at the age of nineteen without ever looking back, I was not exactly prepared for her return. She seemed too comfortable with us, her rhythms in stark contrast to those of Cathy and me. I'll get back to that.

The old farmhouse was in the middle of thirty-four acres that backed up to Beggar's Creek. It was surrounded by 100-year-old black walnut, oak, and sycamore trees, the shade offering the Nineteenth century response to the sweltering summer heat. In some moment of aesthetic rebellion, the gravel drive (recently paved) was not the traditional straight shot off Route 643, but had been laid out in a long "S" curve lined with crepe myrtles which offered a nice view from our bedroom window. Being nowhere near our neighbors and hidden by privet from any sight lines, we had opted for no curtains or window treatments of any kind; mornings, we were bitch-slapped awake when the sun popped over the horizon, nights we took our cue (at least in summer) as the sun dropped. Oh, the rural life. And the chickens.

Joan came home from Ithaca College determined not to return there in the fall. With two years under her belt (including a semester in London), she was in the midst of plans to go to Africa in the fall, do some "hands on," shoot some photos, get credits with the Anthro- and Sociology departments. This was going to be tough: the only way Joan didn't get her way was when she changed her mind of her own accord. We talked about the difficulties involved, health concerns, the likelihood that she might not be able to transfer out the units of credit she hoped to get; that she couldn't transfer to a less frigid climate and do Africa, too; and the cost.

Joan gave her personal responsibility argument, I said okay, ms. responsibility, let's see it. I said "chickens."

Joan said "oh, dad," laughed, tossed some chicken feed at Napoleon and Co. Joan started working days at soccer camp, nights waiting tables at Good Fellas. Joan said it was all a money issue, not about chickens. So did her mother.

They were right. Nothing is about chickens, chickens just are. They are neither form nor function, they are feed. Doing chickens gets you nothing but eggs. Eventually.

Only I saw life through the eyes of chickens. Fowl eyes. I discussed this issue (Ithaca vs. Africa; or London; and, finally, Rome) in some detail with Napoleon, who decided to consult Red (of Rhode Island fame) and Salt and Pepper (perhaps Cornish? I'm not sure). Though there was little agreement, there was great concern, clucking, and clawing.

One thing I learned about chickens; great source of sympathy and empathy, *sans* understanding.

Again, like daughters? Let's dwell on that later.

Joan did come around, though. Determined that Africa was impractical (after Cathy researched living in London, then Rome); then, recalling the hot young guys in Italy, she initiated and finalized the transfer from Ithaca College to American University in Rome over the internet in two days. Then began her interminable process of packing. Clothes strewn all over the house, it was a process I would not have recognized but for being told.

"I can't see your bedroom floor, Joan."

"I'm packing, dad, you silly goose."

"Close," I said; "chickens," I said, "not geese. But fowl." The joke was getting old.

Even though Molly wasn't working and wasn't seeing much of her friends in Williamsburg, we weren't seeing that much of her. She had carved out some space on the front porch where she could smoke, read, do crosswords, and drink wine. After Cathy and I were off to bed she would watch movies until around 4 A.M., then sleep in until mid-afternoon. On those occasions when she did go into town it would usually be after dinner, then she'd take a car and be gone for several days. When we saw her, Cathy and I would mention the "J" word and the "R" word (job and resume), but try not to beat her up too much over it. Caring parents, but not nags. A difficult line to discern. Or a distinction which was quickly disappearing?

Molly was a strong and vocal opponent of the chickens from the outset, based solely on a rooster's timetable. She immediately began compiling a "Chicken Causality Report" when two hens were killed by one of the dogs, Penny or Marcello. She posted the causality report on the refrigerator replete with the dying declarations of distraught fowl; had long whispered conversations with the dogs about the rewards of consuming white meat on their blood cholesterol levels.

Cathy and I were working up strategies to move Molly into the workforce. The fear was that she would roommate up with a friend in Williamsburg, end up waiting tables, or some such. Worried about a double standard: that it was okay for Joan, but not for Molly? Actually, with Joanie, the idea was that it was too hard for too little money, that it would encourage her to get on with her degree. With Molly, though, hard work and instant cash, none of the terror involved in jobs requiring resumes and entry level skills, it was too easy. We needed to move her ass outward and upward. No good program was in sight, however.

Well, one was. Evenings, Cathy would watch *Under The Tuscan Sun*, drink wine and cry. She had family from Umbria, was fluent in Italian, and recently back from a year in Rome with Anna (thrown into the seventh grade school year in an Italian language school). We often talked about moving to Orvieto, a villa with olive trees, a few grape vines (sounds almost too trite to mention, but, hell). Now, the idea was to move during one of the days when Molly was off in Williamsburg, leave a note with a forwarding address. Force her to do something. Kill two birds, etc . . .

And speaking of killing birds, Molly was busy many afternoons developing exquisite torture devices for our fowl friends. It seemed more aimed at Anna, friend to all creatures, who would retaliate and redirect Molly's aggression away from the chickens. One of Molly's plans involved the labeling of the chickens, by means of Anna's paintball gun. Anna —the only one of our children who was usually armed (God knows why: that's a whole other story) pulled out bow and arrow and threatened Molly's favorite pair of shoes. Not an idle threat, nor one to be taken lightly. By the time common sense (i.e., their mother) intervened, there was one shoe, hanging from an arrow wedged into the far chimney, while Molly had fashioned a hangman's noose around a limb of an old apple tree, but was still trying to determine how to round up a chicken without, in fact, actually touching it.

Two Molly legends: first one, Anna and Cathy are in Rome, I'm late at a VASAP Board meeting, Joan arrives home late with several friends to spend the night. Notices a squirrelly looking dude standing in the field, watching the house. Before I was compelled to carry a cell phone. So Joan calls Molly at Georgetown, describes the situation; Molly instructs her NOT to pull down the driveway but to proceed to the end of the road, turn around and drive back down 643 until a police officer arrives.

Then, with Joan still on the line, she grabs the phone of one of the rugby players who she's partying with, dials Mathews county 911, tells the dispatcher what's up and has a deputy down there before Joan is a half mile past our place. Turns out to be a "drunk and wanted." Good call by Molly. Good call by Joan.

Other legend happened at the same rugby house, another party going on, and a car alarm goes off. Car belongs to one of the rugby players, they respond en masse to attempted break-in, chase dude down an alley that ends in a wire fence, pull dude off the fence as he's trying to scramble over. Torn shirt, some scratches where fence meets skin. Molly goes to the street end of the alley for telephone reception, calls the police on her cell. Apparently, two rugby players are holding the dude by his back pack when he slips the shoulder straps, races down alley towards Molly. Molly standing there, cell phone to ear, cigarette in mouth, giving directions to the police dispatcher. With culprit racing towards her, she recalls basic soccer moves, feints right, kicks left, trips dude at full speed. He does a flying one and a half, lands on his back, wind knocked out of him, a few more scratches, scars, and road rash. Down for the count. Police arrive, wonder who beat the kid up. Decide not to arrest if he agrees not to return. Of course he agrees.

You don't mess with Molly. She didn't even lose her ash.

So Anna was wise not to cross the Moll without armament. The rule is, no bloodshed in the house and no dismemberment outside. But even Anna knows you can't hide behind a chicken.

My idea was to settle it on the basketball court. Anna was a player, Molly had been a Dennis Rodman clone, owned the backboards until she fouled out, usually in the second quarter. Joan wanted to be on my team because the last time she wasn't I had clothes-lined her and she didn't even get any foul shots.

I suck on the basketball court, but I sweat so much no one will guard me. We did it for a while and then something clicked when Anna said "foul shot" and Molly raced for the paint ball stuff yelling about fowl shooting and shooting fowl. There was wickedness afoot and no time to round up the chickens; we—the defenders of the fowl—shifted into crisis mood. I went to lock up the dogs, Anna and Joan ran after the chickens.

Except, as I said, you can't chase chickens, you have to coax them. And who can coax in times of panic? It was a two pronged attack: Joan from the left of the shed, Anna from the right. But the number of prongs necessary for twelve chickens are not contained in a drawer full of forks. Chickens, otherwise such flocking fowl, flew, fled and generally made themselves impossible to corner or catch. Anna dove for the Guinea, missed; Joan slid past two roosters.

And Molly reappeared with only her new cell phone, using the video function to record the fowl round-up. She caught twenty-second spurts of Anna and Joan leaping, sliding, falling, and, generally, missing every chicken they reached for. With the audio portion up high, I noted that Joanie did in fact know how to use the "F" word in proper context, not the testing nature of her weak attempts she occasionally tried in our presence. Make a father proud.

It was an extraordinarily hot summer. There seemed to be a temperature barrier in the house: Molly and Joan preferred an ambient eighty-five degrees, Cathy and Anna needed New England cool, no more than seventy-five. Molly kept to the front porch, Joan cross-humidified her space by opening windows on the north side and south side of her room. Played hell with the central air, led to a lot of window slamming when the thunderstorms rolled through, much rain-drenched drying out when planning failed. The deck covered with sopping throw rugs, clothes, towels, etc. The climate change walking through our house could induce fevers and chills in the most seasoned travelers.

When Chip came to visit for a week. Chip was a whippet, skinny greyhound-like dog with no body fat and little hair. Chip had little tolerance for summer-time cool, liked the heat and humidity. Which would have worked but for Joan's dislike of the "skeleton dog." Anna of course took to Chip, but her room was too cool; so the compromise was (again, without my consultation) that Chip slept in our room; mine and Cathy's. On the bed. Under the covers. Between Cathy and I. I will speculate no further. But boy, that dog could fly!

Chip was so quick and so active that the other dogs, Penny and Marcello seemed fat and old. And seemed to feel fat and old. With Chip in our room, Penny and Marcello couldn't decide whether to stake their territorial claim by maintaining their position on our floor, or to seek solace with Molly or Anna (Joan's room being too seasonally warm for any but the most tropically inclined).

And Molly saw her opportunity. She conferred with Chip, determined that his quickness could foil any fowl, and, while the chicken sympathizers were busy elsewhere, she sicked the whippet on our barnyard brethren.

What Molly hadn't planned on was that Chip was more border collie than wolf. Rather than attack the chickens, he chased and cornered, barked at and bothered, harassed and herded the dirty dozen, engaged in a one-dog circling action, and, ultimately, while not so much terrorizing the birds, was able to coerce their compliance into the coop. We extended Chip's invitation for the remainder of the summer.

Thwarted in her attempts to diminish the chicken population, Molly redoubled her efforts in other areas. While I had not been entirely convinced by her assurances that resumes were being drafted and e-mailed, I did give her the benefit of the doubt. Did continue to ask to review the resume: "What, you don't trust me, dad?" Well, dear, it's not really a matter of trust.

Then what is it? That I had some skill in this area, that I could help craft an effective resume, that my experience in short fiction might help her redesign the outline of her life in a manner that was more suitable, to what? To me? And who was I hiring right now?

All good questions. Why not be terrified of the real world, it was all pretty terrifying. Thinking back, I could recall . . .

Let's not do that. Looking at Molly's book collection acquired over four years of classes, I noted that, for a self-proclaimed atheist, she had consumed more volumes on Catholicism, Islam (all makes and models), Orthodox Christianity, Judaism and the like than most theologians I have known. Perhaps I should consider that she knew what she was doing, had good reason to fear the work-a-day world.

Nah. It was all about chickens. Raising chickens, not daughters. And what did I have to offer, or know about either?

Traditionally, I would sit down and write four pages of single spaced letters sharing the great wisdom I had acquired over the years, and challenge my daughters to pluck the gems from these lines. As if ancient wisdom would carry the day. But Molly was the one with whom I always came across with the wrong message: like I was disappointed in her, not proud. Maybe because she beat us over the head with her bad habits: her smoking, her drinking, her nocturnal hours. Maybe it was her own competitive nature, especially now that she saw her sister going off to study in Rome, thinking that it should be her. It could be her, too.

Cathy said that the kids knew all about what a blazing success I was, that they were all well-instructed in how I'd pulled it all together, laid it down trim, neat, straight, and narrow. But, she said. Maybe, she suggested. What Molly might need to hear about were those times, however rare they might be (batting her eyes), when I had not been quite so successful; when I had, in fact, gone down in flames, she reiterated, getting into the subject matter, those occasions when I had fucking failed flat on my flaming ass. She said, alliteratively. Eyes still aflutter.

"I can't tell her about my sex life!" But she told me to shut up and go to sleep. She said, you know what I mean.

Okay.

What did I know about failure? This from the guy who ran cross country for four years in high school and did not see another finisher from either team until midway through junior year. Truth. Who had not failed exams at Wake Forest, but missed them (Mardi Gras). I could go on.

But I won't. We had the talk. No visible effect. No surprise there.

But then the great chicken coup (my one pun permitted). Critters were perched on the lower branches of the fig bush: shelter and shade. Ninety-five plus temperature, humidity felt like twice that. Standard issue August. Dogs had gotten out, but it was just too damn hot to gnaw feathers. Every living thing was pooped, sweating, lethargic. Except the reptile.

Have I told you about the reptile? The shed, which is definitely coming down the moment we build the garage, has a long-term resident which leaves its shed (ahem!) skin hanging from a nail or rafter each year to announce seasonal change as well as evident growth spurts. This year, said skin was over six feet long, further convincing the womenfolk that they had absolutely no need to ever enter the shed—ever—where I kept my stuff, including spare bikes and bike parts. My grandfather was a herpetologist, had written *The Reptiles of Virginia*, had acclimated me to the scaly crawly creatures. Especially because my own father hated them.

So Boris the boa constrictor (he was really a black snake; but I am permitted poetic license, at least around the shed) and I had worked out a system: we both occupied the shed, but we avoided one another. At least that was my understanding.

I blame the chickens. Obviously they had no understanding with Boris. I had two flat tires on my Italian road bike, had the bike upside down while I replaced tires as well as tubes, looking for something a little more road rugged and oyster shell repellant. Nappy and Red had come into the shed, seeing me, thinking food. Hmmm. Like daughters? I explained, in very patient tones, that food delivery was a chore to be completed later that afternoon, and was not now eminent. Nappy began to get a little agitated (well, actually, quite agitated) and my patience began to dissolve; a little background thunder presaging afternoon boomers, Penny skulked into the shed, trembling in fear from the thunder. I assumed, therefore, that Penny was the cause of Napoleon's tantrum. As any new age multi-tasking pioneer would, I attempted to comfort Penny, scold Nappy, and reach for a bicycle tube curled on the floor.

Realized I had my hand wrapped around a six and a half foot black snake with an eye for white meat hissing like a pin-pricked tube under ninety-five pounds of air pressure. Not part of Boris' and my understanding, nor did it lend itself to inter-species détente. I adopted some of Joan's language, dropped the snake and jumped back. Didn't think to defend Nappy or Red: every chicken for himself!

A six and a half foot snake can be a very terrifying creature: thicker than my forearm, mostly muscle, a mouthful of sharp teeth and a hunger unabated. It turned on Nappy with a heightened hiss, reared back like it was about to strike. Then I saw Penny do something she must have learned from Rosie dog: she grabbed the snake mid-body and shook it.

But Rosie's targets had never been over a foot or two long: with Boris, well, there was a whole lot of shaking going on. And it only seemed to piss that snake off even more. Boris turned on Penny, sized up where to strike her.

And then the next amazing part of this Darwinian protocol: Nappy flapped his wings, squawked, jumped forward and pecked the snake on the back of its head. Several times. Snake jerked back to see where this flank attack had come from just as Penny figured out that Rosie had meant green snakes and corn snakes, not black king snakes. She dropped the creature from her mouth; momentary pause, some trans-species communiqué. Then mass retreat, Penny to the side door of the house with me right behind her.

Penny was not the only one who ceased all attacks on the chickens after that. Molly, too, seemed to have a change of heart on hearing of Nappy coming to the canine's defense. There was a thing between Penny and Molly: they were two of the household princesses. Some sort of farmyard accommodation seemed to have been reached. Or perhaps Molly was too busy with resumes, applications, and the like. I'm always the last to know. (Joan says that, too; but with her, I always said it's just a failure to listen. What? What'd you say?)

With all the packing going on it was hard to differentiate: piles of clothes, luggage, lists, etc . . . I could have looked at the initials on the luggage, but that would have been like noticing a haircut, just something I didn't normally do. Joan was in her separation anxiety mode, Anna was angry at everybody for leaving (or not leaving soon enough? She wasn't exactly forthcoming). And I was riding my bike, 80 to 100 miles a week, cranking, spinning, looking good, and sweating something awful. And avoiding what I couldn't digest.

Molly wanted to talk; I said okay, when I get back from a quick twenty-five. What, she wanted me to recite more failures? And with all those to chose from.

I turned into the driveway still doing about seventeen mph (could do that now that it was paved), and just before the house ran into a pack of chickens running across the driveway: missed Red, missed the Guinea, but slammed into Napoleon, bringing up the rear, herding the others to the side yard. A real mess of feathers, chicken blood, cracked and bent body parts. Nappy didn't stand a chance against my Moser Leader AX. Molly and Anna were there immediately, then Joan; two in tears (Anna doesn't cry); Molly venting on me, my bike, Spandex in general; Anna saying it wasn't my fault, just an accident; Joan shedding tears for all mankind. Molly saying (Not a prayer!!) but a memorial, remembering Nappy saving Penny, recalling past deeds of distinction, suggesting a possible recipe. Anna saying No! We can't eat him, need to bury him with Rosie and Max and Moon dog.

Molly had her bags stacked neatly, apart from Joan's; she explained: Condé Nast, entry level, Dad, New York, but working for an editor mom's friend Linda knew, highly recommended. Good opportunity, I'll be back, Dad, don't you cry too. It's what you wanted, isn't it?

The Skirt

Elaine Habermehl

Fairhaven is the county home. It is a haven for some and a prison for others. For Olivia it was both. Ms. Olivia Hughes spent the latter years of her life dealing with the elements. In doing so I believe she came to appreciate the seasons and was the reason she spent so much time near the doors and windows at Fairhaven. Olivia was a street person waiting to go outside.

When Olivia could no longer push her grocery cart she picked through her meager supply of clothes and blankets selecting the ones she wanted to save and gave the rest to her friends.

Through the winter nights she rode the buses. In a back seat she cocooned herself in brown wool blankets and pressed her face to the cold glass. The bus driver never asked for money. He turned the sharp corners of the Chicago streets gently while Olivia dozed.

In the morning when the busman's shift changed he would stop and let Olivia off in front of a diner. Inside there would be a pot of tea, scrambled eggs, and a stack of toast with jam waiting for her.

I met Olivia soon after a winter's ice storm. A bus driver simply pulled bus 362 up to the double doors of Fairhaven and escorted a limping Ms. Olivia Hughes to the front desk.

There were little blue marks along her right side from a fall on the ice. On closer examination there was a bruise under the painted butterfly pin she used to secure her great mane of hair. Her skin was wrinkled from long days in the sun and the harsh winds of winter, but her body was lean and amazingly agile, even after a fall that would cripple one of her age.

It was during the unpacking of her clothes that I learned about Olivia's life. When I asked about her family she said that she was alone, except for friends, who also wore blankets like coats and eyed large pieces of cardboard with special interest.

She pulled the cord on a traveling bag slowly as if she wanted to prolong the anticipation of seeing its contents. As the bag fell away, little bits of dust floated towards the florescent light. She shook out each piece until the room glittered with bits of white fluff. Olivia spent some time gazing at the floating specks as they drifted towards the shaft of sunlight from the window. Fairhaven was their prison too. Not even dust could escape the windows and doors. At the bottom of the pile rested a black skirt. It was long, made of taffeta and crackled to life as she picked it up shaking out the deep ruffles. Something special from a former life I thought. Instead of putting it in the closet she pulled it over her head, settled it on a girlish waist, and spun around the room despite her bruises. It was a moment I will not forget. The glittering sunlit dust circling the room kept in constant motion by Olivia twirling around it in her black skirt. She sat down hard in the chair by the bed and puffed out the words, "That skirt is my freedom, my wings." She leaned back in the chair and giggled like a young girl.

Although there are what we orderlies refer to as "wanderers" at Fairhaven, I did not believe Olivia Hughes to be one of them. So, on a spring morning I signed the paper that would grant Olivia permission to enjoy the yard. Now I would be the one watching from the other side of the glass. Mostly she walked the gravel paths, sometimes trying to skip, or run into a leap but soon stopped and favored her right leg.

Olivia picked up sticks from the grass after a windstorm, looked for weeds in the well-tended flower beds, and sometimes napped on a wooden bench. No doubt habits left over from long days and nights of living on the street. A butterfly once landed on her sleeping form. He came to rest on the brown blanket that covered her knees. When she awoke the creature fluttered up and attached itself to her hair, becoming a live barrette for her graying locks. It shared its secrets only with Olivia before it flew to the flowerbeds, then disappeared over the east gate.

In the early morning hours of April 24th an alarm sounded in the building. A door to the outside was open. There were exactly twenty seconds to punch in a four digit key code, but it was seemingly absent. The floodlights to the grounds flashed on.

From the windows at Fairhaven we watched Olivia dancing

in the black taffeta skirt around the flowerbeds. Our floodlights had become her footlights. Her words echoed in my head, "This skirt is my freedom." While we watched, she pulled the skirt inside out. Across the fabric was blazoned a black and orange butterfly in flight. The skirt waist fit neatly around her neck, and what were pockets became armholes. Her right leg had apparently healed. With her arms out to her side she skipped then ran the length of the yard taking a leap and disappeared just past the beam of the floodlights.

Our search began in the woods, then the buses, park benches, the diner, and a painstaking search of steam vents and the cardboard homes of her friends. We did not find Olivia. That morning the food on her breakfast tray went untouched. The oatmeal under the silver dome cooled. The seeds in the orange juice settled to the bottom of the glass, as the butter on the toast dripped onto napkins. I cleared her breakfast tray away the morning she went missing. On a napkin in pencil the words: "the skirt is my freedom, when I wear it I feel I can fly." It was signed simply, "Your friend, Olivia." Beside it rested the painted butterfly pin from her hair and a yellowed press clipping from a Russian newspaper in St.Petersburg. On close inspection of the picture I saw a young woman wearing a black taffeta skirt featured as the principal dancer of the Bolshoi Ballet.

What Olivia Hughes needed did not exist inside the walls of Fairhaven. I turned out the light in her room and closed the door. I posted the yellowed newspaper to the bulletin board. In front of the mirror in the hallway I clipped her butterfly pin to my hair and felt an unexpected urge to dance.

New Life

George M. Hagerman

Harvey Goodyear, late of Poultney, Vermont, six-feet-tall with a thatch of white hair above a perpetually-tanned face punctured by two dark eyes surveyed his new Hanover Acres retirement home on the outskirts of Richmond, Virginia. He watched as his daughter Jean hung the last picture. "Pops you're finally settled. Now relax and have some fun. Heaven knows you've earned it."

Dang it, thought Harvey, I'm tired of everyone telling me what I've earned. Besides, I love my life, my farm.

Jean sat on the sofa across the room from the window and patted the seat beside her. The sofa had been reupholstered in subdued beige and blue stripes. As Harvey walked towards her, he thought how much cozier the old mustard-colored sofa had been.

He was touched by Jean's resemblance to her Irish mother: soft wavy hair, round face, green eyes, freckles, and a dimple in her chin, but she was built like him, tall and thin. He said, "I don't know what I'm doing here. I love Poultney, I love the people there, and if it weren't for you, I'd still be there."

"Pops we've been through this hundred times. You simply cannot live alone. The fire in your kitchen last spring should have convinced you of that."

Anybody can forget to turn off the stove. I'm only eighty-two."

"It wasn't just the fire. What about leaving the engine in the car running and leaving the lights on all night? Your fall was the last straw. Besides, I love you, Pops. I want you nearby."

"O.K. Jeannie, I'm here, but I'll always miss my life in Poultney."

"Pops, look on this as a great adventure. Here nobody knows you. You can be whoever you want to be, do whatever you want to do. Enjoy life. Take each day and make the most of it. Think about the interesting possibilities."

Harvey thought, she's just trying to cheer me up. Dang it! I don't want to think about possibilities. I want to be back in Poultney.

Jean got up to leave. As she opened the door, she said, "I really must go, Pops. Brad will soon be home. You'll be O.K. as soon as you meet some nice people here."

"Thank you Jeannie, you've been a good daughter even though you're stubborn." Stubborn like me, he thought.

He closed the door behind her and surveyed his new and yet familiar surroundings. His eyes focused on the corner cupboard of good Vermont maple that had been his grandmother's. His easy chair that his father had given him when he went to the University of Vermont, stood across from the sofa. The sofa looked comfortable opposite the chair and window. In the dining alcove was a small mahogany drop leaf table that had been in the front hall back home. He didn't realize how much he loved it until it came time to part with it. He insisted on bringing along the two dining room arm chairs that matched eight side chairs. Jeannie said it was a shame to break up the set. Break it up for whom, he had argued. Some one would be glad to get eight straight-back chairs and would never miss the ones he insisted on keeping.

He walked over to the window and looked out. His apartment overlooked the front lawn of Hanover Acres, the driveway lined with dogwood trees. The fuss these Virginians made over dogwoods, you'd think they were something special. They had small leaves, no fruit and weren't much good for shade. Beyond the lawn and the driveway stood a grove of trees. There were no birch trees and only a few maples. Mostly there were pine trees, but they didn't resemble New England pine, not enough blue.

How did I let myself get talked into this, he thought for the hundredth time. Last year there had been a small fire in the kitchen when he slipped and broke his wrist. Fortunately, his neighbor from across the road had seen the smoke from her porch before any damage was done. Jean had insisted that he move to Richmond where she could look after him. Suppose a fire started right now, he thought. She couldn't dash across Richmond to put it out.

He sighed and turned into the bedroom. The big four-poster double bed took up most of the room. When Jeannie mentioned the desirability of a smaller bed, he refused to discuss it. He and Grace had slept and loved in that bed for forty-two years. God, he had loved her and had become very dependent on her. She had died in that bed, and he planned to die in it too. Before that his father and mother had used it. When Grace was dying, although she hadn't asked him, he promised her he would never touch another woman. He had kept that promise, although it had not been easy. His neighbor, Clara Bartley, had been sweet on him ever since high school. She had started to look after him right after Grace died. Clara was a pretty woman, but when things took a romantic turn, he put his foot down and took charge of his life.

He opened the dresser drawer to get out a clean shirt. The dresser had been his since he was a boy, and Ma and Pa allowed him to move into the empty room over the kitchen that had been added to the house at the turn of the century. As he started to dress he felt nervous. He was a stranger here. Now he was preparing to eat in a new dining room where he didn't know a soul. Fortunately, they ate early enough to suit him. When he stayed with Jeannie, she never had dinner until after seven o'clock. Here he could at least eat as early as five-thirty.

He wished he didn't have to put on a coat and tie for supper. Back home he put on a clean pair of overalls, and that was good enough. He was tempted to go to the dining room in his shirt sleeves. Maybe they would throw him out. No, that wouldn't do, it would just create more problems for Jeannie, and he couldn't do that.

He walked into the bathroom to comb his hair. He chuckled as he looked at the Jacuzzi in the corner. Hell, he and Grace had used a galvanized tub in the kitchen and an outdoor privy for the first five years of their life together. Grace would get a kick out of the Jacuzzi. It sure beat the Saturday night bath in the galvanized tub. After one final look in the mirror, he returned to the easy chair. He'd wait a bit. He didn't want to be the first person in the dining room.

The ringing phone startled him. It could only be Jeannie. It was. "Pops," she said, "I just had a call from Emma Cartwright. You remember her from your visit last summer? She moved to Monument Avenue. Three months ago, she moved to Hanover Acres. I told her you would be coming there. She wanted to know if you had arrived yet. I told her this was your first day at Hanover Acres. She insisted that she come by your apartment and show you how to get to the dining room for dinner."

Harvey's heart sank. He remembered a small woman with dyed hair, a made-up face and a tight-fitting dress. She didn't pronounce her 'r's. He'd had trouble understanding her.

"Jeannie, I don't need a strange woman escorting me to dinner,"

"Pops, remember what I told you a while ago. Make this the first day of your new life."

"Jeannie I can find my own way to the dining room."

"Emma is probably on her way to your apartment right now. Just tell her you're an old fuddy-dud and can't go with her. I love you, bye." The phone clicked.

He hurried to the bathroom, put on some more after shave lotion, smoothed his hair with a brush and straightened his tie.

The doorbell rang.

He thought, now don't be nervous she won't bite. Then he opened the door.

Standing outside was the petite lady he remembered. She had blue-white hair and wore a formfitting blue and green print dress which emphasized her figure. A blue scarf around her neck matched the color of her eyes ringed with makeup. She held out her hand as entered the room.

"Mr. Goodyear, welcome to Hanover Acres. Jean has told me so much about you that I feel like we're old friends.

Harvey felt a little squeeze as he took her hand.

"It's real nice of you to see that I get to the dining room, Mizz Cartwright." He wasn't sure if she was a Miss or a Mrs.

"Oh, do call me Emmie. What a lovely apartment you have. That cupboard and table with the two chairs make a wonderful combination. Did you bring them from Vermont?"

Harvey thought, well at least she knows good furniture when see sees it.

"Mizz Cartwright, I grew up with that furniture." He could not suppress a quiver in his voice. She said, "Harvey, I know how you must feel. Your daughter has brought you a thousand miles from home. You don't know a soul; you don't know how you'll survive. We all feel that way at first, but let's face it, we'll be here a long time—I hope, so let's make the most of it. You're only young once," she added with a laugh.

My gawd Harvey thought, "Is this little Virginian trying to cheer me up?

Harvey looked at her. She was right, he couldn't stay mad at Jeannie, but who was this woman to lecture him?

Emma could see that she had touched a raw nerve, so she

said "I think we have time for a drink before dinner. Do you have any bourbon?"

"I don't think so. Jeannie brought me some groceries and Cokes."

"Most Yankees don't like bourbon, so I brought my own—here."

She took a pint bottle of Virginia Gentleman from her bag and handed it to him.

As he took the bottle into the kitchen, he mumbled, "Who in the hell does she think she is bringing her own likker to my house?"

Back home most people drank rum and Coke in the summer and hot rum toddies in the winter. Only Sam Owen, president of the bank, drank Scotch. Most people never heard of bourbon; a few drank Canadian Club. He called from the kitchen, "What do you like in your bourbon, Coke?"

"Heavens, no! Make mine in the rocks with a splash of branch."

"Branch?"

"Yes branch, like a small creek: water, you know."

Harvey kept mumbling as he poured the bourbon over the ice and added some water. "That woman is taking advantage of me, whoever heard of a crick being called a branch? These rebels don't even know how to speak English."

He poured himself some Coke over ice cubes and as an afterthought added some bourbon. He took a swallow of the odd combination and grimaced at the sugary, sickening taste.

When he returned to the living room, he stopped dead in doorway. Emma sat in the corner of the old family sofa with her feet tucked under her, and shoes neatly placed on the floor. When Grace had been younger, this had been her favorite posture. His eyes misted as he remembered snuggling up close to her. Occasionally, he would put his head in her lap. While they talked, she would slowly massage his temples. Sometimes this even led to lovemaking in the big bed.

Emma brought him back to the present by saying, "Hope you don't mind, Harvey, but this sofa looked so comfortable and the room so homey that I couldn't resist sitting like this."

He didn't answer but only nodded his head as he handed Emma the glass of bourbon and sat down in the easy chair across from her. Harvey could not look directly at Emma; the vision of Grace was still too strong. Instead he concentrated on a painting above the sofa. It was a New England scene with a lake in the foreground. Behind the lake was a forest of birch, blue spruce, and white pine. A fourteen-point buck and a doe stood on the shore line staring directly at Harvey.

Emma must have noticed the pensive look on his face. She said "Now, Harvey, pull yourself together. This is only a new place; it isn't the end of the world. From what Jean has told me, you have survived some serious crises in your life like your son's death in Vietnam and later the death of your wife. You come from an old Vermont family, and you are too smart to be taken in by us rebels."

She's bold as brass, he thought, but danged if she didn't begin to sound like Grace. He considered a second before he answered her. "Actually I've been thinking of moving closer to Jeannie for some time," he said with a straight face as he lifted his glass, "Here's to tomorrow."

"To tomorrow," she replied, lifting her glass.

They sipped their drinks, chatted while he studied her without staring. She had more brains than he imagined. She was a mite small, but in spite of her la-de-da accent, she made sense.

Finally, she said, "Come on, Harvey, it's time to go to dinner. You can handle this."

"All right, Mizz Cartwright, let's go."

She turned to him, "Harvey Goodfellow, if you call me Mizz one more time, I swear I'll go to dinner alone. I am M-i-s-s Cartwright. I have never been married, is that clear?"

"Yes ma'am."

She stood up, slipped into her high-heeled pumps and headed for the door.

Harvey put down his glass, followed her into the hall, and as he locked the door said, "Lead on, Mizz Emma." While they waited for the elevator he took a quick look at the nearby mirror and was startled to see the big grin on his face.

The Theatre

D.S. Lliteras

It is some time since I have drunk champagne.
—Anton Chekhov (1860-1904)

"A November wind blows across the harbor and against several figures, who are standing on Pier Eight at the U.S. Naval Base in Norfolk, Virginia, under the limited protection of their umbrellas. The hem of a long raincoat is suddenly forced upward in response to a gust of wind veering in the rain, which forces the annoyed figure to turn away from the weather. It is a legitimate time of year for the day to be grey and these people are withstanding their discomfort with philosophic resignation. The USS Eisenhower (CVN), a mere speck on the horizon, is near the end of a long and lonely nine-month deployment.

"Off-stage, there is a small navy exchange convenience store where most of the waiting crowd is huddled in an attempt to stay out of the rain and remain warm by drinking coffee. The small group of people on-stage are exposed to the elements as they wait for their loved ones."

The director stopped reading the script and peered at the cast members. He stood near the center of an off off-Broadway stage surrounded by a set of circularly-arranged chairs occupied by hopeful strangers.

"This is a nice stage description. But, realistically, what we're going to have during the performance is a bare stage."

The cast members chuckled and shifted uneasily in their seats. None of them knew each other. None of them were getting paid. None of them had future prospects. But all of them possessed transparent attitudes, which betrayed their dreams and hopes and professionalism as they huddled with their cigarettes and their coffee and their smiles.

The director wanted to apologize to them for the lack of budget and the poor conditions and the lack of pay. But since most of them weren't seasoned actors, he hoped that his ability to teach acting would be some compensation for their heavy contribution of time and energy. He passed out the rehearsal schedule. "You need to look over this schedule and note any conflicts." He pursed his lips. "We need to get this straight from the beginning. I won't tolerate any absences or tardiness. There are no excuses. You know what you have to do to get here on time. I live in the same world and I promise you I'll be here before you and I'll be the last one to leave. Understand?"

Everybody responded in some manner: a nod, a mumble, a flick of a cigarette ash, a shift in attitude.

The director knew he had to inspire the gifted performers, guide the lost actors, and teach the poor players. He wanted to tell them that he was more afraid of this new beginning than they were because he already knew the kind of insurmountable obstacles they were facing. But he felt great anyway. And like a captain of a ship, it felt good to get underway and face the vast unknown of the sea.

He already modified some of the show's dramatic complexities because the actor that he needed for one of the roles could not be found either from the available acting pool or from within the auditioning time frame. He knew that a show like this was, theoretically, only as good as its weakest actor. But he solved the problem and the show would work and life was tolerable.

"Okay. No schedule conflicts. Good. We'll do a read-through today, and tomorrow we'll have what I call our family hour, where everybody will have to talk about themselves. This is always a fun rehearsal, because I've never met actors who didn't like to talk about themselves."

Everybody laughed.

"Is this where we're having our rehearsals?" one of the actors asked.

"Unfortunately, no. One of the things we'll do tomorrow is go to the rehearsal hall and set it up. The New Theatre Ensemble (NTE) has a loft down the street. Believe me, it's not much."

"Does it have a bathroom?" another actor asked.

"Yes. And enough heat to take the chill out of the air."

"When you say, 'set it up—'"

"That means we need to sweep the place clean, take over a

few folding chairs, tables, props—you know, make the place hospitable."

"Ahh, my life in art," one of the actors said melodramatically. Everybody laughed at her.

"Yeah, well, it's going to be our home for the next few weeks."

He was sorry he couldn't provide them with the logistic support of a prompter, assistant director, stage manager, and prop master. He was also sorry he couldn't show them design plots, set models, or costume designs. All they were getting was him and one assistant. Therefore, he had to impress the hell out of them with his efficiency and his creativity.

When he realized that everybody was waiting for him to begin the read-through, he cleared his throat. "We're going to have a fine show. I'm certain of that." He reached into his shirt pocket and pulled out a cigarette from a half-empty pack. "What I say, goes. This is not a democracy. And never forget this: I will fire you even on opening night if I have to." He lit the cigarette. "You will trust me because I know what I'm doing and because I care about you. Okay? Okay." He approached the only unoccupied chair in the circle. "I expect all of you to be off book by the end of the week. Now, let's begin the read-through." He asked one of the minor actors to read the stage directions before he sat down. "Begin."

The actor read the same opening segment the director had read to them. The following actors leaped into their characters.

Jenifer:	Nine months, eleven days, eight hours.
Clorisa:	I'd trade the next two hours for another ship deployment. (She reaches into her purse.)
Jenifer:	What an odd thing to say.
Clorisa:	I'm waiting for my ex. Only . . . only he doesn't know it yet. (She finds her cigarettes.)
Jenifer:	You've got a lot of nerve.
Clorisa:	Never had any. (She lights a cigarette.) I can't be a sailor's wife anymore.
Jenifer:	Have you been all alone?
Clorisa:	I'm weak, remember? (She drops the cigarette on the ground in response to several distasteful puffs and crushes it out with her foot.) And we don't have children.
Jenifer:	That's something.
Clorisa:	He'll kill me when I tell him we're through.

Jenifer:	You should have written.
Clorisa:	I should have gone to college.
Jenifer:	(She peers at the distant ship on the horizon.) It's been a long deployment.
Clorisa:	A lifetime. (Bitterly.) One thousand three hundred and forty-six dollars and sixty-seven cents, along with a monthly allotment check, is all I have to show for it.
Jenifer:	(With disdain.) You don't want much.
Clorisa:	I don't feel good.
Jenifer:	Mama can't keep you home from school anymore.
Clorisa:	(She thrusts both hands into her raincoat pockets.) How come it's so easy for you?
Jenifer:	I work at a laundromat six days a week.
Clorisa:	Leave me alone.

(They continue waiting in silence.)

The director appreciated the strength of these two actors. They were going to work well together.

This was a successful beginning in an artistic world that didn't believe in success anymore.

He closed his eyes and listened to the play. He was back in the saddle again, and God help him, he loved it.

-2-

He liked being a theatrical director. He liked the creative responsibility. He liked actors. At the theatre, he was their director, teacher, confidant, and mentor; his directional discipline was razor sharp and supportive. But outside the theatre's rehearsal hall, he kept his distance from actors.

Frederick Balthazar was lean and short and closely shaven. He owned three pairs of slacks and a half-dozen shirts that were kept clean and pressed. He lived alone.

Frederick Balthazar trusted his talent even though he was unable to make a living in this legitimate, but dying, art form. He worked as a night clerk at the front desk of the New York Hilton Hotel because the night shift allowed him the time to conduct his theatrical business during the afternoon and his rehearsals during the earlier part of the evening. Consequently, he slept little: between 8 A.M., and noon, and on the subways.

He was addicted to the theatre, and he was happy because he was not deluded in thinking it was anything other than what it was: desperate, petty, and impossible; dusty, ignored, and broke; irrelevant, disappearing, and ridiculed by the public.

He went into the kitchen of his tiny apartment, opened his refrigerator, and pulled out a beer. He twisted the cap from the longneck bottle and drank deeply.

The beer was cold. This winter was going to be colder. Frederick Balthazar was glad he didn't have to work at the Hilton that night.

-3-

Before conducting the family-hour rehearsal, Balthazar engaged the cast members in the essentials of transforming the nearby loft into a rehearsal hall. Nobody was exempt from the menial tasks required by this poor New York City theatre. In a continuous flow from the NTE building to the loft, they worked like self-sacrificing worker ants to transport the folding chairs and tables, the table lamps and props, the cleaning equipment and detergents—even coffee mugs and a percolator.

He wanted to tell these actors that it was never going to get any better than this. The magic of the legitimate theatre was sinking into the mud and—well, what the hell did he know?

At the rehearsal hall, he handed one of the actors a broom and a dustpan for the floor and handed another actor a can of cleanser and a brush for the toilet. Essentials. Everything was reduced to its essentials.

-4-

"My name is Jonathan Binghamton." The actor squirmed in his seat. "I'm from Indiana. No use telling you the name of the town because I know none of you have heard of it."

The entire cast chuckled.

According to their resumes, none of them were native New Yorkers, all of them had gone to a state university, and each of them was devoted to the theatre.

Balthazar studied their mannerisms and attitudes as he listened to their personal histories.

The grit and grime of the city had penetrated deeply into some of them, which produced a cynicism equal to a native New Yorker. For others, like the married couple, the unrelenting urban grind as a waiter and a waitress made them appear harried and haggard before their time. Finally, the one Balthazar was looking for revealed himself—the crazy one, one who was going to be trouble and threaten the safety of the show; the nut, who managed to camouflage himself during auditions.

His name was Pete Gustafson and he played Mr. McCue, one of the important roles in the show. Gustafson had a string of divorces and was too old when he decided to be an actor two years ago. To this man, acting was not an art; it was psychotherapy.

Balthazar slumped in his chair. He realized he had to understudy this role as a precaution against this actor. He inhaled. There was one small comfort: the threat of firing was a remarkably effective tool against an actor, normal or psychotic; actors were desperate for performance showcases that would expose them to powerful agents, producers, or directors. He exhaled. But show-business VIPs, who could make a difference in their acting careers, would never use the complimentary tickets set aside at the NTE box office. He felt guilty.

-5-

Balthazar was glad to be home. The night shift at the hotel had been as dull as the biographies he had to listen to before beginning their first blocking rehearsal.

He was getting ready for bed when somebody buzzed him from downstairs. He went to his intercom and pressed the button. "Who is it?"

"It's me, Cloi."

"Come on up."

He pressed the entrance buzzer to let Cloi into the building. Then he unlocked his apartment's door and left it partially open while he started a pot of coffee.

Cloi was the artistic director and producer of the theatre. She also knew his sleep schedule. This had to be urgent.

Cloi pushed the door open and remained standing at its threshold. "Hey."

"Come in."

"Sorry about bothering you like this."

"No bother. Coffee?"

"Sure." She closed the door.

"Make yourself at home."

"Thanks, Fred." She took out a pack of cigarettes and a

lighter before she laid her purse on his couch. "I'll be glad when this winter's over." She took off her coat.

"Yeah." Fred set the percolator on the gas stove. "Care for a muffin?"

She draped her coat over the back of the couch. "No, thanks."

He pointed at the kitchenette table. "Have a seat. Talk to me. You didn't come here for coffee."

She sat down, then fumbled for a cigarette before setting the pack on the table. "It's bad news."

"Yeah, well—I've heard bad news before."

She lit her cigarette. "The theatre's going out of business." She placed the lighter on top of the cigarette pack.

"So? What's new?"

Cloi shook her head. "No. I'm not speaking figuratively, Fred. We're bankrupt. You're out of work."

He sat down on the seat adjacent to hers and snagged a cigarette from her pack. "I keep trying to quit, but this damn business of ours keeps driving me back to them."

"This is not a business anymore. It's a joke."

He lit the cigarette with her lighter, inhaled deeply, then exhaled thoughtfully. "I don't know why I've bothered to stay with it so long."

"Love."

He looked at his smoldering cigarette. "I didn't know I was so transparent."

"The reason why I see through you is because I travel on the same path."

The coffee began to perk. Fred went to the stove and lowered the flame. "I'm glad you came by."

"Yeah. Well. I felt you deserved hearing this from me." He returned to the table and sat down.

"Thanks."

"You deserve a hell of a lot more, god damn it."

"Nobody owes anybody anything."

"You're one hell of a theatrical director. You've got real talent."

"Big deal. Everybody's got talent." He snickered. "Talent won't help you make a living."

"I'm sorry, Fred."

"Hell. You've given far more to the theatre than I have. At least I can walk away from NTE clean."

"You're broke."

"But you're below broke. NTE is costing you, well, bankruptcy—whatever that is." He took a hard drag from his cigarette. "What's it all about, Cloi?"

"If I knew, God, if I knew."

They concentrated on their cigarettes. They stared at the ashtray between them.

"Is there life after theatre?" he finally asked.

Cloi laughed caustically.

Fred rose from his chair, went to the stove, and turned off the gas. "You like your coffee black."

"Yeah."

"Good. Black and bitter and hot is how I feel." He poured the fresh coffee and brought the mugs to the table.

Cloi flicked the long grey ash of her cigarette into the ashtray. "Thanks."

"For what? I thank you for giving me a job this year. It was good." He raised his mug. "It was real."

She raised her mug. "It was great theatre."

"Yeah."

They clinked their mugs together and sipped their coffee like a pair of street urchins wondering how to get out of the cold.

Fred crushed out his cigarette. "What happened? How did it happen?"

"Does it matter?"

He shrugged his shoulders and sighed. "Not really."

"Would you like me to call your cast members?"

"No. I can do my own dirty work."

"Not so dirty."

"Sad."

"I know."

"Damn. This was going to be one hell of a good show."

"Yeah. Well."

He studied Cloi.

She was older. Tired. Worn out. Disillusioned by the dark and dirty wooden interior of the New York City theatre scene. Her eyes still shined because of her artistic brilliance. But the lack of makeup exposed her lost youthfulness and called attention to her fading beauty.

He rose from the table. "Care for more coffee?" She nodded. "I almost went to a bar for a drink this morning."

"Ouch. No good." He went to the stove. "You need to get out of this town."

"I guess."

He brought the pot to the table and refilled their mugs.

"What about you?" she asked.

He set the pot on the table and sat down. "Me? I don't know how to do anything else. I don't want to . . . to do anything else."

"It's a hell of a thing to be who we are."

"You need any money?"

"No." She pursed her lips. "I'm sorry, Fred. Really. Your talent is going to waste."

"Don't be melodramatic."

She crushed out her cigarette. "I'm giving you the credit you deserve." She gazed steadily at him. "You never gave me any trouble. You kept your shows in control. And you never asked me for a penny. You're the best staff director I've ever had."

"Yeah, well, you keep talking about my talent, but what about yours?"

She averted her eyes. "Ahh."

"You're a brilliant director."

"Now who's being melodramatic?"

"Just accept a compliment for once."

"Yeah," she whispered. "Thanks. But my gratitude won't get you very far."

"I'm not going anywhere."

"I hope, for your sake, you are. Because the theatre is dead. Morally bankrupt. Economically impossible. Artistically shallow. And not relevant anymore."

"I don't want to believe that."

"I don't know why. You lose every day you continue your association with this non-existing art form."

Fred snatched a cigarette out of her pack and lit it. "I don't care."

She rose from the table, picked up her lighter, and went to the couch to get her coat. "You will." She draped the coat over her arm and picked up her purse. "Keep the cigarettes." Then she went to the door and opened it. "Thanks, Fred. You were a good colleague and I love you for it." She walked out of the apartment and closed the door behind her.

Fred felt empty. Dislocated.

He rose from the table and went to the telephone. He picked up the cast roster and peered at the first name on the list.

She would have been a great Jenifer.

The Game

Shirley Nesbit-Sellers

Come in, dear. Yes, I'm admiring the beautiful day. But, actually, I'm at the window because I'm expecting someone. No, don't leave. It's not time yet.

I see your eye on those candies. Have one. No, wait. Not the one that's red-wrapped. That's the only red one. Have one of the others. They're all green, but they have the same candy inside as the red. Why do I want to save the red one? Well, I need it. That's a little story of mine. Sit down and I'll tell you.

When I was a child, one of the most enjoyable things we did as a whole family together was working on the annual flea market in the parking lot of the hospital. You'll remember. Right by the first old Willow Oaks nursing home. Our house was within walking distance, and my little brother, Billy, and I loved to help Daddy carry donated things over to the flea market on the day of the sale. We helped set up, too. That way we got to see what we were going to buy with the money Mother always gave us for helping.

I always wanted books. I'm afraid I got distracted from helping whenever we started unloading the books. But one time, when I was about, oh, twelve, I decided I'd like to buy a game instead. As people began to arrive, I thought it best to get over to the game table before I lost a chance to get something I'd really like. A word game, perhaps.

While I was standing there, poking around in the boxes of games, I noticed a little white-haired lady just standing there, leaning on her cane, and looking at me with a sweet smile. I smiled back and her grin broadened.

"I love games, too," she said

I didn't want to break the moment of companionship by saying that I really hadn't played many games and usually wanted books, so I answered, "I'm looking for a word game. You know, the kind that makes you learn new words. The kind you can win if you know a lot of words."

Her bright little eyes sparkled when I said that, and she came over closer to the table to help me find one. She scanned the pile and then she lifted her cane and pointed with it to a box that had pictures of books on it.

"I'll bet that's one," she said. "Anyway, it looks interesting."

At that moment, Billy came bounding up and, just like a pesky little brother, he grabbed that very box and said wickedly, "I think I want this game."

Before he could bring the box from its place, my new friend firmly laid her cane down on his reaching arm and said, "Oh no, young man. That was my choice."

Chastised, Billy withdrew his arm and hung his head. I laughed.

"That's okay, Billy. You can play the game with me when you're old enough. This is my brother," I explained to the lady.

I lifted the box and, with Billy and my new friend peering with interest, I opened it. It was a board game. It had piles of cards with words on them and a spinner with numbers that led you to different colored cards that had sentences with one word missing. At first I thought it would be too simple for me, but a glance at some of the words told me that it was not as easy as I had thought. I really didn't know some of those words, but I knew I'd learn them by playing the game. It was just right.

"Where are the men pieces that travel around the board?" asked Billy.

We took everything from the box, but found no trace of the players. My friend came to the rescue. She reached into the knitted bag on her arm and pulled out four or five pieces of candy gaily wrapped in paper of different colors.

"You see," she explained. "When your game is over,

you can have a treat. Here are four different colors for you. I'm sure you can find more when those are gone."

"Oh boy!" exclaimed Billy and reached for the candy.

"No, Billy" I said, holding them tightly away from him. "We'll get you some other kind. These are our playing pieces."

Billy frowned. "You know that game's too hard for me."

"You know, Billy," said our friend, "you could learn a lot by trying to play the game. Besides, it's like the game of life. It may be hard at times, but what really counts is who is playing the game with you."

Turning to our benefactor, I thanked her for helping with such generosity. She sparkled some more and then looked over to the gateway as though searching for someone.

"You children enjoy your game," she said, as she turned on her cane to leave us. "I see my son waiting for me."

I followed the direction she had taken and was surprised to see a school classmate, Sally, coming to meet her and help her back to a tall man, who must have been Sally's father.

They were gone before I could claim acquaintance-ship.

That evening, after we had all shared our purchases, I told my mother about knowing the girl whose grand-mother had helped us.

"I would really like to see her again, Mother. I know now that her name must be Mrs. Prescott, since she's Sally's father's mother. They live just a short way from here."

Mother was pleased with the idea of such a visit, and soon I was making two or three trips a week to play my game with Mrs. Prescott. Sally played with us at first, but it was not her kind of game; she said, and she soon wandered off to other pursuits.

The friendship between Mrs. Prescott and me developed into a lovely bond. Even when our game times began to be rarer as I grew older, we both looked forward to our sessions. And we never tried to secure new game pieces. We always played with the candy and enjoyed it afterward.

The time came when I had to curtail my visits even more, because old Mrs. Prescott had a stroke and was bedridden for many weeks before she could even sit up. Then she could only use her hands. She would never walk again. When she was able, she played the game with me, but I could see that it tired her. So we sat quietly while I read to her, or told her what was happening in my life. Sally was off to college and I was going to the local university, so I was an especially welcomed visitor.

It wasn't long before another stroke sent her to be cared for in the Willow Oaks Home.

She did not know who I was when I carried my game to play with her. So, when I visited, I just talked to her instead. After she died, I put the game away, until one day Billy came in after track practice and asked me to get it out so he could play with me.

"I need to beat somebody at something!" he said. But I knew he was really just trying to cheer me up.

Oh, I'll have to ask you to excuse me, dear. There's Billy's son getting out of the car. I keep my game here with me at Willow Oaks. I would ask you to play it with us, but I have only the two colors for the pieces. He comes often, though, and we'll ask you to play next time. You'll love my grandson. He's a dear little boy. Mrs. Prescott was right, you know. What really counts is who is playing the game with you.

Daybreak

Lynn Stearns

Always was my favorite time of day, this old concrete bench under the locust trees my favorite spot to watch the gray of night give way to blue. Papa's parents and others on his side of the family buried here before I was born, Chesapeake Bay stretched out in front, waves rolling in, hugging the land day after day. Papa used to say sometimes the bay was rough, sometimes calm, but it had a soul, just like people, and it would never die. Something reassuring about Papa's words, the way he'd stand at the edge of the water, looking out and nodding, so sure that what he'd said was true.

Need all the reassurance I can get before Amanda arrives. Said she wants to show me pictures of my ninetieth birthday celebration, but she's been making noises about how the old farmhouse requires a lot of upkeep, I could get snowed in next winter, she and Frank have plenty of room at their place in Annapolis, want me to move in with them. I don't want to be a burden though, and don't intend to leave Ebb Tide Island.

Checked with the lady at the new Senior Village down the road, and they have a room available on the bay side. Told her I'd have to think about it. Lived on this island all my life, on this farm most of it. Don't want to go any farther then necessary. Earliest memories are of playing on a blanket here under the trees, Mama weeding the garden, shelling peas.

She'd look out from under her sun hat, checking on me I suppose. "Sing with me, Carrie Ella," she'd say and launch into one of the old hymns. "When the roll is called up yonder, I'll be there." Told me everything important in her life happened right here. It's where she met Papa, had all four of us children. Never tired of hearing about the day Joshua and James were in school, she pulled three-year-old Daniel to the family cemetery over there in his little red wagon, a flat of petunias on his lap.

"I was down on all fours," she said, "working the ground by the headstones when I realized you were about to arrive, a good two weeks early. Told Daniel to keep his eye on the soil I'd turned, look for earthworms for fish bait, while I yelled for Papa in the barn. Came just in time to catch you on your way out to greet the world, kept smiling, saying we had a beautiful fair-haired baby girl."

"Girlie," I can almost hear him call. "Go get your bucket, Girlie." I'd run for the pail by the kitchen door, dance in circles as we crossed the field, happy just to be with my Papa. Made our way down the bank and took off our shoes, waded in the edge of the bay to follow some old horseshoe crab's trail or collect clam shells, periwinkles, anything that caught my eye 'til the dinner bell rang.

Mama would have something good waiting for us—oyster fritters and fresh greens, corn on the cob. We were on the porch husking corn the day she told me Indians used to live on Ebb Tide Island, made a meal out of whatever they caught in the bay and grew themselves, buried their loved ones in the field just like us. That night when the windows in the upstairs hall rattled, I pulled the covers over my head, cried about Indian ghosts trying to get in. Papa came in and sat at the foot of my bed, told me it was only the wind. "Blows across the bay like this every fall, reminding us it's time to let the land rest." Fell asleep with him reciting, "To every thing there is a season, and a time to every purpose under the heavens . . ."

I've seen a lot of seasons come and go, a lot of changes around here. A bridge built all the way to the western shore, ferry boats gliding across the bay one day, gone the next. Only a few farms left on the island now, so many people have passed on. Never thought Daniel would be the first one. Seemed like he had a whole lifetime ahead of him.

Joshua and James always tried to see who could run faster, jump higher. Had their share of scraped knees and broken bones. Daniel was as likely as not to start the race with them, then drop out to follow some dragonfly across the cow pasture or study a sprig of clover or Queen Anne's Lace at the side of the lane. Had the same wispy brown hair and clear dark eyes as the others, same sturdy build, but he was quieter, more studious.

After their chores, the older boys took their salted eel down to the shore and set crab lines, then climbed back up the bank to a rope they'd tied to a tree here. Held tight while they took a flying leap, and let go once they were over deep water. Again and again, one after the other, hooting and hollering every time. Daniel chuckled, said they were scaring all the crabs into the next county.

He'd sit here in the shade, content with a pad of paper and pencil or a piece of charcoal, drawing Canada Geese, sea gulls soaring overhead, canvasbacks bobbing in the waves. Gave me a sketch he made during a dead low tide once—a piece of driftwood out on the sandbar with branches like arms pointing in opposite directions. Said the next high tide would take it some place where we might never see it again. "Sometimes, Carrie Ella, the only way to hold on to things is to keep them in our minds."

Another time he found a piece of green glass the shade of a Coca Cola bottle washed up on shore. Held it in the palm of his hand while I ran my thumb over it. Told me time is what wore down the sharp edges. Somehow, even as he sent it skipping across the waves, I knew I'd never forget the cool smoothness.

Joshua and James were married, living up the county when I started falling in love with Carvel, the only man I ever cared to court. Daniel was back home after going to college, teaching history at the high school. Enjoyed teasing me about packing Mama's fried chicken and potato salad for picnics with Carvel. Claimed I was trying to pass it off as my own cooking and he was going to tell Carvel I didn't know how to boil water yet.

Sat on this old bench waiting for that little blue rowboat to come around the point, then hurried down the bank and climbed in. Set the picnic basket next to Carvel's fishing pole and took off my bonnet as we shoved away from shore, let the sun bathe me in warm yellow light. Wasn't long before he proposed marriage.

Had the wedding in this very spot, overlooking the bay. Pleased me no end when Amanda's daughter wanted hers here, too. Told her the same thing Papa told me, "As long as the preacher does it, long as you're married in the eyes of God, not just man."

Mama and Papa were church-goers all their lives, started taking us soon as we could sit up on our own. Heard a lot of sermons I couldn't recall the next day, but Mama's crystal clear voice, the words of the hymns she sang always stayed with me. Should have asked her to sing at our wedding. She made my gown, cooked for days to get ready. Filled every vase she owned with wild roses from the woods, mixed in some lavender from her garden and set them by the trees here where we'd say our vows. Daniel put folding chairs from the church hall in rows facing the bay for the guests. Gravestones of Papa's family off to the side bore silent witness to the event.

Carvel and I were happy as could be on our own farm farther

up Route 8, 'til that day I was putting up stewed tomatoes. Amanda wasn't three months old yet, sleeping in the laundry basket on the pantry floor. I was thinking how blessed we were with a healthy baby and fertile land, a truckload of soy beans ready to go to market. Closed my eyes to say a little prayer and opened them to find the sky dark as midnight, middle of the day. Wind picked up, brought the rain across the field all at once, hit the roof like rocks, left dents in the ground. I scooped up Amanda fast as I could and Carvel ran in from the barn, steered us to the closet under the stairs.

"Hurricane must have changed course," he said. "Wasn't due to make landfall 'til tomorrow, and not this far north. Could have some twisters in it." Stared at me as he closed the closet door behind him like it might be the last time we'd see each other.

Sat on the floor inhaling the scent of furniture polish, vacuum cleaner hose coiled at my feet like a snake, wind howling, rain pounding nonstop. Asked Carvel if he thought it would ever let up, the words barely out of my mouth and there was a crash—wood splintering, glass breaking. Carvel put his arm around me, trying to keep me calm while I held Amanda tight as I dared. Come daybreak, the wind had finally quieted and rain slowed to a drizzle. We left the closet to survey the damage. Weeping willow had fallen through the pantry roof, the basket where Amanda slept the day before was covered with tomatoes, broken glass.

Thought we were going to stay with Mama and Papa just long enough to repair our place, but ended up never leaving. Daniel was headed home from Gettysburg during the storm, the only vacation he ever had. A tractor trailer's brakes locked and nearly folded his car in two. Mama never got over losing him. Went to bed and developed pneumonia that fall, died in January. Made sure to sing her favorite hymn at the funeral, "A rose is blooming there for me, where the soul never dies, and I will spend eternity, where the soul never dies."

Papa went soon after, in March. Found him in his chair, reading glasses still on, Bible open to Ecclesiastes: ". . . a time to be born, and a time to die; a time to plant, and a time to pluck up that which is planted . . ." A shame they couldn't be here with the others. Now there are even laws against being buried on your own land.

Spent the better part of a year on this bench, wishing for things that couldn't be, complaining to God that it was too much to bear. One morning Carvel carried Amanda down the bank, put her on the sandbar. Barely walking on her own, she spread her arms apart like she was ready to fly away. Reminded me of Daniel's drawing of the piece of driftwood, him saying sometimes the only way we could hold on to things was in our minds, that time's what made the sharp edges of the green glass smooth. Seemed like only the day before, I was walking on the beach with Papa. I knew I'd always miss those times, the people who'd left me, but I needed to get back to caring for the ones still here.

After Carvel's first stroke, I came down here again when I could. Watched the waves drift away from the shore, gather strength, come rushing back in again. Prayed he would do the same, but knew in my heart he'd be gone before it was time to harvest what was already growing in the fields. Thinking about Papa saying the bay had a soul and would never die, the same as people, gave me some comfort. Still, it wasn't easy to continue living myself without my dear husband by my side.

A year after he passed on, a developer bought the farm next door. Before the ink on the deed was dry, heavy equipment rolled in, men were pouring concrete where corn once grew, putting up pink and yellow boxes for houses. "Bay Shores," they call it. Like Papa, we left a strip of woods down both sides of the property, with a rough road through the middle, just wide enough for the tractor, for times when we needed to help our neighbors.

Bay Shores people no sooner moved in when they started riding bicycles and walking dogs through the woods like they were at a public park. My heart ached so for Carvel, I wanted to withdraw from the human race, but having that dirt road there turned out to be a blessing. People mostly just wave when they come out in the open, yell, "Hey Miss Carrie," and turn around and go back home. Now and then one comes all the way to the porch with cookies or to ask me how to make crab cakes, and once a little girl gave me a bouquet of clover and Queen Anne's Lace she'd picked from my own land. Had a good laugh about that. Turns out, they sort of kept me connected. Time to let go now, though.

The lady at the Senior Village said people bring some of their own furniture, make their rooms as much like home as possible. All I really need is my memories. Have more good ones than bad. Trust they'll take me back to the times Mama's sweet voice floated across her garden, I skipped barefoot on the beach with Papa by my side, sat in a little wooden rowboat, soaking up the sun.

Sun's chased away the gray now. Sky's blue and clear. Time for me to go to the house, call the lady and tell her I'll be taking that room.

Riverview Road

Shirley Wilson

The view had sold the houses. It was legendary how quickly they went, once on the market. The river seduced all. Sometimes calling a prospective buyer's attention totally away from walls that might need painting or certain repair work that would have to be done, to a fantastic sunset, just beginning. Times like that, the buyer, mesmerized, wandered through the rose-colored rooms in a daze. Or, if another came by at high noon to look the house over with a more careful eye, the lulling sound of soft lapping at the shore line came through open windows, and caught that careful eye, taking it beyond, where the breeze rippled the water and gulls screamed *buy it, buy it.*

The river brought them all together. Sunsets too beautiful not to celebrate brought them out with wine and cheese, and sometimes even a jazz trio. They also celebrated weddings beside the water, and the river's breeze would ruffle the colorful tents set up for food and drink and touch the bride's hair like a blessing. "We are gathered together," the minister would say, as the gulls hollered their approval. On the 4th of July they brought fireworks and sparklers and wore red, white, and blue sun dresses. And of course, on Labor Day, they gathered for a final outdoor celebration—a lavish picnic—all tan and happy from a summer of swimming and sailing on the river, talking of the big fish they had caught this year, or the new dockside restaurant, or a midnight ride when the moonlight on the river had nearly hypnotized. The children, too full of picnic food, and tired of adult talk, would wander down close the river's edge, squishing their toes in the wet sand, wishing they could go swimming this day but having to keep their clothes dry and pert for the occasion, often just looking out or skimming a stone, as if listening to something only they could hear.

The river had another side, particularly during bad storms when lightning cracked the black sky over the darkened, churned up water, and the sound at the shore line turned angry.

It had even flooded once, back in 1942, and stories about this terrible flood, once told, remained in a listener's ear. Especially if the listener's house happened to be in the section that was somewhat low and rain had been coming down heavy for days and days, causing the river to move swiftly in a menacing fashion. But this was nothing to compare with an approaching hurricane, where some unseen thing seemed to wait, way down the river, ready to pounce at any minute, ready to roll through the water like a Loch Ness monster, causing the dreaded high tide to rise higher and higher, as they held their breath and the wind tore at the windows and rattled their doors. Times like this, the river was like someone in the family, suddenly gone mad.

A rare fog, resting on the river like a silver shroud, could be especially beautiful. It would move in quietly in the morning, staying long enough to prod reflection and prick their memories, an occasional fog horn accenting their thoughts, saying look here, see it as it was, don't lie about it.

Besides the children, there was one other who understood the language of the river: the artist who lived near the end of the road. It was she who set up her easel in the sloping yard and captured all its changes. Her house was like an extension of the river, its walls hallowing those waves and white caps, as well as a day without a ripple, a day when you could even see crabs moving slowly, just under the surface. Her walls had brought the fog inside, the rain, the incredible sunsets, the storms. And when it was her time to have them all over (she chose winter), they always wandered through the rooms, glasses in hand, and looked quietly at the new work she had done, displayed on the walls. Gatherings at her house were always more subdued, almost reverent, and the topics more serious. Once, someone said suddenly, "It's as if this house *moves*," and then smiled as if embarrassed, and walked on. But the words hung in the air and a few people, only half in jest, steadied themselves by touching the shoulder of a nearby chair. They saw that the artist had captured on canvas the thing they could not quite express themselves. And though the gatherings at her house were not as much "fun," they were really preferred. It was as if she was some sort of mediator, between the river and themselves. The children, however, hardly noticed the paintings.

In 1982 everything turned around. The river took one of their own, little Bobby Conner, out with his father for his first fishing lesson. A sudden storm churned a water spout that came rapidly down the river, straight for their little boat and capsized it. And Robert Conner never found his boy. Nor did the Coast Guard. After that, almost no one wanted to go to gatherings at the artist's house, and Robert Conner became a recluse. The artist, however, painted even more, and one who had seen it, said this last painting was beautiful " . . . but terribly violent."

Then, in 1990, Mary and Ben Champion's son walked into the river as if called, and never came back. They knew the young man had emotional problems, knew he had come home from college to "rest." But they never, in their wildest dreams, thought he would take his life. There were not quite as many fireworks at their 4th of July gatherings after that, although the children (now grandchildren) enjoyed the sparklers just as much as ever.

The few weddings that took place, generally were now held in churches, some distance from the river. But by now, most young people simply opted to live together without nuptials.

In 2001, Mark Harrison, who had invested almost all of his money in computer technology, lost most of it in the stock market, and had to sell his house. An Asian doctor bought it and brought his three children and mother-in-law to live on the river. There were few children on Riverview Road then, and they were ecstatic to have new friends, and were playing at the river's edge in no time. But some of the older adults said their gatherings would never be the same, that "the closeness was simply gone." Others took immediately to the newcomers, making sure they were invited to all the functions.

The river seemed especially hospitable to the new family's obvious pleasure: "This wonderful water, and right out in our back yards!" When they got into their boat and ventured out, they had a great time in what seemed an unusually long spate of perfect weather and calm waters, just for them. And soon, their pleasure reminded those who watched behind curtains, or on their long sun porches, of their own earlier joy. And, in some small way, brought it back.

But always some sadness would temper their joy—as when Mrs. Simmons died of a heart attack, and for some long months Mr. Simmons sat facing the river in his Adirondack chair, not noticing them wave from their boats though he was looking straight out in their direction.

It was sad, too, to pass by Jenny Moore's house and see her out back trying to work in her beloved garden, with a turban hiding the head now bald from cancer treatments. All these things reminded them that they, too, were getting older—brought their eyes to the windows, where they looked off long and hard over the water. And caused the fog to seem intensified, the fog horns especially jarring.

Boats were sold as some got too old to handle them, and their children either had their own or had moved far away. And another new family moved into the neighborhood.

In the fall of 2001, when they watched the twin towers collapse on their television screens and realized that it was not drama after all, but real, Riverview Road got quiet again. *What's happening?* they asked themselves, taking in the mail wearing plastic gloves. *What on earth is happening?*

Someone started an Easter Sunrise service on the pier that following spring, and what was left of the old group and some of the new, attended. They would not witness the sunrise, but would be able to see the purple and pink hues spread over the water from the east side of town, when the sun came up. Almost everyone was there—even Mr. Simmons who stood with his new granddaughter in his arms. And even Jenny Moore, who had, miraculously recovered, her hair blowing slightly in the breeze, her flowers gracing the cross at the entrance of the pier. They stood in the early morning darkness and lit candles that the breeze threatened to extinguish, and laid out the bread and wine. The bread caught a seagull's eye though it kept a safe—if somewhat noisy—distance. The priest handed out copies of the service and they began singing, "Welcome Happy Morning." Someone had a diabetic attack during the service, turning pale and holding on to the side of the pier, but a whispered plea for sugared mints brought success, and they were passed down swiftly—the Priest, all the while continuing on with the liturgy, as was the canon: In the midst of all, life goes on.

So it went that morning, and while the folded newspapers in their driveways told of stocks still down and fighting continuing in Afghanistan, and how they should still store bottled water and canned food just in case, they passed the cup, Mr. Simmons little granddaughter beaming happily at each, her white blanket turning pink with the now rising rays.

And all the while the river—showing itself between the planks, just under their shoes—slapped rhythmically against the pilings, its water beginning to recede for low tide, its rising sure to follow, as it always had.

And always would.

Choices

Dating a Roman

Matt Cutugno

Something was not right. Saphrax pulled at the hilt of his gladius, nervous. A soldier next to him in line noticed and gave a look that said stop it you're making me nervous. Saphrax and his cohorts had begun their march around the edge of Lake Trasimeno at sunrise, and there was something in the air that morning; not simply a thickening fog but a foreboding. Nearby, a centurion rode on horseback alongside his troops and addressed them.

"Look men," he began, and pointed up to the hills that rose in the distance, "the fires still burn, that's where our enemy is and that's where we are going." And with that he gave his mount a kick and he advanced along a line of common soldiers that seemed to stretch to eternity.

Yes, I see the fires from the Carthaginians, Saphrax thought. But that morning he did not trust the evidence of his senses. He had been a soldier in Consul Flaminius' legion for six weeks. He was a good soldier (a born soldier a superior told him), tall and lean, with fierce black eyes and quick reflexes. He had fought stubborn Etruscans the winter before and though those simple farmers were no match for legionnaires, it had been a good introduction to warfare and Saphrax had fought well. But the Carthaginians were not farmers, and the Consul, the honorable Flaminius, was not equal to the already famous Carthaginian general, Hannibal. Flaminius was a somewhat experienced soldier but a more experienced politician, and when he assured the Senate of Rome that he would pursue Hannibal, find him, and defeat him; he was believed.

But now as the mostly green soldiers headed deeper onto the valley floor, Saphrax wasn't the only one who felt uneasy. The Romans were in a line, two abreast, hardly a formation to fight in. The first thing they learned in training was the invincibility of the Roman phalanx. To fight in such a formation was to not fight alone, to be part of a moving, fighting machine that had defined the Roman military. But now the legion was ambling along the lakeshore in a simple line. Saphrax did not like it. Yes, something was wrong.

Could there have been two archeologists as different as Raymond and James? They were both middle-aged, both suitably overeducated and dedicated professionals, both good men. But the similarities then came to a sudden stop.

Raymond was tall and thin, with thinning black hair, deeply-set eyes, and a ready smile. James was shorter and might be described as stocky, with a wild head of brown hair, and a quiet, almost sleepy demeanor. Raymond was a twice-divorced single man who liked to go out and dance (though he seldom drank). James was happily married enough, and after long days at his lab, his pleasure was to return to his wife, evening TV, and a couple of beers.

An interest in ancient history brought them together years ago, and they had remained partners and friends. A grant from the Ford Foundation (God love it) had taken them to Italy the summer before, where they both worked on a wonderful find: that of the remains of two Roman empire-era men, one partially mummified; miraculously preserved by dry air trapped in a closed-off portion of an underground cave.

The site was near what is now Lake Trasimeno, in the province of Umbria, in central Italy. Many years ago, in antiquity, the lake was larger than it is today, and so what had been a cave along the shore was now in foothills, half a mile from water. The area had been the location of one of Rome's most famous battles: a catastrophic defeat suffered by the empire at the hands of Hannibal, the Carthaginian general in 217 B.C. Some 15,000 Romans lost their lives in a day-long summer slaughter, and the lake was referred to as Sanguineto, blood water, for generations afterward.

Raymond and James had a rare opportunity: to excavate the cave and examine the remains of two men they came to believe had fought in that famous battle.

The line of the legion stretched for a mile, making it impossible for Saphrax to be sure what was happening. Then a cry of voices echoed from the front: an attack had commenced. At first, it was of little concern to the portion of the army near him, the end that trailed from the southernmost hills of Montigeto. Perhaps it was Etruscans, a nuisance and nothing more, or maybe it was a small portion of Hannibal's army, caught out of position. But the sound of the cry grew within minutes and Saphrax and his fellows saw a long and thick line of men, armed and screaming, poured down from the fog shrouded hills before them. Then the concern of the Romans was magnified: from behind them they could first hear and then see another line of Carthaginians approaching.

Legionnaires are taught not to panic and none did. A centurion reared his horse up for a better look while drawing his sword. "Attention soldiers," he yelled, "our enemy comes to us." Saphrax' mind raced fast and he didn't care for his thoughts. Obviously, the great fires his army saw in the distant hills were a ruse. Hannibal wanted Consul Flaminius to think more than a day's march separated the two great factions, and indeed the Consul had sent out no forward troops. The Romans had fallen into a trap: Carthaginians and their allies on three sides and Lake Trasimeno on the fourth. Great noises were thrown into the air as man and beast readied for battle.

James was not a natural public speaker, but occasionally the role came with the job. He was attending the twelfth annual state Archeological Society conference, and, at a podium, he was about to address a small but interested audience. Raymond was seated nearby, and they exchanged a glance. Then James cleared his throat and began.

"It's ironic," he said, "that the discovery I'm speaking about was made possible by an earthquake." He paused, there was no reaction from the audience, and Raymond smiled and shook his head because he had urged his friend to begin with a joke about two archeologists and a traveling saleswoman. Undeterred, James continued.

"The earthquake that struck Umbria last spring caused slight destruction, but it also opened up a cave hidden in a rock formation in an area that in antiquity was part of the shoreline of Lake Trasimeno. In that cave, this is what we found. Lights please."

The room darkened, a slide projector was turned on, and a single slide appeared, then in a cadenced series, others.

"These remarkable slides show the remains of two males who undoubtedly fought in the battle of Lake Trasimeno that your handouts refer too. The year was 217 B.C. In addition to a rich sample of organic matter, we recovered a nicely-preserved gladius, the weapon of choice for Roman legionnaires, two partial breastplates, one of metal and one of leather, and some bits of pottery."

The most startling slide was the first—that of a partially mummified man, buried in sand for over two thousand years, a skeletal face looking up at the camera, arms extended from his body. The second slide was a close-up of his right arm, and a crusted, pitted, and broken, but visible sword nearby.

"After we view these slides a second time, my colleague will speak on our chemical analysis of this extraordinary find."

Chaos! The word pressed into Saphrax's brain like a hot brand. His portion of the army was in a hopeless position. The Carthaginians and their allies were upon them quickly, the fog was too thick, the marshy land beneath them too wet to allow proper deployment, the cold water of the lake nearby, and his cohorts, in general, too inexperienced. Immediately after the initial attack, the Romans were thrown back. The Carthaginians were quicker, more prepared, and attacked with wild eyes. Saphrax fought back, and after the shock of the thoroughness of the ambush, he settled into a deadly rhythm of his own. He represented Rome, his family, friends, and a woman named Stearia whom he hoped to marry after his time in the army. He fought for them. He fought for himself and his fellows too, because the battle was serious indeed. Positioned near the end of the Roman column, they had been attacked from behind by light cavalry. The riders on horses moved through the Roman lines like farmers with scythes through fields of wheat. For every cavalryman dismounted and killed, a half dozen Romans lay on the ground. And blood—it flowed in every way imaginable, from every part of a human body, and at one point Saphrax slipped in a warm, red pool.

A centurion on horseback tried to form a fighting line nearby, but he was felled by arrows. Oddly perhaps, the Carthaginians were not content to kill, they stopped to dismember the dead and stab the wounded again. They fought with hate, while Saphrax's fellows fought merely to survive.

The enemy was talking too, yelling out to each other and the Romans in several languages that Saphrax had neither ability nor interest in understanding.

"Damn you all," he answered to no one in particular and continued his slashing and stabbing, even as he stood among a quickly thinning line of Romans. There was a small hill nearby and Saphrax saw the Consul Flaminius himself, surrounded by his personal guard and some of the legion's more experienced soldiers. They were fighting well, and the Consul was calling out to those around him, trying bravely to reorganize the ranks. Saphrax fought his way to the hill. "If I'm dying," he thought, "I'm dying alongside our best."

Raymond couldn't resist a wisecrack. "It's great to be here this afternoon," he began, "with people who know how much fun a logarithm can be."

The crowd laughed because they were mostly scientists and scientists in general like to laugh at themselves. Raymond's subject was a short background to the radiocarbon testing process used on the Lake Trasimeno artifacts, but he was inclined to minimize the science part.

"Our dating methods were complete," he said, "relative dating was essential since we knew we were dealing with the battle of Lake Trasimeno and artifacts had already been recovered from the plains where most of a Roman legion died. As you know, many types of rocks, as well as pottery, record the Earth's magnetic field at the time they form, and so paleomagnetic dating confirmed the age of the cave's contents. Amino acid racemization yielded the changes through time in the organic matter, but then your handouts explain all that well enough." With that he paused and removed his reading glasses and ran a hand through his hair.

"But what I'd really like to talk about are the men, the two soldiers we found in the cave and how they came to be there. One, whose remains were partially preserved in a bed of dry sand, was Roman. We know that from his armor, his sword. The other was either a Carthaginian, or one of their allies that day, perhaps a Celt, or Lombard, at any rate, not a Roman. We know that by the amounts and kinds of leather found around and among his bones."

The audience listened attentively, but off to the side, James watched his colleague with a rueful look. Raymond had now left the field of science and was freely surfing in the waters of speculation. Not good research, James thought, but he could tell from the faces of listeners that it made good theater.

How long did the battle last that summer day? Saphrax didn't know. It was hours, it must have been, or was it days, it might have been. It didn't matter. He now found himself flat on his back, in and out of consciousness. He had been struck by an arrow, had his side pierced with a pilum lance, and his left hand had been nearly severed at the wrist. He had wrapped his wounds as best he could, he was nearly covered in blood, most of it was not his own. The battle had moved past him, past the hill where the Consul Flaminius had fought and finally been slaughtered with his best troops. There were still cries all around him, but they were of the wounded and dying. Men, mostly Roman, crawled past him, over him and several times he kicked or pushed them away. "Leave me," he managed to say, "let me die in peace." He lay not so far from the Lake's edge, he could hear water sounds, splashing, then flailing, as men drowned in redness. After what seemed like an eternity of staring at the darkening sky, he turned his head slightly and saw a man he knew, a common soldier like him by the name of Cato, lying not six feet away. The man was missing half his face, but with one bloodied eye caught Saphrax's glance.

"We're dead," he said.

"Not yet."

"We're dead," Cato repeated.

"Don't talk, the enemy will return."

Saphrax's comrade laughed, if the bloody gurgle and cough that came from his throat could be a laugh. "The Carthaginians have better men to kill than us," he said.

And then he died, and Saphrax turned his gaze back up to the sky.

Raymond was on a roll: "How did two men, one Roman and one Carthaginian, get into this cave where they both died? Geologists tell us that the grotto was at the shore line of Lake Trasimeno in 217 B.C., so we can postulate that as the Romans were pushed into the water by the onslaught, fighting spilled into the cave, where perhaps the Roman fled to escape. In fact, a portion of metal, an arrow or lance head, was found in the rib cage area of the Roman, suggesting he was killed by the Carthaginian. Fascinating to note is the position of the Roman's body, as he came to be buried in sand. He died on his back, looking up at the cave's ceiling, surely wondering what had happened that Summer day as one of Rome's greatest legions, led by the Consul Flaminius, suffered such a terrible defeat."

James had to laugh. His partner was setting new records for speculation, postulating this, theorizing that, and to punctuate his final remarks he showed the first slide again, that of the man in the sand. Some in the audience took notes.

"Two men," Raymond said in closing, "in a gruesome ballet amidst an entire day's dance with death." And with that he smiled, and thanked the sponsors and attendees and his partner James, and the presentation was over, and there was applause.

When Saphrax awoke, there was silence. It was complete: not men, nor beast, nor sky, nor lake was making a sound. Or perhaps Saphrax couldn't hear. It didn't matter. He rolled his head on his shoulders and looked around. It was day, it must be the day after the battle. An odor, the most awful smell he could imagine, was everywhere, the smell of every vile and deadly thing in the world mixed together, it forced him up on one elbow.

There was fog in the valley leading from the lake. Everywhere, on every patch of earth as far as he could see, there were dead bodies, many of them Roman, faces frozen in masks of death, their white service tunics dyed red. There were men and parts of men, horses and parts of horses, weapons of every description, bloodied. He reached out with a hand (the one that remained useful) to steady himself, and the very ground was soaked. Saphrax wasn't afraid to die, but he didn't wanted to die like this, bathing in blood and horrific stench.

It was then the rain started, slowly at first, sad drops of water from heaven, and the sky darkened. I've got to move, he thought, somewhere else, anywhere. Then he saw a formation of rocks near the Lake's edge, and the small mouth of a nearly-hidden cave. I'll die there, he decided and with a mighty effort he stood up. There was the entrance, was it yards away or was it miles? He stepped forward, over one body, over two more, over a pile of ten. Slowly, slowly, so as not to slip, if he fell he wouldn't get up. It was raining harder now.

Then he was inside the cave. Daylight lit the entrance, then darkness inside. But it was warm and dry and it didn't smell like a thousand dead men, like it did at the Lake's edge. Quiet, there was quiet, it was a good place to lay down. But there was something else, though it was so dark, and the pain inside him so profound, he wasn't sure. He heard breathing that was not his own. Saphrax was not alone in the cave. His sad eyes began to adjust to the light and he saw a man, a solider, a Carthaginian, lying against a rock on the cave's floor. He was hurt badly but alive and he was looking at Saphrax.

The twelfth annual Archeological Society conference was ended and Raymond and James were staying at the local Holiday Inn. Now they were having a drink in the lounge: James with his usual beer while Raymond was enjoying a cappuccino.

"Dance with death," James laughed, "that was quite a turn of phrase."

"I missed my calling," Raymond answered.

"Why don't you give up science and take up marketing or advertising?"

"Well, I know one thing, people would rather hear inter-esting speculation than uninteresting science." Raymond was only half-serious but James understood his point. That's what made them a good team. James was the bookworm, Raymond told jokes, but together, they got the job done.

At that point a well-dressed man approached the two at the table where they sat. He nodded at them and smiled.

"Excuse me gentlemen," he began, "My name is Evan and I was at the conference this morning, I saw your presentation."

"Ah, a science lover," Raymond said, "Have a seat." The man sat. James did the introductions.

"It's a pleasure," Evan said. "Actually, I'm in a different line of work than yourselves." He presented a business card. "I'm with United Pictures," he said, "you know, movies."

The cave mouth was darkened; Saphrax knew it was night. Had he been there a full day, or two? It didn't matter. Both he and his companion were on the cave floor, propped against rocks. They simply sat. Both seriously wounded, both aware they were dying. The Carthaginian said something to Saphrax when he arrived, though neither spoke the other's language. But the enemy had offered him a drink of water from his leather flask, and the Roman accepted. A truce had been declared: neither had come to the cave to fight.

"Will Hannibal attack Rome?" Saphrax said in a near whisper. "If he does he'll be defeated."

His companion coughed, and said something. Red dripped from his lips. Saphrax wanted to answer with defiance, to demonstrate that only a battle had been lost, not a war. There was no strength.

"I'm in development," Evan said, "I look for story lines, good ideas, and I really liked your battle tale, two survivors, one Roman, one Carthaginian, dance of death and all that."

James and Raymond shared a look, but they resisted the temptation to snicker. They were scientists and they were mature men, they knew they weren't screenwriters. But Evan anticipated what they were thinking.

"Listen, I know you guys aren't screenwriters, but if you ever want to write down a few ideas, a treatment we call it, fire it off to me, who knows where it might lead?"

Evan was a personality. He had an engaging smile, bright eyes, and he talked fast. Before James and Raymond knew it, he had them thinking of Hollywood and movie stars, notoriety, and royalty checks.

"Hey listen, I have to get going," Evan said finally. "If you're ever in L.A.," he said, leaving the sentence unfinished and just like that he was up from the table and gone. The two archeologists sat a moment in silence. Raymond held the movie man's business card.

"United Pictures presents: The Battle of Lake Trasimeno," James said in a low voice full of portent, like the coming attraction in a movie theater.

"Starring Bruce Willis and Samuel Jackson," Raymond added, in the same tone.

Then they both had a good laugh.

The Carthaginian was dead. The cave was dark and Saphrax heard no breathing but his own. He finished a last sip of water and threw the leather flask across the cave floor. He was tired, had he ever been so tired in his life? His clothes were soaked, had he spilled water on himself, was he sweating? No, it was blood.

He was on his back, staring up at blackness, thinking about Stearia. She had a mole, a beauty mark she called it, on her upper lip. He could picture it perfectly. He remembered walks they would take in the gardens behind her family's estate. It was spring and the smell of flowers was so strong it made a man believe in love. Stearia smiled at him and gave his hand a squeeze. She was so beautiful, wasn't she?

The Line

W. Michael Farmer

Paris in July— it's all tourists strolling the Champs Élysées, the Eiffel Tower dressed head-to-toe in brilliant light standing tall above myriad streetlights, and, motoring on the Seine, long boats filled with couples watching only each other as they pass under centuries-old bridges, by Notre Dame and the Tuileries Gardens. He and his friends wandered its streets, sniffed gorgeous faint vapor trails of vivid perfume left by elegant women, sipped wine in the bistros, snapped a thousand ordinary travel pictures, and stayed in an old hotel with an elevator that could hold no more than two and one large bag.

They were returning home from a business trip south of Paris, playing tourist for a few days in the "City of Lights" before their flight to New York. "Business trip" meant three weeks in the Loire Valley living as only the French knew how—pastries with *café au lait* in the mornings; two hours of work before lunch; three hours for lunch with red wine, steak tartar, and exquisite vegetables; two hours of work after lunch; little breaks for wine and cheese in the afternoon; a little of this or a little of that; and, evenings spent on specially arranged visits touring wineries or castles.

She had been there in the south with them—one of the interpreters hired to ensure that rarely used English and unintelligible French was clear to both sides. There were wrinkles around her eyes, a once girlish figure was growing wider, and gravity was doing bad things to her breasts. Still, her brown eyes, quick smile, throaty laugh, and quick-witted repartée made her charming. Although she stayed at the same small hotel as the Americans, he rarely saw her except when they left on the bus that came for them in the mornings or when she traveled with them on the evening tours, and he didn't pay much attention to her then except to marvel at how facile she was with simultaneous translation. Her delay in translating French or English as it was spoken was never more than a second or two—no worse than the delay between parties in a transatlantic telephone call.

On the return from their last tour, one to a winery far up the valley, he sat by himself near the back of the bus. Most of the Americans were having a raucous good time after enjoying a little too much wine, goat cheese, and a five-course dinner topped with cherries jubilee and numerous toasts to their hosts. The bus lights cast a warm yellow glow against the windows, black mirrors in the dark, as the tour guide and driver consulted a map for the best way back to the hotel over narrow, winding country roads. She too sat by herself a few rows ahead of him and across the aisle. Glancing toward the back, her eyes met his. He smiled and nodded. She smiled back smoothing a strand of her dark auburn hair away from her face.

The train back to Paris left on a bright, sun-filled morning and whizzed past huge fields of golden sunflowers, ancient villages, and dark green forests. As its passengers disembarked at the Gare du Nord, he offered to carry her valise to the cab queue. She thanked him with a nod and warm smile. They exchanged business cards and promised to stay in touch as the interpreters and the Americans stood waiting for their cabs. She wrote her home telephone number on hers. Handing it to him, she said, "Call me, Cheri. If you need help finding places in Paris I'll be pleased to direct you. Bon voyage!" Smiling his thanks and nodding, he held the cab door open for her as the cabbie tossed her valise in the trunk, took a few murmured instructions from the back seat, and roared off into the chaotic traffic.

The Americans checked into a small hotel wedged between two ancient businesses on a street near the Eiffel Tower. In his third-floor room overlooking the street, he unloaded his pockets and tossed the detritus of their train ride on his dresser before hurrying down the steps to join the others. As he closed the door, he saw her card on the dresser staring back at him. He paused, but decided there was no need to bother her for advice. They sat outside a bistro under an umbrella alternately colored red, white, and blue. Their waiter was a stereotypical snooty Frenchman who wrinkled his nose in disgust at anyone eating beef that was cooked beyond rare. Over chocolate mousse, their conversation was filled with suggestions about what to do the next day. Staring at the amber cognac in his snifter, he thought again of the card on his dresser. It would be great fun to see Paris through the eyes of a Parisian.

The next day, amid the crowds waiting to enter the Louvre, he found a payphone and learned the protocol for getting a call through. Three rings burbled on the line before she answered.

"Bonjour?"

"Uh . . . bonjour, Madame. I hate to disturb you, but I was wondering if it might be convenient for me to take you to dinner this evening?"

"Ah! Monsieur! It's so good of you to call. Did you have some place in mind?"

"Well, no . . . I was hoping you might suggest a place."

"I travel so much I stay home as often as I can. Why don't you let me fix you dinner here? The view is superb from my apartment balcony and I can point out many interesting places."

"Oh, but that is way too much trouble!"

"No, no. It will be my pleasure. Come around six o'clock. Oui?"

"Well sure, that's very gracious of you."

Before he rang off, she gave him directions to her place, requiring only that he take the Metro from the stop in front of his hotel, get off in four stops, and walk a block.

The rest of the day he was in high spirits and felt like a teenager planning a date with a prom queen. How great to learn about Paris from a charming French lady who spoke excellent English! Why, he assured himself, after this he'd be the office expert on Paris.

He didn't have any trouble finding her apartment, and on the way bought her a dozen long-stem roses as a hostess gift. She met him at the door wearing wonderful perfume and an elegant cream-colored dress. Delighted with the roses, she carefully put them in a crystal vase, hung up his jacket, and gave him a tour of her apartment. The walls, covered with a park mural in pastel greens on a light background, held a couple of expensive abstract paintings and several black and white photographs of young women on the streets of Paris during the Second World War. He was impressed with her large floor-to-ceiling library of books in French, English, and Spanish. He noted the threadbare first edition of Proust; she was surprised and pleased that he even knew who Proust was, much less that he had actually read *In Search of Lost Time*. Crowded into a corner of her small office was a large organ with complex sheet music on its rack. His admiration for her grew as she told him over cocktails about her adventures as a translator. The sun faded as though in a dream, the nightlights emerging in the twilight. She served him Brie, paté, and red wine while telling fascinating tales about fooling the Germans during the resistance. Then came a steak dinner with a nice Soave Bolla. He drank more than he intended but didn't care. They were having a wonderful time.

It was completely dark as the last drops of the tart orange flavor of Cointreau trickled down his throat. Arising from their candle-lit table, she stepped out on her balcony. Looking over the city, she motioned him to join her. "Come, mon ami, come and see this sight!"

Stepping into the soft night air, he gasped at the lights spread out before them. Nearly speechless he could only murmur in his best French, "*Sacré bleu!*"

"Look, there." She pointed to the Eiffel Tower, rising in brilliant majesty, sparkling against the clear black sky. Delighting in the scene spread out before them he hugged her. She turned and hugged him. They kissed, first gently, and then with the passion for which the French are famous.

She laid her hands on his chest and looking in his eyes whispered, "The bedroom is just down the hall. I'll be right back." She swished passed him toward the bathroom. He stared after her, his mind in turmoil, the bright light of sudden recognition glowing in his brain. He was at a milestone in his life.

He knew if he stayed he had crossed a line, a line he had not crossed in fifteen years of marriage, a line over which there was no going back. He could walk out the door or he could stay. He made a fist and thumped his jaw to think. Why had he come? What was he expecting? He had fantasized this might happen, but had denied to himself that he was even thinking about it. He paused and stared at the door across the dimly lit room. He heard a voice in his brain saying, Run, fool, run! But another whispered, You only live once, take what life has to give, it's the price of living.

Turning slowly, his feet feeling like they were made of lead, he walked down the hall and found a neatly-made bed with the coverlet and bright white sheets turned back. He sat down feeling very old and very world-weary. As he began taking off his shoes he told himself he was going to Hell. Well, if I am, he thought, gritting his teeth, I'm going to enjoy the trip. He crawled under the sheets and waited.

She appeared out of the soft summer darkness in a light, lacy dressing gown.

"Forgive the narrow bed. It is a small apartment and I have no room for a large one."

Smiling at her, he said in a voice so low she barely heard him, "We won't need a large one."

Sitting on the edge of the bed, she turned her back to him and let the gown slide from her shoulders as she slid over beside him. They kissed and then again—deeply. He felt desire spread across his body like the warmth of a swallow of good bourbon. He was filled with wonder that she desired him.

Their passion lasted into the late hours; he left her only to avoid his friends seeing him come back at an hour that would generate speculation and gossip. The Metro didn't run after 1:00 A.M.; she had to call him a taxi. He kissed her good-by and thanked her for a wonderful evening. She kissed him back murmuring, "Farewell, Cheri."

A few short hours with her erased a lie he had believed for years. The revelation made him angry. He could not believe he'd crossed the line after all those years of fidelity. He knew there was no going back. But what she taught him! Things he'd never imagined a woman did with a man. He wanted to hit himself in the head with a brick for the lie he had come to believe about himself. Over his married life, his wife, in her cold reluctance for intimacy, convinced him he wasn't much of a lover. All those years he believed what she told him! It pained him like an old war wound that didn't heal. Now he knew he could pleasure a woman, even one that was much more experienced than he, pleasure her often, and pleasure her well. All those years of what might have been with his wife—wasted!

In the taxi back to the hotel he wondered, if in crossing the line, he had lost his soul. It didn't feel like it. He wasn't about to leave his wife. They had children and he loved her. The French woman had wanted only a brief moment of intimacy to warm the chill of her solitary life, not a lifetime commitment. She didn't want him to leave his wife. She didn't even want an affair. What was wrong with what they did? Had he, had they, actually done anything wrong? He knew he was playing with fire, but maybe, this one time, he hadn't been burned.

He flew back home determined to improve his married life. From the moment he walked in the door, and to his amazement, his once distant wife was as enthusiastic about their marriage bed as he. Their lovemaking was more passionate than he could ever remember—even when they were first married. It was strange and wonderful. He couldn't imagine the source of his wife's epiphany. She denied there was one, and he believed her. The guilt he felt for being unfaithful was like a fog, it came and went with the tides of their desire. However, any guilt he felt virtually disappeared when the ardor of their lovemaking cooled in a few months. Drinking a little more than usual, but not getting drunk, sleeping more and exercising less, gaining weight, he recognized he had all the symptoms of stress and depression. Now, however, the dark fog that use to drift into his mind wasn't as thick as it was before France. He now had, at least, good memories of lovemaking, and he didn't blame himself for being a bad lover.

The hard carapace of morality that kept him protected from tempting liaisons cracked after his trip to France. As his wife's ardor cooled and the months flew, he survived several temptations to cheat. But, he had crossed the line; temptation's pull was stronger, the desire for forbidden fruit a taste on his lips that wouldn't go away. Within two years he crossed the line again, and then again. Each time he expected to be caught, steeling himself for years of grief and embarrassment, and marveling that he wasn't. He loved all his lovers. They knew his situation, demanding in return for his attention nothing except a little of his time and his heartfelt care.

As the years passed, he began to understand the meaning of hell. He hated himself for sneaking around and lying to his wife and knowing his colleagues knew what he did and still tolerated his peccadilloes. Earlier in his life, he had always spoken the truth. Now he lived in a world of secrets, a cheater with no morals, the worst kind of fool. He had nightmares of being caught *in flagrante delicto* and escaping through public places naked, exposed for all to see. He and his wife drifted further apart, still cordial with each other, but living in different worlds sharing nothing about what was happening or true in their lives.

The day came when he could no longer live a life filled with lies and determined to change regardless of the cost. He had to tell his wife what he had become, beg her forgiveness, and try to make things right. She might never trust him again. She might kick him out. He only knew he had to try.

Their lives were so separated and independent from each other that he literally had to make an appointment to talk with her. Two days, two days of agony, two days of wondering what was going to happen, passed before he finally faced her.

Feeling his pulse thumping in his ears, he swallowed down bile as she sat down across from him at the kitchen table, her face a picture of curiosity.

"I . . . uh . . . I don't know any easy way to tell you this so I'll just spit it out. I've had several affairs in the last few years. I'm truly sorry."

Her expression changed from one of curiosity to a smile, to a giggle of relief.

She said with a broad grin, "Oh, yeah? With who?"

He was so relieved she wasn't outraged and playing the part

of a wronged woman, he rattled off their names—all, that is, except the first one, the one in France. She was acquainted with them all, one or two she even knew socially. She continued to smile and look pleased, as though she was proud of him. He was mystified at her indulgence. Just so all their cards were on the table, he asked in wonder at her reaction, "Have you had any affairs?"

She nodded, still smiling. "Yes."

"When?" Surprise leaped from his voice.

"About ten years ago—you were in France." She named the date. It was the same day he had been in the French woman's bed, perhaps even the same hour.

Guilt lifted off his shoulders like a hot air balloon rising into blue infinity on a cold autumn morning. He saw she felt the same way. He suggested they seek counseling; she shrugged and said, "Let's think about it, counseling is expensive and it takes a long time." They hugged and he whispered again that he was sorry. She nodded, but said nothing. They didn't say much the rest of the evening, wandering about the house and yard alone in their thoughts. When they slid into bed, she gave him a peck on the cheek, their only touch for the rest of the night. He lay awake a long time staring into the darkness, hands clasped behind his head. She peacefully snored.

They stayed together another year. Counseling didn't put them back together again. Their grown children were confounded that they were married so long and then fell apart. None of their half-lie explanations for what was going on between them rang true, and the children knew it, but it was all the truth they could face, then. He moved into an apartment. She got the house, half his retirement, and some alimony. He wanted it that way, even when he learned that she had a lover during all the years he'd had his affairs.

He changed jobs and moved far away. A young woman convinced him he couldn't live without her. They were married. In her bed, the pleasures of his first affairs returned. On warm summer evenings when the peepers and crickets sang and frogs croaked, he liked to sit watching the lights twinkle across the river while he sipped Jack Daniels neat. She often sat with him, keeping his musings company.

One evening she asked, "How did we ever get to be so happy?"

Smiling, he took a sip of the liquid fire and felt the warmth spread down his throat. "Oh, sometimes, but not often, it's across the line."

The Nail Dream

W. Michael Farmer

On the way out of Albuquerque, a golden oldies radio station played Bob Dylan's *With God On Our Side*. Teresa, her mind zoned far away, was resting her head against her hand, her elbow propped against the open window of our old Ford truck. The wind streamed and whipped her long hair making it look like raging black fire. From the corner of my eye, I saw her slowly turn and stare toward Dylan's sarcastic, atonal lyrics. After awhile she said, "Do they? Do the whites have God on their side?"

We rattled down the two-lane a few more miles before I said, "Let me tell you a story."

You know great grandfather's stories of his life in the Indian School. Whites ripped him from the arms of his parents and held him against his will. He was forbidden to speak our language, his hair was cut short, his clothes were chosen for him, he wasn't allowed home visits— even for summer vacations, and he was beaten for breaking rules. When I heard those stories, I was outraged, just as you were.

The Indian Schools have been closed for over three generations. For our people Charlie Lummis battled the Bureau of Indian Affairs to make them change. The school in Albuquerque, it changed a lot—for the better. Still, when I was a young man, I believed a debt of justice was owed great grandfather who was *educated* before Lummis came. I schemed and dreamed, with no success, about how to right the wrongs done to him. A dream many times came to me when I studied how to make things right. I didn't know if it had anything to do with great grandfather, but I decided to ask his interpretation anyway.

He was nearly a hundred, and blind. We talked together often, and drank grandmother's strong black coffee. One day I said, "Grandfather, I have a dream. It comes many times. There is a wooden stair step with a nail sticking up through it, and a big black boot is about to step on it. But I always wake up before the boot hits the nail. I don't understand this dream. Somehow, I feel, it is about your Indian School days. Can you explain it?"

He nodded slowly, thinking, his head bowed. Then, looking straight at me with his sightless eyes, he said, "Old Braddock was the meanest man I ever knowed. He had many years. His bald head, big hooked nose, and big empty eyes made him look like a buzzard. He used an ol' fishin' cane stick to beat us on the hand when any of us crossed him. Every mornin' when the wall clock pointed to seven, he was at the door of our classroom on the second floor. First, he made us answer questions about what he showed us the day before. If a boy give a wrong answer, Braddock whacked his hand with the cane while he told him the right answer, and, then, made him repeat it.

"One Saturday, Braddock caned Charlie Rope's hand to bloody meat. Charlie give the wrong answer three times in two days. Charlie, two other friends, and me, we sat out behind the shop building next day to figure out how we was gonna stop old Braddock from beatin' us. Charlie, he wanted payback. He was wantin' to stick'm with somethin' sharp. Hurt him good, but he didn't want to go to no jail neither. It got late and we still didn't have no good ideas about it. We decided we'd talk the next Sunday after we thought about it some more.

"Monday, old Braddock come stompin' down the second floor steps leadin' us to the dinning hall for lunch. He got about five steps down, yelled, 'Damn!' and rolled down the steps all the way to the bottom. His arms and legs was a flyin' ever which a way."

There was a big smile on grandfather's face. He was wind-milling his arms about like he remembered Braddock as he fell down the stairs.

"When Braddock hit the floor, his neck was broke, and he was dead. We was all glad. Life was better at the school after he fell."

"What made him fall grandfather?"

He shook his head. "Don't know for sure. I think it was the nail, it tripped him up. I seen a big shiny one stickin' out when we was comin' down the stairs. I was careful not to step on it. When the Superintendent and the doctor looked at the steps they didn't find no nail like I seen. I looked at the step the next day. There was no nail, not even a nail hole. Your dream says there was one."

He shrugged his shoulders and shook his head. "Don't know where it went. The white man's God, sometimes he's on the side of the Indians, too. That's what the padres say. Maybe God, he tripped up old Braddock with the nail, and then hid it. I don't know."

"Grandfather, who put the nail there? Was it Charlie Rope? Did one of his friends stick old Braddock like Charlie wanted?"

"I don't know my son. Maybe Charlie did it. I never heard him say. Maybe Charlie's boy, Joe Foot, he knows. That's all I have to say."

I knew when great grandfather said that, it was the end of the story.

Joe Foot was in his late seventies, clear-eyed, and very active. I stopped by his fifty-percent off Indian jewelry store in Old Town. He knew who I was and talked freely.

"Do you remember Charlie talking about a man named Braddock who taught at the Indian School?"

"Old Braddock? Sure! Real mean. Charlie said he looked like a buzzard flapping his arms when he went flyin' off them steps and broke his neck."

"Yeah, that's the man. Did he ever say anything about Braddock stepping on a nail just before he fell?"

"Why?"

Joe squinted at me, his mouth drawn in a tight, straight line.

"You ain't plannin' to get nobody in trouble are you. It wasn't Charlie's fault."

"No! Look, I've dreamed many times about a boot about to step on a nail. Great grandfather says that maybe the dream is about Braddock stepping on the nail. The nail's what made him fall. He said when he looked at the step the next day there wasn't even a nail hole in the wood! Curiosity's eatin' me alive. I gotta know what happened."

Joe smiled. "Yeah, there was a nail. Charlie saw it, too. He didn't do it though! Wished he had. He liked to say, *Fifth step'll get you ever time.*"

"Fifth step?"

"Yeah, there was fifteen steps in them stairs and the nail was on the fifth step down. Old Braddock just wasn't limber enough to roll down ten steps without killin' himself. Charlie said that he fell down the entire fifteen steps a couple of weeks before Braddock stumbled, and that he only got a few bruises and a twisted knee. He had to use a walking stick for about month though. Guess that's the breaks—no pun intended."

I laughed. "Yeah, that's the breaks. Is there anyone else who might know something about that nail?"

He stared at the ceiling for a moment thinking, and then rattled off some names of the children or grandchildren of our father's and grandfather's friends. I talked with them all over the next few days. They remembered hearing stories about Braddock. They all remembered hearing about the nail. Some saw it, some didn't, and if it was seen, it was gone when they looked for it later. Some said a nail hole was there others said it wasn't. The story was a pile of contradictions. It didn't make any sense.

The nail stories chewed at my mind for a week. It was like trying to weave a blanket without knowing the design first. I thought about the threads that went into it. The nail was in the fifth step down. That meant, at eight inches per step, it was in a step eighty inches off the floor. The children in that class were only ten or twelve years old, which I took to mean they were less than five feet tall—sixty inches—they couldn't reach the fifth step to drive in the nail without standing on something. They'd surely have been caught if they'd tried. An adult must have put the nail there. Was it one of the teachers? I doubted that. Putting a nail in the stair and expecting Braddock to step on it sounded more like a childish prank than something an adult would do.

Some claimed they saw the nail and walked around it and some said they didn't see it. How could it be there for some and not others? Then I thought, *What if someone pushed the nail down out of sight before they all saw it?* It couldn't be done with a shoe, the nail would just pass right through the sole like it had for Braddock. I chewed on that one for a few days before I had a head slap. I called Joe Foot. His old gravelly voice answered on the second ring.

"Joe, do you remember saying Charlie fell down the same steps just a couple of weeks before Braddock, and that he used a cane for about a month?"

"Yeah?"

"Do you know what the cane looked like? Did it have a metal cap on its end?"

"I don't know. Charlie never described it. The Superintendent lent it to him, and Charlie returned it when he didn't need it no more. I remember him saying it was so long he used it more like a staff than a cane. It might be in the Indian School Superintendents exhibit over at the Pueblo Center, if you want to see it. I was just over there last week."

I felt my heart beat a little faster.

"One more question, did Charlie ever mention any adult Indians living at the School?"

"Naw, don't think so. They was all kids . . . Wait . . . Yeah! There was one. He was the janitor and handy man. I know his youngest daughter, Clara Ruth. Nice lady. Must be close to eighty now. Lives over on Menaul."

My heart rate went up some more.

"Thanks Joe! You've been a great help!"

"Bueno! Adios!"

I found the telephone number for a Ms. C. Ruth on Menaul. I was about to hang up when a yawn-filled voice answered. I explained who I was, and asked if I could visit in a couple of hours to talk with her about her father's life at the Indian School. She said she'd be glad to have some company.

At the Pueblo Center's exhibit showcasing the history of Indian School Superintendents, great grandfather's Superintendent stood in a large, free-standing photo blown-up to life-size, cane in hand. The cane had a shiny metal cap on the end! I stared at it wondering how I could be so lucky to find its picture. Then I noticed it in the case at the foot of the picture along with a big gold watch and chain, and a few other personal effects. I had to get down on one knee and twist my head around a sign to look at the end of the metal cap. Right in the middle was an indent— just like someone had pushed it against a nail! I felt like I'd just discovered a gold mine. People must have thought I was a little tipsy when I ran out the door shaking my fist rushing to get over to Clara Ruth's house.

Petite, white-haired, sparkling eyes in a face that had seen hard times and good, and a smile never far from her lips, Clara Ruth answered the door before I knocked a second time. She showed me into her kitchen, walking down a little hall whose walls held some really nice blankets she had made. I sat down at her table; she poured us tea from an old copper pot puffing on an ancient but clean stove and studied me hard as I told her about Braddock and how I was trying to find out about my nail dream.

Staring at my eyes through her round, silver-framed granny glasses, she listened, her head cocked to one side to catch all my words. When I finished my story, she nodded.

"Yes, my father was the janitor at the school in those days. He was trained at the school. When he went back to the pueblo, the people shunned him. They said the white man had tainted him. He had to leave. He was very angry with the people and the school, but the school took him back. He had to earn a living. He had suffered much to learn the white man's ways. Old Braddock, he made them all suffer. I can't tell you about the nail. If Braddock's relatives find out, they'll want my house, maybe even my life in payment for his."

I begged her to tell me what she knew. I had to know, and I promised I'd never breathe a word of what she told me.

Her eyes looked through mine searching for a lie. "You promise not to speak of this to anyone?"

"Yes. I swear I'll not say anything."

She stared out the window for a moment, and then murmured, "It was an accident."

"What! You mean your father didn't deliberately put a nail there to stick Braddock?"

"Yes, that's what I mean. He stored his tools under the stairs and drove the nail into the stair step so he could string a piece of wire between the steps and the wall. He wanted to hang some wet rags up to dry. The wood was soft, just pine, and one hard hammer stroke sent it all the way through the step. He was just comin' out from under the stairs to drive it back down, when old Braddock came stompin' down the steps, stepped on it, and went crashin' to the bottom. My father, he didn't like old Braddock 'cause he was so mean, but he'd never kill him. One of the boys followin' Braddock, he saw the nail and figured out why Braddock tripped. He had this big cane, and quick as a snake he took the end and pushed the nail down out of sight. Father ran back under the stairs and pulled the nail all the way out, and then ran to get old Braddock help. It was too late. Braddock's neck was broke. That night father replaced the step so there wasn't even a nail hole to give away what happened. It was easy because several of the steps were replaced after the kid with the cane fell down the whole flight a while before. Remember now, you promised not to speak of this to anyone."

I promised her I wouldn't tell, and I never did. She went to the Grandfathers several years ago and none of her family is left so I guess it's okay to tell you now. After she told me what happened, the dream never returned. But, once in a while, the words of great grandfather float through my mind, "The white man's God, sometimes he's on the side of the Indians, too."

Teresa twirled a piece of her hair around her finger as the vermillion haze on the horizon disappeared into the sun's vanishing light. After awhile she smiled, and started humming, *With God On Our Side*.

Country Road

Keppel Hagerman

The old man stirred, snorted, and woke himself up. Already daybreak he could hear sparrow's chirping and the raucous of crows. He lay still trying to remember where he was, what day it was. He wondered why he didn't hear the rattle and chatter of his wife and daughter in the kitchen. His thoughts cleared and he grimaced with pain. His wife was dead and Molly had run off with a strange man years ago.

The noisy crows distracted him. By hell, he thought, I'll blast those suckers clear out of my cornfield.

"It's gonna be a scorcher today," he muttered out loud while he searched for shoes and overalls. He grabbed his wife's old straw hat remembering the doc's warning about keeping his head covered in the hot sun. Then he picked up his shot gun from the corner of the room, stuffed some shells in a pocket and finally popped a big chaw of tobacco in his mouth.

Today the sun seemed hostile to him. The corn was pitiful, dried up, and picked over by the crows. Already the familiar throb in his temples had begun. He fired at random. His aim was way off, but the shot-gun blast startled the crows away. Frustrated and angry, he threw the gun down then pushed it under a row of stalks. He looked up to see a silver-blue convertible come to a screeching halt across the dirt road. Through cataract covered eyes he made out the form of a tall, thin, black-haired man wearing a red sport shirt.

"City slicker," the old man snarled to himself.

In the car he could see a bare-shouldered woman. Her long blonde hair glistened like corn tassels in the sun and she wore dark glasses. "Bet she's got on them durned short pants," the old man growled.

"What can I do for you, Mister?" he said to the young man who had gotten out of the car. The girl walked over to the old man. A short green skirt rippled above her knees. She sure smells good, the old man thought. Her perfume prodded a memory of magnolia and Molly. She had been a handful to raise but it was that slick-talking salesman stole her from him and her Ma, well nigh killed them both.

The man from the convertible spoke again, "Old timer, we're lost. Maybe you can help us."

"Shet your mouth, you don't know me well enough to call me old timer." He spat out tobacco juice which barely missed the man's shoes.

The girl smiled up at the old man.

She's sure pretty, the old man thought to himself—little biddy white teeth, eyes blue as field flax. He and Ma had loved her so much, and that city bastard took her away.

"I ain't telling you nothing, Sonny", the old man said.

"Come on, Jill let's get out of here," the man shouted to the girl. "This old crab is too ornery to help us. We'll find a filling station and get some decent directions to Richmond."

The old man was bent over scratching around in the tall corn stalks.

"You're goddamned right I'm ornery. Now git! You git the hell out of here."

He pulled the shot gun up through the corn stalks. The girl gasped and began to run toward the car.

"Molly, you're my daughter and you belong here. You ain't going no where this time," said the old man grabbing her arm.

The girl whispered, "My name is not Molly, and I'm not your daughter." But the old man didn't hear her. He was glaring at the man in the car who jumped out and yelled, "You old fool, put that gun down."

"I swear to God I'll blast the guts out of you if you come any closer."

The young man stood still. The girl looked from one to the other, hesitated, then turned to the old man.

"Pappy, let me go with him," she said. "I need to go, Pappy. I got young 'uns in the city. They'll be getting hungry. I got to get home to them." She reached up and put her arms around him.

The old man scowled, his face twisted with pain. He rubbed his head, looked hard at the girl, then let her go.

"By gawd, you could always wheedle anything out of me gal. You swear you'll come back to see your old Pa?"

"I swear it, Pappy."

The old man moved aside. The girl walked steadily to the car. She got in the convertible, then turned and waved good-bye, as the driver revved up the engine. The wheels spun and they bolted off. The old man stared a long time at the speeding car, until all was left to see were layers of dust filtered in the sun settling on the empty road.

Solatium

Lawrence James

The thin man hopped from the tracks to the wooden platform, opened his black cardboard suitcase, removed a clean, discolored handkerchief, patted his forehead, looked at the town below, considered the long walk back, and smiled a thin smile. There was really no choice. Never had been.

Beneath his yellow straw boater, a head too small even for his thin body craned forward above a wide, red tie with a yellow horn of plenty swirled down its center. His small chin backed away from two great white teeth. This apparition stared down from the platform of the deserted station on the side of the mountain. "Hello, people. Yes, yes, it's me. I have returned. Come to kill the fatted calf."

Gripping the black cardboard tightly, the thin man made his way down the uneven wooden steps, toes tapping ahead for safety. Reaching the bottom, he walked in the center of the street toward the blackness of the pool room door, suitcase flopping loosely against his leg.

The books with the belt around them slapped Thomas Jefferson O'Hara's back as he bounced through the forest. The flat side would slap against him, then another step and the sharp edge of the books would dig into his back. Thomas tilted his tiny face back to the sun, walked into a tree, laughed, aimed at an opening, tilted his head back and launched himself again.

The chunk of mud whirred by in front of his face and spattered through the bushes. A short, fat boy crashed to a stop in front of Thomas' face.

"I'm King Dennis. I own this forest." He stepped with his feet wide apart toward Thomas until his sneering lips were all the boy could see. "What're you doing in it?"

"Walking. Walking home. That's all."

"I don't care." Dennis blinked and licked his lips. "I don't give a damn. This is my forest. Get out."

Thomas said nothing. A bird called once and then was quiet. Dennis' breath was hot and fetid against Thomas' face. "Get out!"

Thomas started toward where he thought the road was. Dennis jumped in his path. "You make me sick." His yellow shirt had flower designs and stains scattered over it. His denim pants were worn and old, the cloth, like his round face, soft and mottled. Thomas stared at the bulge in the fat boy's crotch. A feeling of jelly put its soft fingers onto his muscles, radiating weakness. Dennis whispered. "Maybe it's too late for you to get out."

Thomas tried to jump to the side but the fist blinded him, sending him reeling to the ground. He was covered by Dennis, the denim of Dennis' trousers somehow stuffed into his mouth, blows beating on Thomas' silent body.

Dennis writhed on top of Thomas. Then his body became limp and silent. Suddenly, he jumped up, screeching, and bolted away through the trees.

For a long time, Thomas whimpered in the broken leaves. He pulled himself up, put a hand against a tree, and threw up. Then he shuffled blindly from the secret place to the road, his books beneath the broken leaves in the clearing, free from their belt, their white pages smeared with black loam.

The wagon rattled up and stopped. The hard, black hand gripped his collar and pulled him squirming into the air, onto the roughened seat. "Now what the hell you been into?" The dark hand coming out of the sky, slapping his face. "Stop that blubberin' and answer."

"A fight." A fight.

"Well, stop that damn blubberin'." A rough hand slapping his head lightly. The wagon clattering toward home.

The wagon snarled and rattled into the short main street where Thomas stood. Thomas saw the black hands first, then eyes looking calmly down, shoulders rounded and back bent against some unseen weight.

The old man's smile squared his face into black furrows that had, with the wagon, grown old in wind and rain. He stirred slightly with the waiting and then murmured, with the familiar slow smile, "Son."

Thomas' jaw worked wetly, his head bending up, bulbous eyes turned to the blazing sky. "Yes, old man, the sun is certainly very hot today, isn't it."

The old man frowned, snapping his head back to a stared-out spot on the horse's back. He clucked his tongue and the wagon jerked forward. Thomas watched it until it disappeared.

The sound of ivory cracking against ivory shot into the street. Thomas breathed deeply, aimed his body toward the black maw, and leaned carefully in.

A fat man wearing a baseball cap with a broken bill sat on a stool that creaked unsteadily beneath him. His left hand was clenched around a bag of peanuts and the other clutched a bottle of cola. He turned the pages of a magazine by jamming his fist across it. Then he tossed his head back with the bottle aimed into his throat. His left arm remained tense and, as the bottle came down, the peanuts were rocketed up to the red fleshy cheeks that surrounded his waiting mouth. The bottle missed the counter. It smashed on the floor, dark liquid spilling free.

Two sharp faces, battered brown felt hats and overalls, turned from their game, laughing. "Think you'll starve, there, Silo?"

The fat man growled. "Shut the face." He kicked the broken glass under the counter.

The two farmers gurgled to each other and slapped their knees, small clouds of dust puffing from their mud-caked overalls.

"What the hell you two doing?"

Instantly there was silence.

"Oops."

"Oops, hell!" The fat man wheeled around facing the stranger in the doorway. "Yah, you! Whadda you want?"

Thomas fell backward stumbling into the street, his suitcase springing open. On his knees in the dust he stuffed handfuls of underwear and bottles and dirt back into the case, jammed it shut, and jumped to his feet. Without brushing off, he hurried, running toward the mountain depot. Behind him, one of the farmers in the pool hall yelled, "Hey, Dennis! Hey, fat man! Come rack `em!" Thomas slowed and stopped. Within an hour, he had rented a never-used room above the stores across the street from the pool hall.

The next morning was clear and bright. Thomas emerged

from the rented room. An old impulse gripped him. He placed his suitcase in a narrow slit between two buildings, covered it with leaves, and began running, laughing, careless, crazy-legged through the town and into the forest through the cool glade and onto the bridge over the brook. He stomped to a halt among the covering green of the cool and shaded bridge and shook the dust off his suit, breathing hoarsely, clearing his lungs. A light cool breeze played across his face, drying it, pulling the skin tight. Eyes closed, he threw his head back and turned it, this way, that, trying to catch each shifting breeze.

In a forest clearing below, the spring paused to form a waist-high pool. The girl stood at the edge, sheltered by surrounding leaves.

She smiled, peered into the water, and removed her dress. Thomas choked back the fear, the impulse to run, and knelt down behind the wooden railing.

The girl gazed into the cold, dark water. Finally, she stepped into the shallow edge, delicate fingertips touching her throat. Silver scales flashed in the water and she stepped quickly back. As she knelt for her dress, wisps of bright hair falling from her shoulders caught the sun. She shivered and laughed as cold leaves touched warm skin. The young girl walked into the woods, her dress in her hand trailing along the ground.

Thomas closed his eyes tightly, trying so hard to hold the image against the darkness in his mind that tears struggled out and fell onto his hands clenched in his lap.

"Pretty, ain't she."

Thomas fell back, scattering dust as he shuffled to his feet.

The wide-brim hat, khaki, the boots, hard metal star and, like part of the uniform, the mad fixed, staring eyes. Always there, all of it, always. It held Thomas' suitcase in its hand.

"Like some of that, wouldn't you, nigger." Closer.

Thomas waited, silent and motionless, as it edged near. The insane face came within the length of Thomas' arms. Just before it spat, Thomas' hands snaked out and caught the compressed rush of air in its throat. Almost at once, Thomas felt the popping and snapping beneath his fingers. Thomas pressed the side of his left knee against the holster. The suitcase dropped and the body began to fall. It clawed at Thomas' arms and Thomas felt the searing pain spread from his genitals as its legs kicked below. He watched the surprised face begin to craze with blue lines. Then it went limp in Thomas' rigid arms. Thomas pulled back his hands and the bubble of air wetly rattled from its throat. It had died.

At dark, Thomas emerged, sweating, from the forest. When he returned to town, the night was pitch black and he stumbled frequently over wood, brick, and stone. He bumped along the fronts of darkened buildings, past the building with the rented room, pushing through the town, breathing hoarsely. "That was stupid. That was wrong. That is not what I came for, not what I came for."

Grandmother sat on a wooden plank in a shed smiling at the ads in the catalogue that bespoke the wonders of porcelain and copper. Maybe someday. The stroke signal came in two streaks up to her brain, terminating the left and, a moment later, the right side of her exhausted body. She died where she had crawled on the bare path, her ragged britches still hanging on her bloated ankles. Grandfather, leaning on his plow drunk in the noonday sun, looked out from his field to the far place she had fallen. He called her name.

"I ain't cuttin' your hair in here." The head with the scissors and the head beneath his hand both glared at Thomas as he planted himself at the center of the shop. Thomas' eyes roamed the room. He took his time, then returned to stare back evenly at the two men. This much I can do, he thought. He stared. The barber's eyes began to water and then he spoke, softly. "I don't know how to cut hair like that." Almost apologetic.

"Oh, that's okay. I just came in to . . ." Thomas' eyes searched quickly and saw the old man hunched in a corner of the shop, the small black face a scarred mask of many old arguments. The face was pleased at what it had just seen. ". . . get my shoes cleaned. Can he do it?"

"I can do it."

Both white men looked in surprise at the small black man. Thomas sat down in the old man's chair and put his foot on the box in front of it. The old man worked smoothly, wheezing, running the cloth again and again over already-glistening shoes.

Night came. Thomas looked through the window. The fat man was perched on his stool flipping the pages of the magazine. The rest of the long, hazy room was empty.

Thomas swung his suitcase through the doorway and bounded in after it yelling. "Hi!"

The fat man's feet went up in the air and he screamed, his

hands pawing wildly as his body thumped onto the concrete floor. With an agility that surprised Thomas, the fat man jumped back to his feet. "You crazy sonofabitch! You . . ."

"Sorry."

"Sorryzizass!" The fat man came forward, his fists raised above legs spreading for battle.

"Hey, stop, stop it. I came to offer you a drink."

Dennis stopped, still snarling. "What?"

Thomas turned to his suitcase and opened it. "I didn't mean to make you angry, certainly." He turned back with the pint dangling from his fingers. "I'm looking for someone to share a drink with."

"This is a dry county." The fat man paid homage to the law, eyes fixed on the pint bottle. "Where'd you get it?"

"I have several. And more in my room. Have to carry a lot. You know, in case I hit a place like this." He waved vaguely at the dry county and smiled. In charge. In charge now. The beginning. "Take a drink. If you wish."

The fat man looked curiously at the stranger for an instant and then shoved the bottle, and part of its neck, inside his mouth. He put the bottle down at his side, hiding it from the window's view. Whiskey sparkled at the corners of his lips. "You may be cracked, Mister, but you sure can spot a man's weak points." He laughed. Thomas laughed. Rain began to pelt the dust outside and run in dirty streaks down the window.

As they drank, the rain fell harder, rattling against the window. The fat man drank, occasionally offering the bottle to the stranger and then taking it quickly back. He stumbled through the room, humming and clanking the bottle along the rows of cues. The stranger sat with his hands cupped around his knees, waiting, and stared out at the rain.

The stranger jumped up. The girl from the forest stood outside in the dim light from the window, her dress and hair soaked dark by the rain. Streaks of black ran down her cheeks from ceramic eyes. "Who's that?"

The fat man staggered to the window. He cocked his head and closed one eye. "She's crazy. I don't know. She likes fat men." He laughed wetly. "She comes here and watches me." He frowned and pouted. "Like I'd done something. Or should be doing something. Or whatever. She caught me once dancing." He grinned. "She likes my dancing. Watch."

The fat man danced, tapping about on his toes, twirling faster and faster until the fat seemed about to leave his body. He bumped against the table and the counter, then fell, then hopped up, grunting. The sound of his scraping shoes and his hoarse breathing again filled the room. He whirled. He yelled. The fat man danced closer to the stranger, laughing and sweating, red cheeks flopping loosely.

The girl, crying, lips distorted, stepped back into the street. She was bent forward crookedly from the waist with her hands clasped together, arms tight against her sides.

The stranger closed his eyes. He pushed back and pressed the side of his face against the wall. The fat man laughed and twirled in front of him, dust swirling around the short, thick trunks of his legs. He stopped, poised on one foot, small, bright eyes boring into the stranger. "You like my dancin' too?"

The stranger struggled to breathe. At last, he was able to suck air. He opened his eyes. The girl was gone.

"You got any more of that stuff?"

"What?"

"Heh-heh. I was just wondering if you got any more of that sweet honey dew laying around in your raggedy laundry box there. It's been a long time since we shared a drink, don't it seem like to you?"

"Let me look." He ran his hand through the suitcase, and turned back with his palms up. "Empty. And I'm dry too." He smiled. "I didn't get much out of that last bottle." Don't say it. Let him ask.

"Didn't you say something about some—uh—some more?"

"Yes. Do you have time?"

Dennis ran behind the counter. "Just lemme close up, darlin'!" He grabbed a straight broom and lined up carefully with it between the wall and the row of tables. Then he pushed the broom before him running, laughing, and dropped it at the back wall. "All clean!" He shut off the lights, locked the door, and they weaved through the mud and mist and up the stairs to Thomas' room.

Dennis awoke to a hot sun bombarding his face through the open window. Gawd! His head ached. His body ached. The whole damn world ached! All the hilarity of last night was mocking now, all the words jabbing at newly-located areas in his throbbing head. His thoughts turned to insects, greatly exaggerated in size and aggressiveness. Last night's joke about the whore who had suffered her last stroke now seemed pathetic and melancholy.

After long reflection on the necessity of it, he tried to heave his aching body up off the bed. His body didn't seem to be working. He couldn't raise his arms. He couldn't raise . . . He couldn't raise anything! Coming up over the side of the bed, over his belly, down under the bed, up over his arms. Ropes. Over his thighs, around his ankles. Ropes. Crazy. Crazy! Tied to the goddamn bed! "Hey!" No answer. He was alone in the room.

Dennis tried to remember if this had been a result of last night's rollicking. He couldn't. For the most part, his memory stopped somewhere about halfway up the dark flight of stairs. He remembered giggling when the stranger had pulled out his shirt-tail for Dennis to hold onto after Dennis had stumbled and fallen on the steps, and he could remember dancing again when the guy had asked him to. That was all.

Where is that damn guy? He tried to wriggle around to see if he could free something. No luck. The damn ropes were really tight. It was hot and sticky underneath the blanket. Dennis was still frowning and muttering to himself when shoes scraped up the steps. Dennis craned his neck, staring over his head at the door.

The stranger burst through the door cradling a pyramid of leaves in his arms. He spilled the leaves over Dennis. "Phew. There." Dennis sputtered and blew a dry leaf off his mouth only to have it flutter down on his eyes. He shook it off. "Look, what—" The stranger turned his back and walked over to the dresser. He ran his hands carefully through the top drawer, found what he wanted, and turned back to Dennis. He smiled.

"Look, man, what the hell's going on?"

The stranger sighed and shook his head. When he turned to sit in the chair, something flashed in his hand. Steel. A knife! "Jesus!"

"Pardon me?"

"What're you going to do?"

The stranger sat in the chair smiling at Dennis. For a long time he said nothing. Dennis' eyes were fixed on where he held his hand at his side, hidden between his leg and the chair. The stranger's head nodded slowly forward but his eyes were wide, staring at the floor.

"You gonna cut these ropes, man?" Silence. "Ahk," Dennis grunted with disgust. This was silly. But a new, immediate fear began groping through Dennis' body, making him forget all earlier pain. The sun shot straight down through the window into his eyes and voices murmured up from the street. Dennis opened his mouth wide. The stranger sprang up from the chair with the huge bayonet raised above Dennis. The yell came from Dennis' throat as hissing air.

"Look," Dennis whispered, "you mind tellin' me . . ." The stranger slumped back into the chair. His head nodded forward but his glazed eyes were wide, fixed on the floor. "God, man, I'm gonna suffocate here." No answer.

Dennis stared at the bayonet. He tried to think how to get the ropes off and how to deal with the maniac in the chair. Damn! What is this?

The stranger cleared his throat. "The sun's overhead now."

"C'mon, man, what the hell is this? It's hot. I'm suffocating. Let me loose. It's stifling! And I'm dying! I mean—let me out of this! I don't even know what's going on."

The stranger stood in the center of the room with his neck distended to one side, rubbing the black stubble on his chin and mumbling. "He doesn't know what's wrong. He doesn't understand. He's a foggy, foggy man."

The way the stranger dipped his head, as if to move away, stirred in the recesses of Dennis' mind. He studied the black figure intently, coaxing the memory forth. It slipped away, but the taste remained. "C'mon, man," Dennis said quietly, gently. "C'mon. let's knock it off. What say?" The figure in the center of the room craned its neck further, as if listening, but otherwise made no move and said nothing. "Say, you from around here?"

The figure grimaced ever so slightly. "The gentleman wants to know if I'm from around here." He stepped to the bed, over Dennis, his right hand held behind his back. The stranger's voice was a loud whisper but, to Dennis, he was screaming. "You know what, fat man? You know what now?" Dennis shook his head violently, cheeks flopping, and whispered from a dry mouth that wouldn't work. "No." Sound! Make sound! "No! C'mon, let me out of here!"

The stranger stood straight up. He was grinning! "Maybe it's too late for you to get out." Then he strained forward again, jabbing his dark fingers again and again into the bulging flesh beneath the drenched blanket.

The memory again tried to creep from a recess in Dennis' brain, but again slipped back. Into the darkness. But the intuition remained. He could cope now. He was better than this man. "You're crazy, man."

The stranger grimaced. "You can't do anything right."

"You're crazy as hell, mister!" A mistake.

Dennis screamed and blubbered through spittle as he saw the

flash of the raised knife again. The stranger held the bayonet tight in both fists pointed down at Dennis' heart.

The knife did not come down.

Dennis whimpered, trying to twist his head away into the pillow, to the side, against the wall beneath the window. The stranger stood frozen, staring over the fat man through the window down into the street where the girl from the forest stared up at him. Her mouth was open but silent, eyes wide and pleading. She beckoned to Thomas.

"Too late, Goddamit, too late, too late!" Thomas screamed and dropped the bayonet to the floor, jabbing both fists at the forest air. Thomas screamed at the window, at himself, screamed again and again until the soft feeling that had begun to radiate into his muscles was pushed back, contained, until the animal hardness returned to his body and brain. He lifted his seething eyes up to confront an empty street.

Thomas' sister had been gone so long his memory could no longer summon up her face. She died in a strange town from disease, seeking her fortune away from home, still at work with her bent, dead knees pointing up at a sleeping God. Her body should have been brought home, but father just shook his head in tight-lipped silence when her name was mentioned. Her employer, a beefy woman with red face and hair, bore the cost of the funeral with sour piety. The Madam's surviving flesh measured the quality of her mercy soberly, brown fingers folded neatly in their laps.

Dennis watched Thomas stand muttering in the center of the room. "What?"

Thomas shook his head. "Nothing."

"You were groaning or something."

"Nothing." Thomas picked up the bayonet. He looked down dully at the fat man, bayonet dangling in his hand, and then said quietly, "It's no good with the ropes. There were no ropes. You'll have to understand." Muttering. "We need the leaves. Need a book too." He opened the dresser drawer and chuckled. He flipped the Bible toward the bed. It landed in Dennis' crotch, the pages sprawling open. Thomas laughed out loud. Too good.

The last remaining ray of hope died in Dennis' soul. He screamed. "Damn you! You—Goddamn you!"

Thomas spoke softly. "No, no. No, fat man. No." The fingers

of his left hand fluttered gently in front of him, freeing cobwebs from the air. "You don't understand. Not at all." His eyes were glazed and bright. He leaned close to Dennis' ear. "My brother. My brother fell out of the barn loft when he was just a kid and got his suspenders caught on the top of the ladder, and they twisted around his neck. They found him hanging from the loft, strangled with his own suspenders, just hanging there. Just another stupid joke."

As Thomas' insanity displaced Dennis' own thoughts, memory came clearly. A smirk played irresistibly at the corners of Dennis' lips.

Thomas jumped up and looked into Dennis' wide and bulging eyes. "You understand now, a little bit, don't you, fat man." Dennis said nothing. "Yes, you understand." Thomas puzzled as, again, the familiar soft feeling crept over him. "I hope—perhaps—we can do this with some dignity. If you're prepared." And again Thomas desperately fought the jelly feeling down.

Dennis saw the steel flash in the sunlight as Thomas brought the knife around and swooped it down. Dennis squealed. Thomas' arms whirred through the air as he slashed the shining steel back and forth through the ropes, snapping them one by one, slitting lines through the blanket. With the same smooth motion, the knife circled up and over Dennis' heart, the hilt clasped in both of Thomas' hands.

Dennis screamed and heaved sideways off the bed, slamming his bulk into Thomas' legs as the knife came down.

The bayonet tore through the fat man's undershirt and caught in his shorts, ripping the elastic band, as Thomas toppled back onto the floor. Dennis bounced to his feet and leaped and slammed his shoulder through the door panel, rolling out onto the stairway. Thomas came through the shattered door after him, stabbing the knife at the air behind Dennis. "No! For God's sake, no!" Dennis rolled against the wall and struggled to get his legs beneath him. Pushing up, he leaped through the air down the long flight of stairs. Landing heavily on one leg and slamming against the wall again, he pitched out onto the sidewalk and staggered into the street.

He heard Thomas pounding down the steps behind him, gasping and stumbling. "No! This is wrong! Stop! This is wrong!" Dennis skidded to his hands and knees in the street and sobbed, his fat chest heaving, bloated lips sucking at the dust-filled air. Thomas lurched out into the blinding sun. Dust swirled into

Dennis' eyes and mouth. He heard only his own hoarse breathing. And then the rasping breath of Thomas as he shuffled to a stop next to Dennis.

Dennis did not see, but sensed, the bayonet being raised again. And then a roaring explosion filled his ears, filled his head with numbing thunder, but no pain came. And no darkness.

Through the haze of dust and tears, Dennis saw Thomas pitch forward into the dust beside him. Thomas' hand was against his face. The hand fell away and scarlet filled the front of the shattered face. A widening red silhouette formed in the dust. Dennis watched Thomas' chest expand, sucking air through the many holes in the front of his head. Then the air rushed bubbling back out as the body rolled, face down, spraying the redness of Thomas' life into the parched street.

Behind Dennis, the old, black man in the wagon carefully put the shotgun back under the seat.

The two farmers, who had been angrily kicking at the locked back door of the pool hall, ran through the weeds along the side of the building toward where they had heard the shot. They peeked cautiously around the corner. "Land, land! Will you lookit that!" They walked over to Dennis and stared alternately at him and then the dead man. The taller farmer hooked his thumbs in his overalls and started to ask Dennis a question but decided against it.

Dennis was standing on one leg, an obese crane. Dennis' undershirt was torn and falling away, held by a single strap. With one hand, he gripped the old horse's mane. With the other, he clutched his ragged and dirty shorts which hung at his knees. An intermittent, thin and bloody line ran across each of his mountainous buttocks.

The old man in the wagon grimaced as the farmers began to laugh, hesitantly at first, and then raucously, gripping each other for support, pointing at Dennis, and stamping their feet in the dust. The wagon pulled slowly away. The two old farmers rocked and slapped their knees, their laughter bounding down the street, finally fading among the trees on the mountain.

Night. The scarred, black face peered cautiously around the back corner of the barbershop at the body in the street. The small man tiptoed through the dust and knelt by the lifeless pile of sticks. "You ain't shit," he whispered at the dead man. "You cain't give if you cain't live." The old man's eyes burned.

He left Thomas' body and ran stiffly to his hidden place in

the forest on the mountain. He sat between the pines and drank, occasionally crushing the moist and fragrant needles in his hand and rubbing them over his face, feeling it sharp and familiar against his parchment skin. He rocked back and forth on folded legs, the pain of the dry, rebelling bones dulled by the clear liquid from the jar. He breathed quietly and deep. Then he cried out into the yielding air of the dark, hidden place. Silence answered him.

Summer Solstice

Robert Kelly

June twenty-second opens silently. The summer sun rises over Rainier sweeping down on the lower reaches of Puget Sound fanning out over the still water, slumbering islands, drowsy beaches, and lazy coves, searching until it finds my closed eyelids and wakes me on this second longest day of the year. I get up, find my bathing trunks on the line outside and slip into them. They are still damp from yesterday and a little cold but that sun warms me as I walk down to the float for my early swim. Meadowlarks are already singing, roosters crowing, and crows cawing as they search out their breakfast. The morning sun's warmth is seductive. I stop, stretch out in the big wooden chair, lingering in the sun's mesmerizing heat before plunging into the cold water. Once in, I get my trunks off, put them on the float, and begin my swim with the sunfish, salmon, sand sharks, seals, and cod. It is my best time of the day and the neighbors have finally stopped talking about my swimming this way. Plunging underwater, I see scurrying crabs, starfish, snails, sand dollars, and fat sea cucumbers all awakening to this new day, this first day after the summer solstice.

Back in my trunks, I return to the big wooden chair, lean back letting the sun penetrate my skin going right into my anxious soul that needs salving this morning after seeing the "ghost" last night. He was there at the cove's entrance by the deserted cottage. The cottage that we hope will be our honeymoon house. Though it was built in the nineteen-twenties, it is still the newest and most attractive place on the cove. It has been deserted for years since Jim murdered his wife there. That hasn't bothered us. We have rowed up there many times. Mary loves the big front porch that looks out on the peace of Glen Cove and the sweep of Carr Inlet. We've sat on that empty porch and dreamed of just the two of us living there. The nearest neighbors are more than a mile away on either side. It would be our own quiet place to live out the love we have for one another. Just a few coats of paint, inside and out we know, would work miracles and make it our own.

But that's where I saw Jim's ghost last night. I have heard stories about his being there but have never actually seen him. I had to look hard last night to believe it. They say he's a ghost but I saw clearly that he is a living, breathing man. People who say they have seen Jim's ghost never mention his size. I was totally unprepared to see such a large, powerful man instead of a ghost. There he was standing silently on the edge of the woods next to our "honeymoon house", arms stretching up toward the moon. It was unnerving. Then, when I looked back, he was gone. I have an option to buy that house but after last night I need to know more. I don't want him walking around my yard at night scaring the wits out of Mary and he's too big for me to handle. The last thing I want to do this morning is see the Hermit, but after last night I know I must. He's the one who really knows about that house and Jim's ghost.

I row down to the end of the cove, beach the skiff, and walk out on the one-plank-wide float that snakes some fifty feet into the cove to the Hermit's shack. It is a beautiful summer day and I hate to think of even having to get near the Hermit. The stories I've heard about him are ugly. Already, as I approach the door, the smell of decaying seafood scraped from his plate lodged in the logs under his shack assails my nostrils. Just outside his door I call, "Harold, are you there? I need to see you." Silence. Then the shack door groans, moves, and begins to open inching slowly inward. I was hoping it wouldn't—anything to avoid this encounter.

The door opens all the way. "Are you that new guy at the Beamers?" booms out of the darkness of the shack. "What do you want from me? Just finished breakfast. Have mussels left if you want some."

"No thanks. I need you to tell me about the cottage at the entrance of the cove." I say, hoping my eyes will adjust to the blackness of his room so I can see where he is. I continue, "Some people call it Jim's house. Some say it is haunted by Jim. Last night I saw a man, not a ghost, standing there as I came in from Carr Inlet. The man was next to the house with his arms stretched up toward the moon. But when I looked again, he was gone. John Sterling told me you know all about that house and the ghost of Jim. I want to buy that place and bring my bride there. But now I'm wondering about that. What can you tell me?"

"Come in and sit down!"

I see him for the first time. He is huge. He is ancient. His unkempt hair hangs over heavy eyebrows and shaggy whiskers. His stained and matted beard turns my stomach. Some of his breakfast mussels are actually still in it. All I need now is to see is a mouse stick its nose out of that beard and wiggle its nose whiskers at me.

"Thank you. I'm fine out here," I say not wanting any of his mice jumping on me.

"Well I'm not going to blow my lungs out talking to you out there. If you want to talk to me, you've got to come in!" As I step inside his shack, the stench of rotting crab and fish mixed with the sour odor of cat urine fill my nostrils, tighten my throat. My stomach rebels. I'm on the edge of retching. I stand just inside the door gaping in awe at this unexpected sight, this seeming Paul Bunyan of a man sitting before me. Something very soft rubs my leg. I make out two gray cats and hear their purring. An emaciated calico is rubbing my other leg. Fleas bite my ankles but I don't move. A huge gray cat sits in the Hermit's lap. Then I see it. The shack has but one small window right behind the Hermit. It looks down the length of the Cove to its entrance and frames Jim's house.

"Jim hasn't been around here, that anyone knows about for years, let's see, seven at least," the Hermit begins. "That house was built by a doctor in Tacoma for a summer place. His kids grew up and went away. He got remarried and his new wife didn't like it so he advertised for someone around here to look after it for him." The Hermit sees me staring at his beard, stops, looks down and picks the mussels out of it and puts them in his mouth licking his fingers. I gag. "The doctor worked it out with Jim. Jim needed that house then." The Hermit begins to wave his arms with his telling of the story and his acrid armpit odor churns out into the shack. Even though I am breathing through my nose I can taste it on my tongue and now my whole mouth tastes awful. "He had just met Evangeline, the most beautiful girl he'd seen in his life. She worked at the store in Vaughn and Jim told me he didn't know why such a beautiful girl would pay any attention to a guy like him. Jim was plain, you see, but clean cut and strong as an ox having worked timber all his young days. Something about Jim made her dizzy, she said. He proposed, carried her to the preacher, and they settled in that house on June twentieth, so as Jim said, 'They would have the longest day of the year to make love.' It was all love and roses until the store-owner's wife told Jim her husband and Evangeline were at it in the back of the store. She wanted it stopped. Jim lost his temper that night when Evangeline got home." The Hermit looks away. I wait. There is something new in his eyes when he turns back to go on.

"When Evangeline didn't show up for work the third day, the Sheriff went to the house. He found her body in the kitchen with a trail of blood right into the dining room where her head lay. Her eyes were open, looking back into the kitchen. They found the chain painter for the skiff around her neck. Jim must have wrapped it around and just pulled until her head snapped off and rolled into the dining room. You can guess how he felt with her eyes still looking at him. The Sheriff didn't find Jim. Most folk think he hiked out of there to the rain forest on the Olympic Peninsula. But, from time to time people say they see him back at the house at night just like you did. That trail of blood from the kitchen to the dining room is still there in the floorboards. It won't come out. People have scrubbed it with lye. You don't want to take your pretty little bride there, son. She wouldn't like it and neither would you." I think I see the shadow of a smile flash across his face but now he is rising, leaning toward me. He is in my face shaking uncontrollably. The cat screeches and jumps off his lap as an ungodly belch erupts from his gut followed by a monumental breaking of wind.

I fly out of there into the fresh air, row home and dive into the salt water to get clean. Then, up at the house, I get the Lava soap from the laundry tub, turn on the shower, and scrub for my life, brush my teeth with gobs of Ipana toothpaste, but I still feel soiled. I need that Sears and Roebuck Catalogue that Mary brought last week. She saw one of their houses that you can build yourself that she really liked. I find it, just where she marked it, a Sears kit house that I can afford. The dimensions for its foundation are given on the same page. I walk up to the top of the hill behind the house. Look out across the Cove. This is the place where the sun's first rays will wake us in our bridal chamber. With my measuring tape and twine, I lay out that foundation, then I dig the foundation trench all day long spurred on by that horrible tale and his ungodly belch. The physical work helps me get that ugliness out of my system and I finally fall on my bed exhausted.

Mr. Robards comes by this morning to see what all my digging is about. I tell him what the Hermit said and ask him what he knows about a murder in the house. "Oh yeah, he killed her all right, but I don't remember anything about her head coming off. As I recall, he shot her with a gun as she got out of her car coming home from work. They found her dead in the driveway. Jim got out of here fast and I haven't seen him since. He's probably up in the rain forest. Posses scoured the rain forest at the time and found somebody's animal traps but they never found Jim. There have been occasional reports of a big wild man living in the rain forest. Some say Jim comes back to that house to remember her and visits his dad too on the summer solstice."

"You mean he has a family here."

"No, not a family, just his dad, the old Hermit."

"Blast him. That was a smile on his face!"

My Eighth Summer

Donna M. Kenworthy Levy

Summers were like the sound of piccolos playing, filled with jaunty trips to Griffith Park, La Brea Tar Pits, and the Santa Monica Pier. The days in-between those trips were often spent spitting the shells of sunflower seedsdown on the grass while perched on thick branches of our favorite oak tree. We would languish there during the hottest part of the afternoons and plot schemes to dispossess small business owners and kind neighbors from their loose change.

I was the brains behind the swindling schemes. That is not to say that my partner in crime lacked intelligence. Kathy was just short on enthusiasm. Every time I came up with an idea to make us some money, her eyes would move rapidly from side to side. With a pale face and a shaky voice, she'd remind me that all my ideas were sins. "Now I'll have to go to confession again," she'd complain. I felt sorry for her. It must have been tough being Catholic.

"Gosh, Dana, don't you worry about going to hell?"

"Right now, I'm worried about getting some nickels and dimes together so that we can go on a few amusement park rides at the pier next week." I secretly hoped I wouldn't succumb to spending precious cents on the Hall of Mirrors. It was a maze that made me feel trapped and frightened . . . as if I would never get out. But I knew that if Kathy wanted to venture in among the mirrors again, I would once more agree to enter this nightmare world.

On days that the two of us meandered along the lures of the carnival world totally penniless like unclaimed waifs, I would wonder what ideas entertained my mother as she lay motionless on her towel. Did Mama ever think about us as she roasted herself for hours at a time on the hot sand without ever moving or going to cool herself off in the waves? Correction: She did make that one grand flip from stomach to back at halftime. What should have filled her mind was the obvious realization that we needed some coins. A good mother would have given us a few cents to entertain ourselves. Did she even imagine how much we suffered looking at the other kids riding high on the Ferris wheel or descending with titillating screams on the rollercoaster? It was no fun at all just being a spectator.

Apparently my mother was content to nap or listen to the old people tell their long stories about life in Europe as they ate deli sandwiches, drank seltzer water, and played non-stop hands of cards. These old folks brought their own card table and non-matching dining room chairs with them. Whoever heard of bringing furniture to the beach? Even though she was removed from them by at least fifty feet, she could hear every word. Sometimes she would laugh so hard at what they were saying, tears would run down her face.

I was just glad she didn't go over to talk to them person to person. What a sight they were. The men, dressed in wrinkled bathing trunks and black shoes and socks, were so bow-legged, a beach ball could fit between these extremities.

The opposite could be said of the old ladies. Their knees rubbed against each other as they walked. And each of them possessed at least nine million wrinkles spread out all over their far too visible body parts. I made myself a solemn oath that I would never wear a bathing suit in public once I reached thirty-five years of age. Thankfully, I still had twenty-seven years of sun wear fashion to enjoy.

"Mama, don't you get bored lying around doing nothing?" "Not at all," she would reply, while adding, "aside from being a sun worshiper, I am savoring memories of my youth. I'm re-living a past that's gone forever."

What was wrong with the present, I wanted to know.

"Dana, I really don't want to go around to the stores and beg for money again. The last time we did that, the shop owners got a little mad at us when you said, "We'll only leave your store if you pay us." You really went too far. The jeweler even threatened to call the cops on us!"

"Don't tell me you believed him! Just look at us. We're both so sweet and innocent looking! There you are with that cute Irish face full of freckles and dimples, and here I am with my big blue eyes and bright smile. Can you honestly imagine the cops taking us down to city hall in handcuffs?"

"Sometimes I'm afraid you're really going to end up in jail!"

"Fine. We'll stop going to the stores for a while. In the meantime, how about stealing some fruit from the Burton's orchard?

They have so many citrus trees, they won't miss a couple of bags full. Come climb down and help me."

In spite of her protests, my faithful accomplice seemed to perk up at this newest adventure.

As it turned out, we had a tough time selling the lemons and grapefruit. Most of our neighbors either weren't home or weren't interested in buying anything that day. On a lark, we thought it would be really funny to knock on the Burton's door. Mrs. Burton greeted us and patiently listened to our sales pitch. Kathy and I got kind of nervous when she called her husband to come to the front door. "Joseph, just look at these nice young ladies who have come to sell us some fruit. Go get my change purse so we can buy all the lemons and grapefruit they have in those grocery bags.

Kathy and I each walked away with three quarters apiece! This was more money than we asked for! Wow wee!!

We laughed and giggled so hard as we ran down the block that we stumbled and fell into a heap on the sidewalk. Feeling the pain of scraped knees quickly changed our mood.

My friend and I looked at each other sheepishly.

"Say it, Dana."

"It was wrong," I stammered out.

We talked about how it was bad enough that we stole the fruit from the Burton's orchard. Then to take money from those kind people for fruit that actually belonged to them in the first place was a dirty, lowdown scheme. Kathy and I agreed that it was the very worst thing we had ever done. We feared if our parents ever found out about this business transaction, we would never be allowed to play with each other again. So we didn't confess our crime to the Burtons nor return the money they paid us, lest the story got back to our parents.

We chose instead to live with ever-lasting guilt. Our atonement was to make a solemn vow that we would never steal or cheat anyone again. To our credit, we did work up the courage to apologize to all the shop owners for giving them a hard time.

My eighth summer clearly marked the end of my childhood. Life unfolded as a constant array of moral choices. From that summer on, a stern old judge took up residence in my mind. His opinions forever drowned out the sound of piccolos playing.

I dedicate this story to my first best friend, Karen Jean Hall. Our friendship remained strong until she departed this life in 1998 after a protracted struggle with breast cancer. I hope she's found us a comfortable oak tree in Paradise.

Fatal Decision

Betty Maistelman

The young physician turned away from the bed in the intensive care unit, where Brett's mother was lying with a myriad of colored tubes in her body.

He avoided looking at Brett, and, in a tone that could have been discussing the weather, suggested she turn off her mother's respirator. "She's in a vital bed," he said. "The nurses are needed for other patients."

Brett sat up with a start from the nightmare. She knew she had cried out in her sleep, and looked over to see whether she had awakened her husband, Jed. He was still asleep, with a faint smile on his face. He must be dreaming about the white sands of Hawaii, Brett thought, which until two weeks ago they had been talking about as a possible vacation destination later that summer.

She lay down again, every muscle in her body rigid, afraid to go back to sleep, afraid the nightmare was so deeply etched in her brain, she would dream it again, as she had for the past seven nights.

Brett replayed the nightmare in her mind as she curled up under the covers in a fetal position, reminding herself it wasn't just a dream. It had really happened . . .

It began at 4:15 A.M. a week ago, after her father's frantic middle-of-the-night phone call. She booked the first flight she could get to Cleveland out of Boston, kissed a sleepy Jed good-bye and took a cab to Logan Airport, a forty-five-minute drive from their home.

When she arrived in Cleveland, Brett grabbed a taxi from Hopkins Airport to the hospital. She hurriedly walked up the hospital steps, where she found her father dozing in the lobby.

"Hi, Dad," Brett said softly.

Her father awakened with a start.

"Oh, Brett," he said. "I'm so glad you're here."

"I'm so sorry I couldn't get here sooner," she said. "I got the first plane I could out of Boston."

When Brett and her father talked about what had happened, he told her that her mother had complained in the middle of the night about not feeling well. Since her mother had a heart condition, he had called 911, and the rescue squad had taken her to the nearest hospital, the small one across the street from their apartment.

Brett's father said he would have preferred a larger hospital, but since this one was so close, he didn't make an issue out of it. He didn't know if they would have done anything differently, even if he had requested it.

"Tests were done in the emergency room immediately," he told Brett: "an EKG . . . x-rays. The diagnosis was gastronomic upset—upset stomach. Not her heart." He stopped talking and looked down at the floor.

"Then they closeted your mother in a curtained-off cubicle, but wouldn't let me go in with her," her father added in an irritated voice.

He said he *bothered* anyone who would listen every twenty minutes or so, asking if he could go in to see his wife, only to be told, "She's coming along fine." He even walked over to her cubicle, but the curtain was closed, and he could see only her feet.

"Someone in the ER finally told me I could go in," he continued, "and said I could take her home in a little while." Her father paused and looked at Brett.

"As I walked toward her cubicle," her father went on, "I thought everything was going to be okay, and thanked God that an upset stomach was your mother's only problem. I found her on the bed with her eyes closed. I thought she was asleep, but there was vomit around her mouth and on the sheet. I kept calling her name, but I couldn't wake her. I ran out to call for help."

After Brett's father found her mother comatose, she was rushed to the cardiac unit to clean out her lungs. It was a dangerous procedure, the doctor who had just taken over her case, Dr. Barlowe, had told Brett's father. Hours later, he told him she had had a stroke.

Her father put his head in his hands. "They should have let me go in sooner. Maybe then this wouldn't have happened."

Brett got up from her chair and put her arm around him.

A few minutes later she said, "I'm going to go see Mom. Will you be all right alone?"

"I'll be okay," he told her. "You go ahead."

As Brett walked slowly toward her mother's bed in the intensive care unit, she stopped momentarily to regain her composure. Her mother's uncombed gray hair was strewn carelessly back on the pillow. Brett knew she would never have permitted it had she known.

Her face was chalky white and slightly bloated. An orange breathing tube protruded from her mouth. Other tubes were in her arms. To Brett, her once vibrant mother looked alone and helpless.

Brett walked closer to the bed. "It's Brett, Mom," she said. "I love you. The boys and Jed send their love, too." She put the bracelet made out of bottle caps, which her seven-year-old son had made for his beloved Nana, near her mother's hand. "This is from Ronnie," Brett said. "Mom, please move your hand if you can hear me."

Her mother didn't move.

"Can she hear?" Brett asked the dark-haired nurse.

"We really don't know," she answered.

Brett focused on the nurse's features: pretty, but so young to be balancing her mother's life in her care.

She sat next to her mother's bed for a few more minutes, then walked back to the lobby, where she had left her father sitting in a chair.

Is it cold or just me, Brett thought, as she sat down in a chair next to her father to try to put the pieces together and scribble notes. Note scribbling was her way of handling most serious things.

Brett wondered if what had happened to her mother was malpractice. She also wondered whether the outcome would have been different if, as her father said, he had been permitted to stay with her.

Later that morning Brett called Dr. Barlowe's office and persisted until his receptionist called him to the phone. He finally agreed to see her.

Brett told her father she wanted to see Dr. Barlowe alone. She thought he might object, but he didn't. Her first impression was that Dr. Barlowe was too young, too boyish-looking. Or was she just getting older?

Dr. Barlowe confirmed that her mother had been scheduled to be discharged from the emergency room . . . and that she had vomited and aspirated before her father went in to see her.

"She did not develop chemical pneumonia, which is what we

were afraid of," he added, "and her lungs are as clean as they ever were."

Brett had the feeling that Dr. Barlowe was talking about a baseball game, and had just told her that her team was winning. She also thought his young boyish looks—black hair, hazel eyes and perfectly-shaped eyebrows—would be of interest to some twenty-year-old something, but not to her. She felt that he had a Satan-like look, and could almost see horns beginning to grow out of the top of his head.

"Stop this," she told herself. "He isn't Satan, even if he isn't as sensitive as he should be." Brett glanced hurriedly at her questions. She had jotted them down on pieces of paper the hospital receptionist had given her: green paper. Her mother's favorite color.

Although it wouldn't help her mother now, she wanted to know why she had been left alone in the emergency room cubicle with the curtain closed. Did she have a stroke? And had anyone checked on her mother when they wouldn't let her father go in? Dr. Barlowe answered all of her questions, except the last one.

"Your mother did not have a stroke, he told her, but her brain was severely damaged because of loss of oxygen," For some reason, he emphasized that.

As she talked to Dr. Barlowe, Brett had the feeling that the hospital wanted to "bury its mistake"—her comatose mother.

She was certain of it when he suggested she turn off her mother's respirator—because she was in a vital bed—needed for "live" patients.

On Saturday evening Brett and her father went to visit some good friends of her parents.

At dinner, Brett realized she wasn't focusing on the conversation until Bob, their host, suggested she call Dr. Hamilton, a well-known neurologist he knew.

"Appreciate that," Brett said. "But how do I get Dr. Hamilton at 6:30 on Saturday night?"

Brett couldn't, but Bob did, and Dr. Hamilton went to see her mother early Sunday morning.

On Monday morning, Dr. Barlowe met with Brett and her father in the consultation room at the hospital—the "Quiet Room." It had a funereal feel, Brett thought.

Dr. Barlowe didn't mince words. "Your mother's brain is probably dead," he said.

He really is insensitive, she thought. I wonder if he is this way toward his wife?

"Dr. Hamilton saw her yesterday morning," Dr. Barlow

continued, "and came to the same conclusion." His words held no emotion.

When Brett first talked to him, Dr. Barlowe had told her he didn't think it was necessary to call in a specialist. She felt then and still did that he thought she was questioning his diagnosis and treatment. Again, Dr. Barlowe told her she should consider turning off her mother's respirator.

"There's no point in visiting my mother any more, is there?" Brett asked quietly.

"Not unless you really want to," he replied.

Brett went to call her husband, but couldn't remember the number. The decision about the "machine," as she began calling it, had to be hers, Jed told her. He suggested she call their minister.

Brett placed the second long-distance call and cried for the first two minutes. Her minister reassured her it would be all right to turn off the "machine" if there was no hope. Her dad agreed, although she didn't know if he was really aware of his consent.

By Monday afternoon Brett wavered. She had to talk to Dr. Hamilton first. She would have to live with this decision for the rest of her life.

But first she called Mr. Wood, the hospital administrator. She had to get answers as to why her mother had been left alone in the ER cubicle. Mr. Wood was at a meeting.

At 2:15 Brett called again. He had left the hospital. Would she like to talk to his assistant, Mr. Byrd? Brett said yes she would speak to him, and Mr. Byrd agreed to personally walk her through the emergency room.

Brett knew her mother had been in the last cubicle on the left. A man was lying there, swathed in a sheet. Only his feet were visible. She thanked Mr. Byrd and walked out.

Then Brett called her mother's family doctor, whom she hadn't spoken to yet. She had known him for twenty years. He was abrupt. Almost cold. He didn't practice at the hospital where her mother was, but Brett felt he could have at least come to see her. He reiterated what Dr. Barlowe had told her, so he must have talked to him about her condition.

On Tuesday, Brett decided to try Mr. Wood, the hospital administrator again. He was sympathetic and promised to arrange a meeting with the doctor in charge of the emergency room, as well as the one who had been on duty when her mother was admitted.

Not more than five minutes after she left Mr. Wood's office, she was paged. Dr. Barlowe was on the phone. He informed her that the results of the spinal tap Dr. Hamilton had taken were in, and she would be "relieved"—she thought that was the word he used—to know it showed blood in the spinal column. Her mother had had a stroke.

Brett asked if he knew whether the blood was recent or from several days ago. Dr. Barlowe got huffy. "It's several days' old," he said, adding that the EEG showed that she was brain dead.

Brett mentally pictured the horns on Dr. Barlowe's head getting bigger.

She mentioned that she was going to see Dr. Hamilton later.

"I told you what the results showed," he answered sharply.

Brett told Dr. Barlowe she wanted to see him. He said he would meet her in the Quiet Room. She slammed the phone down. Her mother was DEAD! They had killed her!

When Dr. Barlowe arrived, Brett was still numb. She told him not to talk. He put his head in his hand. Maybe he is human, Brett thought. But he didn't know how to handle her. Or the situation. He was still *so* young. He would learn. But she didn't have the time to wait.

Dr. Barlowe suggested an autopsy, simply because she wouldn't believe anyone, and again pressed for her answer about turning off her mother's respirator. She told him to give her a couple of hours, until after she spoke to Dr. Hamilton.

When she got to Dr. Hamilton's office, Brett blurted out her feelings, her anger, and her frustration.

Dr. Hamilton said at first he had suspected Brett's mother may have been given an over-dose of a drug to control her vomiting. He explained that he had taken more than one specimen for the spinal tap. All showed blood in the spinal column, which meant that she had had a stroke.

He assured Brett that her mother had felt no pain, and told her that she was brain dead.

She thanked him for his sensitivity and caring, then asked if she could call Dr. Barlowe's office. Dr. Hamilton's nurse had to dial the number. She couldn't.

At 4:20 p.m. Brett informed Dr. Barlowe of her decision.

At 4:20 p.m. the lights went out in three counties. Coincidence? Brett still doesn't know.

Her mother's funeral was Thursday. And the nightmares began.

Obscene

Lu Motley

Dr. Guthrie's deep voice brought Mary back to the room. Looking at his downcast eyes, which made him seem more deceptive; there were more accusations: "Mr. Sisson and Miss Withrow are here to file a complaint against you Ms. Thompson! You already know the circumstances . . . Right? His voice grew louder!" Yet, he couldn't look her in the face. He knew he was wrong. His constant looking down made him seem guilty. Long ago he'd become Superintendent of Schools for rural Haskins County, West Virginia. His booming voice made her remember tent meetings she'd gone to as a child with a maiden aunt who'd had a crush on the choirmaster.

There was a rivalry between the preacher and the choirmaster. Each tried to outdo one another, resulting in the preacher shouting until he was red in the face. When he almost collapsed one day while preaching, Mary's aunt swore she'd never go to one of those meetings again. She never did. Instead she began to invite the choirmaster to dinner. They were married after nine months of courting.

This taught Mary to distrust loud-voiced people. Yet here she was faced with one of the worst accusing her of using obscenity with one of her students. His booming voice continued as Dr. Guthrie suddenly stood up behind his desk to get her attention. "Young lady, we here in Haskins County do not take kindly to teachers who use obscene language in the classroom; that's not our way of teaching impressionable youngin's!"

Mary stood up to face the little man. "Dr. Guthrie, I am a member of the West Virginia Teacher's Union. Before too much more is said, I warn you that I'm going right out of this room to give them a call. I'm here without representation, and frankly, I don't like what these two (she pointed to a man and woman sitting on the other side of the room) have taken out of context. I would never use an obscenity with a student. You, as a gentleman, should know that!"

Her words were not without effect. Dr. Guthrie almost stumbled backward. He blinked a couple of times before rallying. Then he began to yell again. "Mr. Sisson and Miss Withrow were both witnesses to your usin' an obscene word in front of your class! Before you go callin' outsiders in, you'd better think twice young lady! This whole thing just might reach the newspapers, and you just might never teach again. Do you hear?"

Dr. Guthrie's finger was pointing right at Mary's nose when he stopped. Provoked, Mary couldn't keep from reaching out and brushing it aside before continuing to defend herself. This time she pointed her finger toward Mr. Sisson and Miss Withrow. "For some foolish reason, these two need to distort what happened in my class. They have lied about what I said. I feel I've been slandered; I have no choice but to call in the West Virginia Teacher's Union!"

Mary reached down and picked-up her coat, almost running to the door before she turned toward her accusers. She felt the venomous hatred in Maude Withrow's face. "Goodbye, Dr. Guthrie," Mary tried to control her voice as she backed out of his office, determined not to turn her back on those vicious snakes. That's what they were, two sick, vicious poisonous creatures who had no idea what education was about. Her face was stoic until she got to her rented room, where she made herself a hot chocolate and thought about her grandma's embrace. Only then, could she let go and cry like a hurt child. Growing-up was hard. She had been orphaned early, but, her grandma had raised her well. Her whole life was spent in Richmond, Virginia, until she went to college. She knew Richmond was still fighting the Civil War but there were more historical sites in Richmond than almost any other city. Mary was familiar with and loved them all.

"Edgar Allen Poe is not dead," Mary often told her friends and classmates at the University. Why he's still alive and well in Richmond. He's still courting Elmira Shelton over on Grace Street. Grace Street was only a block from her grandma's house. "Why he goes over there and reads her his poetry and stories." I see him often as he climbs up the hill." Mary preferred to discuss what she felt were the positive points of Richmond's history, rather than dwelling on a war that would not die.

At the university, Mary had excelled in teacher's education. Still, there was no education in any school anywhere that offered a course which could deal with teaching in rural Haskins County, or Maude Withrow and her devious, puritanical mind. She had gotten "A's" in most of her classes, so her advisor assured her that teaching promised security. Still, it was difficult not to blame her. Mary thought back about when she went against her Grandma's wishes by accepting the job in West Virginia. "I'll get home often. There's Thanksgiving and Christmas which will give me long breaks. I need to earn some money so I can pay back those student loans," she argued. Still, she was tempted to wait until the following year when something closer might open; her granny wasn't getting any younger. For the first time since her parent's death granny had a man in her life which Mary knew was one of the best things to happen.

So Mary accepted the job in West Virginia where she was lucky to find a small place right in back of the school where she'd be teaching. She felt positive about the move. Her interview with Dr. Guthrie was late in the season. Her predecessor had died during the summer, leaving the biology position open. The school placement office had called her on Friday with the interview on Monday. School was about to begin the following week.

Mary remembered the Superintendent's words. "These people don't take kindly to outsiders. It'll take a couple of years for them to accept you. Then, all at once, you'll be one of us," he'd said laughing and patting her on the back. His laugh had caught in the back of his throat. It made Mary look back as she went out his door. Now, she knew why.

Still, the students had proved him wrong. They were eager to learn. With their help, Mary went to Harrisonburg and bought an aquarium and stocked it with live specimens caught in West Virginias' wild and blue-green, gurgling creeks. Several parents had volunteered to chaperone when she took her class on a field trip to Trout Stream and Seneca Rocks. They enjoyed the incredible beauty of the nature which surrounded them. The mountains were like a magnificent woman, luring and enfolding, feeding stories about the old pioneers, plus harsh winters, which sometimes made survival impossible. Yet, the streams and mountain fields and woodlands provided a wonderful classroom in good weather. The only problem was Maude. Maude was her teacher's aide, assigned to help with the overcrowded classroom. Mary remembered thinking the only one who overcrowded was Maude.

The old woman would sit in the room and sleep most of the time while Mary read. Once in a while, she would wake and raise her gnarled old head and mutter, "Never heard sech a thing. Don't know whut they'll teach kids next." and then, she'd doze again. The miracle was that the students already had the score. They'd look at Mary and smile as if they knew Maude was typical of the "old ways." Yet, the students made it all worth while. Still, the isolation plus Maude's antagonism made Mary set goals to visit Richmond as Maude kept right on sitting on her little chair in her corner, quietly sleeping, the sound of her muffled snores occasionally caused the students to stifle laughs or to poke each other. Mary thought how tolerant they were.

Sometimes Mary wondered if Maude wasn't "planted" there to keep tabs while she taught since she was an outsider. Then, she dismissed the thought as paranoia. Just before Thanksgiving, as the students were busy helping her clean up after a lesson, Mary had yelled last minute instructions for homework. One was completely absorbed at the aquarium, and that student at the aquarium never been quiet for that long at any lesson Mary could remember. Maude was sound asleep in her corner as Mary started over to see what was holding Cory Higgenbottom"s attention as his words echoed across the room, "Look at those crawdads a "F'ing!"

The class immediately burst into laughter and ran to the aquarium. Sure enough, when Mary reached the aquarium, there were two crawdads obliviously mating mightily. Mary was stifling a guffaw when she saw Maude's eyes fly open. She was afraid the old woman would fall as she stood, shaking, trying to grasp the situation! Then, when Maude looked in Cory's direction, she had fire in her eyes, as she rushed to the door and slammed it behind her.

"That's right Maude," Mary said under her breath. "You all can do it, think about it, even sing about it in your country songs; but for God's sake, don't be spontaneous or talk about it." Mary hated Maude's self-righteous attitude! As she quickly searched her mind, wondering how to deal with this problem rationally, Mary asked herself if it really was a problem. Why shouldn't the child say the "F" word? That's all he had heard all his life. Who was there to teach him differently?

So, taking a deep breath, she tried to focus on what to say to Cory without sounding phony. These students could spot a phony a mile away. "Cory," she began. "Cory," there are other words that explain what those crawdads were doing. The "F" word is not acceptable in the classroom."

The boy's eyes took on an almost wise gleam. "Hell, Ms. Thompson, "F'ing" is "F'ing! That's how life begins!" he blurted out. The other students almost fell on the floor laughing at the look on Mary's face. By that time, she had turned three or four shades of red. Nevertheless, she tried once more to maintain her composure as she said, "You're absolutely right Cory, but there are some people, most people here at this school who don't like that word."

"You mean the "F" word?" Cory yelled again. Cory's voice was so loud its woodsy huskiness could have taken first prize at the hog calling contest at the West Virginia State Fair.

"Yes, I mean the "F" word!" came Mary's reply in the vernacular as the door opened. In came Mr. Sisson with Maude trailing right behind. Her eyes were feverish with gleaming, squinting intensity. Mary didn't think it possible. Her knees almost buckled. The full impact, plus Corey's pronouncement raced across her brain. "Cory, the proper word you want to use is copulating," said Mary feeling stupid and hypocritical.

Still, Cory would not be quiet. Mary felt her fate was sealed as he shot back. "Hell, I know you told the class that before Ms. Thompson. You can't expect me to say, look at those crawdads a copulatin'. No one would understand me!"

With that, Mr. Sisson's voice thundered, "That's all!"

Maude's face was exultant! She loved punishment! Cory was going to get it! Mary never forgot the fear on the boy's face as he was literally lifted off his feet by the seat of his pants and carried from the room by the enraged principal.

Corporal punishment was still allowed in West Virginia, usually inflicted with a huge wooden paddle which Mary had seen hanging like a weapon beside Mr. Sisson's desk. Mr. Sisson's office was just down the hall from Mary's room. She stood with the students in the doorway listening as the man's stern voice, slightly higher and shriller than usual, collided with the boy's harsh resonance. When the whacks began, followed by low, muffled groans combined with intermittent sobs, there was no compassion shown. The whacks continued for a full five minutes. Mary and her students counted each with nodding heads, trying to hold back the tears. Even at their tender age those students knew the punishment didn't fit. Cory was only twelve years old.

After that, Cory was suspended for a week, leaving Mary to

wonder what the other students had learned from the incident. The "F" word "had picked-up in popularity. It appeared on every bathroom wall, dirty rock, dusty car, anything that it could be written on. The seventh grade was the most defiant. If possible, they would have hired an airplane to write it in smoke across the blue West Virginia sky.

Then, when Cory returned he was withdrawn and remote. Mary watched as he got out of his dad's pick-up truck with the Confederate flag. She couldn't avoid feeling responsible. She felt helpless, unable to afraid to reach out or help, fearing Maude's critical eyes were constantly waiting for more to carry to Mr. Sisson. There was no way she would ever believe what happened to that boy was right as she wondered how she could bear to finish her term at the school. Cory and his family had moved to Haskins County from Bloody Mingo. She remembered his telling the students how hard it had been in bloody Mingo County. He loved the history of the Hatfields and the McCoys. When he described Sid Hatfield's being shot in the back on the courthouse steps, she suggested he give a report on it and he did. That was when she realized how talented Cory was in his written descriptions of the rural area and the people. He had earned an "A" on the report "For your use of the English language Cory," she said patting his arm.

So by Friday following Cory's return, Mary could almost breathe normally. Maude Withrow was the only reminder. She kept the incident alive by repeating over and over again: "Some people feel education put them above us normal folks who act proper." Mary felt if she had to listen to Maude say that one more time under her breath as she walked by she'd . . . then she felt . . .Why give the old fool the satisfaction?

The next Tuesday a note from the Superintendent's Office was in Mary's mailbox. She put it in her purse and waited until she was safely home before reading it: "Superintendent Guthrie requests your presence at 4:30 p m at the Haskins County School Board, Thursday, November 12th.". Mary felt sick. Surely they couldn't fire her over such a little thing. Yet, deep down, she knew the seriousness of the matter which made her long for Richmond and her grandmas' loving arms.

November 12th came quickly. The West Virginia Teacher's Union had intervened which resulted in another meeting in Dr. Guthrie's office. He had seemed almost fatherly when he offered to destroy Mr. Sisson's reprimand. "I wanted you here to watch me tear up this reprimand, Ms. Thompson."

Mary had won! At least on the surface. So she decided not to continue past Christmas. She hated the anger which showed in her face as she replied to Dr. Guthrie's remark. "What's to keep you from writing another one and putting it in my file after I leave Dr. Guthrie?" That hit the mark! An astonished Dr. Guthrie jumped up and walked out the door! He left her to find her own way out.

The last day of school there were tears as Mary said goodbye at Christmas break. One little fellow, aptly named Tom Wolf, yelled from a safe distance, "I'll bet you never say that word again." Mary met his smile thinking how right he was.

Later, driving toward Richmond, she wondered how she had survived the farewell without breaking down. Back home, there was a good job working in a laboratory, but it would be a long time before Mary stopped thinking about Cory and the other students. She had learned much from them. Also she knew she would miss the beauty of those glorious mountains which lured and enfolded, almost like a grave. "I thought they needed good teachers," she said out loud.

The Rescue

Virginia O'Keefe

Douglas Packney drummed on his desk as he waited for his mother to answer her phone. It had rung at least six times. He'd wanted to install another one next to her favorite chair in the sunroom, but she was as stubborn as ever. "No need for that, dear," she'd protested. "I've already got a perfectly good phone in the kitchen."

Half way through the seventh ring, he heard her tentative, "Hello?"

"Mother," he said sharply, nerves stretched to the limit. "I heard you were in town with some strange guy, took him to the bank. Who was it?"

"Oh, now, don't worry. Woody's a nice young man. It's nothing for you to fuss about."

"Woody!" He practically screeched the name. "Who's Woody?" It was sad how quickly she was slipping into her second childhood. She'd started to wear red lipstick and rouge her cheeks as though she were forty years younger.

"He's just giving me some advice."

His palms went damp. It was the classic con—gullible widow, a schemer. Mix the two and . . . the money is gone before you turn around. "How'd you meet him?" he snapped.

The other end of the line went silent.

"Mother?"

"Oh, yes, dear. Sorry. A car just pulled into the driveway. I'll have to answer the door."

"Wait," her son demanded. "Tell me, now. How'd you meet this—Woody?"

He heard her speak to someone. Then she was back. "Let's

see. I guess he called like all the rest. But, Woody's the nicest. I've got to go now. We'll talk later."

The situation was even more critical than he had anticipated. She had said "the rest." Jackals were circling around his seventy-year-old mother who was so trusting she'd give up her life savings for any kind of a story.

Douglas gave his secretary a buzz. "Liz, I've gotta meet my lawyer." He didn't mention he also would see his mother. There was no need to start another rumor flying in West Carrolton about Gladys Packney.

A touch of guilt slid down his spine. Maybe her problem came from his neglecting her since his father's death. Grant Packney had always dominated their home. A self-made man, he'd transformed his farming interests into a tidy fortune. Between beef cattle, lumber, and good investments, he'd built a considerable estate. That was what troubled Douglas. His mother didn't know a thing about handling money. While his father was alive, he'd handled all of the finances. Now she was being as stubborn about letting him manage her assets as she was about the telephone.

That long overdue arrangement would change today. The rumors embarrassed him. His mother had been seen at lunch with a flashy-dressing man, probably this Woody character. And, Hal, the vice-president of the bank, had made a crack while they were playing golf. "Looks like your mother's making up for lost time, isn't she?"

"What do you mean?" Douglas had asked, uncomfortable to discuss his mother in public.

Hal whistled. "Those withdrawals are impressive. She must be really buying some fancy jewelry."

Douglas choked, "Withdrawals?"

"Oh, sorry, pal. Thought you knew," Hal had smirked as he got into the cart and took off down the fairway.

He'd told Liz, his wife, that night and moaned, "God knows what she's done with it."

"Ask Hal to give you an accounting," she'd suggested.

But he couldn't, not without a power-of-attorney. That's what he intended to get today. Jerry, his lawyer, was going with him, taking the proper papers. Douglas also planned to put her into a good retirement home, one close by where he could visit often and keep an eye on her.

In the past, every time he'd suggested she move into a senior residence, she'd balked. "No, this is my home. I want to stay here." He refused to put up with that stall any longer.

Her argument was that she was as physically fit as ever. He had to agree. It was her mind. She'd slipped into her dotage after his father's death, wearing too much makeup and shorter skirts, acting like she was still the head-turning beauty of her youth.

Douglas knew he had to stop her. Liz would have to handle the kids' soccer tournament details, and he would miss the Rotary Club meeting, if necessary. This was an emergency, he thought, feeling ever more guilty about his lack of attention to his mother's obvious needs.

"Are you ready for this?" Jerry asked as he slid into the passenger seat. "It could get nasty."

Douglas had thought of nothing else. "If you're there, she'll see it's the right thing to do," he said with more assurance than he felt.

When they arrived at the handsome white house banked with huge magnolia trees in full bloom, Douglas's attention riveted on a silver Mercedes parked in the graveled circular drive. "This should be interesting," he said, slamming the door shut.

Gladys Packney's face lit up in surprise when she answered the door, and Douglas noticed her new more flirty hair style and the scent of some exotic perfume.

"How nice you've come, Dougie, and your friend, Jerry, too." She patted him on the cheek and gave him a peck.

Douglas cringed at the pet name she never gave up calling him. "I haven't seen you for quite a while, Jerry," she said taking his arm. "You're both in time to meet my good friend Woody Turner. He's about to leave."

I bet he can't wait to get out, Douglas thought, especially when we've shown up.

"I hope you boys can eat supper with me," she chirped. "I have your favorite homemade apple pie, dear. It's Woody's favorite, too, but he can't stay."

Gladys introduced the men, seemingly unaware of a tension so thick you'd need a laser to cut it.

The tall, tanned man in a perfectly tailored Armani suit extended his hand. "Woodruff Turner. My pleasure, Mr. Packney. Your mother has told me quite a bit about you." He lifted one eyebrow toward Jerry in recognition. "You must be the famous lawyer everyone in town talks about. I'm sorry I have to run."

"Not so fast," Douglas said. "We've got some things to settle."

Turner gave Douglas a cold stare. "She'll tell you about the deal."

Douglas blocked his way. "Oh, yeah! If you leave now, I'll have the police here so fast your head'll spin."

Gladys gasped.

The other man raised his eyebrows in mock surprise. "On what charge?" he cracked. "Visiting a lonely woman?"

"Try fraud. Or embezzlement. I don't think it'll be too difficult." Douglas fought for control over the rage boiling through his veins.

Turner glared at him, jamming his hands into the pockets of his fine, unwrinkled gabardine suit.

Douglas stared at the bulge in the man's right pocket, and thought better of challenging him any more. If he was carrying a gun, and it looked like he might be, it was pointed right at him. His mother was mixed up in something really nasty, something that might be better handled by a professional in law enforcement. He slid to one side so Woody could pass.

Woody cast a cold threatening look at Douglas and then at Jerry. He meant business, and Douglas was having trouble remembering the number 911.

"I wouldn't call in the law right now if you know what's in your best interests," the man in the beige suit growled. Turning, he spoke kindly to his mother. "Thanks for the contract, Mrs. Packney. You made a wise decision. If you want to get in touch, you know how."

Stunned, Douglas watched helplessly while the man who had defrauded his mother sauntered down the steps and drove away in the sleek Mercedes.

She sighed. "I'd hoped you two would get to know each other better."

"I'll get to know him well enough when we take him to court," Douglas said, heading toward the phone to alert the police chief about a silver Mercedes with an out-of-state license.

"Don't, dear," his mother said, closing her hand over his as he began to dial. "There's no need. It's all right. Trust me."

Reluctantly, he hung up the phone. From the corner of his eye he'd seen Jerry pull the power-of-attorney from his briefcase and give him a wink.

She shook her head. "He was such a nice boy. I'll really miss him. I guess that's why I took so long to make up my mind."

"He's a crook, Mother," Douglas snorted, motioning for Jerry to hand him the document. "He was out to get your money. How much did you give him?"

Gladys Packney's face crumpled. "I was going to surprise you, dear."

"Look, let's stop playing games. I know you withdrew thousands. How much did—Woody get?"

"None, dear. I just invested it in stocks."

"In that—in Woody's company?" His throat grew dry.

"No. I forgot to tell you, dear. I joined a girls' investment group. We meet for lunch and discuss which stocks are the best. It's really working out quite well."

"And Woody?" Douglas choked on the name.

"I had to disappoint him," she said quietly. "And I was sorry because it might have been a good investment."

Douglas and Jerry exchanged glances. "I don't understand. What was going on?" Douglas said. "What was he trying to get out of you? What's the contract he was talking about?"

Gladys shook her head. "You see," she said confidentially, "I found out something about Woody. He wasn't what he seemed."

"You figured that out?" Douglas dropped one of the papers in surprise.

"Oh, yes. But I didn't want him to know right away. I was having a little fun." She sat down and smoothed out her skirt. "That's all right, don't you think, dear?"

She looked so pathetic, his heart stopped for a moment. She really was quite vulnerable. "Sure, Mother. Look there's one little favor I wish you'd do for me. Sign this paper, right here. It's for your own benefit. I'll help you take care of your affairs from now on. I don't want you to have to bother your head about money anymore." He shoved the document into her lap and forced the pen into her hand.

She took the pen and held it suspended over the document. That disturbing faraway look he remembered from his youth had come into her eyes. "I was thinking about your father and what he would want me to do. It was so difficult to make the choice."

"I know, Mother. If you sign here, you won't have to think about things like that any more. I'll take care of you."

She lay the pen on the end table beside her and touched his hand lightly. "You're a good boy. I know you want to do the best for me, and I hope you're not upset. I wanted to hold out until the price was right, you know. Fifteen million dollars did seem right." Distractedly, she set the power-of-attorney on the table beside the pen.

Douglas swallowed hard. "Fifteen million dollars?" She didn't have that much money in her investments. What kind of papers had she signed?

"Yes, dear. I figured he could afford it after I learned how he was a front man for Jackson and Wheeler, that big investment company, and they were trying to broker a deal for a new world-class theme park. My property was the last one they needed. They'd bought my neighbors' farms for peanuts, you know, so it only seemed fair."

Jerry and Douglas looked at each other again. They were quiet for a minute and then Jerry asked, "Are you saying you sold the farm for fifteen million?"

She turned to Jerry. "I think my husband would be pleased, don't you?" she said, tapping her fingers on her knees.

He swallowed. "Fifteen is well above market value . . ."

"I'll miss this old place, but maybe it's time to move into town, anyway," she continued, giving Douglas that patient smile he remembered so well from his childhood. "I've started enjoying having lunch with friends at restaurants. Now, what did you boys want from me today?"

Douglas sat down in one of her flowered chintz chairs and nodded to Jerry as he picked up the papers from the table.

"You mean you're going through with this?" Jerry blurted.

Douglas stared at the paper. "I just didn't want to alarm you, Mother," he said. "Crooks try to take advantage of people, especially the elderly."

"I know, Dougie. The girls in my club talked about that. I promise I'll be careful."

He winced at the nickname, but cracked a small smile. "Fifteen million, you say."

"Then you think I did all right?"

Douglas carefully wadded up the power of attorney. "I don't think I need this anymore, do you Jerry?"

The lawyer dropped into another of Gladys's flowered chairs and sighed. "I'm having a terrible craving for homemade apple pie."

"Me too," Douglas said. "And I'd like it smothered with ice cream."

El Jugo

Daniel Pravda

—Gratias, Agent 1903

Manny's On/Off was the first bar to reopen after the hurricane. It wasn't the worst storm of all time, just kinda blew and screamed for a few hours in the middle of the night. Keeping kids up. Scaring people who thought their lives meant something.

I was the third to show up, after Manny and superwaitress Tamra. We all lived within walking distance. Bobby the bartender wasn't going to make it. He lived a few miles north, and was flooded in.

I was the first to get a drink. A cold beer.

Manny was a smart son of a gun. He'd been through plenty of storms, but you'd be surprised how many beach people live with hurricanes and nasty gale-force storms, but never get it. He always knew the weather forecast. He also knew weathermen were half-guessers and half-readers of information. He was still thinking ahead. For a guy who never spent a day in high school in his life, he was pretty damn smart. He kept around a lot of extra liquor. Extra beer. Extra wine. And maybe some other intoxicants for his friends. He also stocked ice. By the ton. Had three ice makers going full tilt the night before the storm. And he had cold storage. Places he could keep ice for days on end. And when you have ice, you have cold beer and drinks on the rocks and even iced tea for sober suckers.

Looked like Manny was gonna have to work the bar, since Bobby was trapped. He did it at least one night a week anyway. But not usually on Fridays, my day to impress local chicks and disc jockey drunks with my guitar skill and songwriting bullshit.

I always wondered why people liked my songs. I played some old favorites like "Knockin' on Heaven's Door," but mostly I played my own songs. They were slow rock'n' roll, with a little blues and a little more booze. And my sipper was bourbon. Jack. Jimmy Beam. Turkey. Kentucky Gentleman. Old Granddad. I didn't care. Just as long as it wasn't in a shotglass.

Cabin fever sets in quick after a hurricane. Real fast for me. After storms, I like to see the damage. The pain. Destruction at a level no tiny human can achieve. Sounds cold, but I ain't above it. If I was sitting at home in a hurricane, any storm, plicking on my wooden woman and the roof caved and killed me, I'd die happy. Not in one of those nursing home nightmares. Not at some company job. Not hanging on till I can't hear or see or figure out what's going on.

But if the storm doesn't smash me like an ant and carry me out to sea, I'll be out there. Checking it out. I love the ruin. Obliteration. People looking at what was and wondering what will never be again.

So before I came to Manny's, I walked through town. Couldn't drive; stoplights were on the street, buzzing, daring you to touch them. Telephone poles smashing in roofs of cars. Trees down. Trailers on their sides, a couple black from fire. Windows taped up. Some broken. Branches blanketing the road. Leaves. Pine needles. Sand inland like drifts of snow. Trash blown everywhere. People's minds windswept and soaked and scared and happy-blessed just to be alive.

You could see it in their eyes. Where to get help. Food. Water. Power. Most folks are wimps. Can't live without Walmart and Exxon. Wimps. Bitches. That's why I liked Manny. He was tough. A brick. A charred log. He didn't need electricity to open his bar. He needed cold beer and plenty of change. And he wasn't one of those bastards who'd raise prices in the toughest of times. He was still running a business, but he was there to help too. That's part of what a bar is, a place to come for help: advice, forget, escape, a smile. And cerveza.

And Manny liked me, because I was on time, I could play all night long, and I didn't need any power either, just my acoustic, my windpipe, vocal chords and an I.V. of alcohol. See, being a guitar player ain't easy. It's real hard to play and drink at the same time, so either you don't drink as much or you drink more before, between, and after. That's why I liked 80 proof gold—fast. In a short glass. Instant. Fire in the belly, not far from the heart.

My parents long passed. One brother married and moved to Colorado. Other brother dead. Heroin. So the only person I hurt is myself, they say. My opinion, if I didn't drink and strum my baby at the bar a couple nights a week, *then* I'd be hurting myself. My songs help me. Heal me. Or keep me from the darkness.

I know the darkness though. Saw my brother shooting up. Saw my dad sick from cigarettes. Saw his oxygen mask. Saw his weak breath. And his black lungs turning him into nothing. A pile of bones in a dirty bed.

I know darkness. Fights at the bar far beyond words or a girl. Drunk driving. Arthritis. Impotence. Rotten teeth. Tumors. Cold. Manic depression. Sadism. Suicide. Numbness. Not caring about nothin.'

I didn't concern myself with any of this artist shit either. No goatee or ears pierced. No thin glasses or combat boots or silver rings or spiked leather. I never gave a squirt about how people looked at me. When I got up on stage, I wore a t-shirt, shorts, flips, maybe, and my six-string on a plain black canvas strap.

So that afternoon, I knew Manny's door would be open. I walked in and Manny was there. Smiled at me. Knew I would show. Knew I would play.

You're like the sun, he said. Every morning.

More like the moon, I said.

Even if it's cloudy, sun or moon, still up there, he said.

Yup. Still there.

Thanks for coming, he said.

I looked at him like he was crazy.

Huh? Thanking me? Thanks go to you for opening this place and keeping it open!

He smiled.

Got a drink for you, Six, he said.

He pulled a bottle from under the bar. One I had never seen. It said *El Jugo*.

I picked it up. Old and dusty. Brown glass. Had what looked like a Mayan temple on the label.

What is this? I said.

Couldn't read it at all. He looked entertained by my confusion.

The juice, in Spanish, he said. Got it from my brother down in Arizona. He finally got out of the military.

Is it tequila? I said.

No. Agavé with some extra ingredients. I was saving it, but every time a big storm comes through, I think how stupid it is to save things. No point saving something if it gets destroyed or spoiled or you get dead before you can taste it.

Before you can enjoy it, I said.

He nodded. Manny understood things. He called Tamra over. She skated over and slapped my arm.

Hey, Babe, I said.

Hey, Six, she said.

Everybody all right in your house? I said referring to her two cats.

Yup. Just another leak in the roof.

This night is going to be different, Manny said. Gonna have a lot of drinkers here tonight. They got no power at home. No tv. No computers. No refrigerators. They're gonna wanna get out. So we're gonna get busy. But . . .

But what, Manny? Tamra said.

But we have *El Jugo*. This stuff is lightning trapped in glass. Not just strong. Makes you strong. Gives you juice. Energy. Blood.

Manny went off in Spanish. I don't know what he said, but he meant it. He was smiling, but it wasn't something funny. It was excitement with a teaspoon of the unknown. There was wonder in his eyes.

What's in it? Tamra said.

What's in dirt? Manny said.

Tam looked confused.

A thousand years of Aztecs and Mayans and Spanish hate, he said. Labor and patience and local knowledge passed down through the centuries like a proud family name.

All right, Manny, I said, don't overhype.

I ain't, he said. I ain't had a drink of *El Jugo* for at least ten years. Cause I ain't no medicine man. I don't talk to spirits and all that stuff they tell you out West.

Sounds like peyote, I said.

This ain't about hallucinating, Manny said. This ain't some hippie Grateful Dead shit.

Don't talk bad about them, I said.

We've sang plenty of Dead tunes, Six, Manny said, but *El Jugo* is different. This is intense clarity. More intense than anything you ever drank, smoked, fucked, whatever. It's not a trip. It makes the real realer.

Whoa, Tamra said. Sounds heavy.

Is heavy, Manny said. Kinda like speed, but not as synthetic. Not so chemmy. This shit here is organic, made from the earth.

Manny, I said, enough. Pour us a shot and let's go.

Okay, Manny said. People will be coming soon, so let's do it.

Manny reached behind the bar and lined up two double-shooters and a short glass for me. He broke the seal. I could smell it instantly. It was like smelling fire. It smelled like I was about to cough. Hard.

Let it hit you for an hour or so, Manny said. If you want another one, let me know.

He was looking at me.

Don't assume, Six, he said. More ain't always better.

I think that every time I throw up, I said.

Exactly, Manny laughed.

He carefully filled each glass. It seemed if he spilled, it would eat through the bar or something.

He then uncapped three Pabst Blue Ribbons.

Gonna need a chaser, he said. Ready?

We each lifted a glass.

To power no hurricane can handle, Manny said.

We clinked glasses and shot.

It made sense that the stuff smelled like fire. Tasted like it too. Like nothing. I've drank 190-proof grain. Straight. No contest. Grain is like dropping a match in your stomach. This was like dropping a comet. Tamra started coughing and spitting up her beer. As his eyes teared, Manny took a couple gulps. I downed the whole beer in five seconds. It helped.

When I belched, I expected fire to come out. Manny handed me another PBR. We all sat in silence. Breathing deep. Slow. Swallowing saliva by the gallon.

Damn, Manny, Tam said.

The pain passed. We were okay. Time to wait. Time to wonder what was coming. Knowing it was serious and deep and way down beyond the liver and kidneys.

Manny hid *El Jugo* and swept the glasses into the sink.

Wasn't long till the regulars started to come in. Eyebrow Meadows was first. Then Jeff Wall, the big bouncer from down the street. Then Mike McCovey with his girl Jo. Then Alabama Jane and her neighbor Jenni Griggs. Ditch Coleman with a couple of his boys. Murphy came in with Brick. They racked up a game of pool.

Manny started mixing as Tamra started zipping from table to table. That woman was a ballet dancer with a tray full of glasses. I talked to Eyebrow for a while. He was talking about a prize-fight he hoped wasn't canceled by the hurricane. Seemed like he had a bet down.

Normally, I would get down a little bourbon before I went up on stage. Even though I didn't feel *El Jugo* yet, I held off. Manny handed me another beer, and I went up.

Just a step up from the floor of the bar. But it was like a wall between me and the crowd. Wasn't always though.

I took my baby from her stand and strapped in. I started to tune her, comparing fifth fret to open string, except on the G, where you tuned the fourth fret. I tuned with harmonics. She was ready to wail.

Manny was right. The bar was full in no time. I went up and sat on that shaky stool. Tuned again.

Manny was rocking behind the bar. Little grin on his face that said, I knew it. I liked nights like this. Cause no one gave a shit. No one was prettied up or clean-shaven. This night, it was all right to be ugly. Wasn't even ugly really, just oneself and cool with it. More like beautiful.

I could feel *El Jugo* building. Going to work on my temples. My teeth. Jaw a little tight. Palms cool.

See, people used to say I coulda made it big. Record deals, tours, the whole reeking pile of crap. I guess part of me woulda liked that. I'd be lying if I said otherwise. But it bothered me sometimes, late at night, when a half-gallon couldn't knock me out. Did I not reach far enough? It was always there. Somewhere down there.

So I was up there, playing for the friendly, mellow crowd. Strumming true and smooth like you barely know you're doing it. I wasn't drunk. Just a couple beers. As I warmed up, it was like clouds parting up there. Like wide doors opening, sparking off dark tar. I looked at the fretboard and it seemed magnified. Like my glasses were microscopes. The guitar felt a mile wide, like I couldn't miss where I wanted to put my fingers. I didn't think about playing at all. Just did.

I usually worked up a good sweat playing in front of people. But not this night. It felt almost cold, like late November. I smiled and flirted with the crowd. I told them I wouldn't do a request, and they ate it up. I jammed out some rock and went off on a few solos I never thought could come out of me. Didn't take a sip of beer the whole set.

I left them wanting more. Waded to the bar in a sea of handshakes and backslaps.

Damn, Six, Manny said. You were up there forever.

I was?

Yup. How long's a normal set?

About fifty minutes, I said. How long was I up there?

Two hours, easy.

What?

I looked up at the clock above the register. I couldn't believe I had played for almost two and a half hours non-stop.

Damn, Manny.

Damn straight. Best you've ever played. Tightest. Sharpest. Funnest. You gonna get laid, for sure. Look out there.

I looked at the crowd. People were happy. Quite a few were looking at me, pointing, and talking. I felt weird, like I was a little bit famous. I wanted another taste of *El Jugo*.

Pour another, I said to Manny.

What?

El Jugo, my savior.

Manny looked at me funny.

Have one with me, I said.

His expression disapproved.

What's the matter?

Manny's a friend. And a good man. So he said nothing. But I knew he didn't think I needed more.

He poured anyway. And like an idiot, I drank it.

Sometimes, I came here drunk as hell. Just had those days, where either everything went against you or you ran into the right/wrong people swinging bottles around their heads like whips intended for themselves.

I still got up there and mumbled through the songs. Spitting on people. Spilling my drinks. Spilling other people's drinks. Knowing you shouldn't be like that, especially at work. Trying to play cool, but everyone knows you ain't even close.

Truth was, I wasn't trying to get drunk every day. Didn't want to. Wasn't fun. Sitting around alone. Asking the bathroom mirror why I was like that. Why I did that.

I saw that bathroom mirror on Manny's face. But I bottomed *El Jugo* quicker than a blink.

I relaxed for a while. Talked to Jenni Griggs and Alabama Jane. The roof on Jenni's place had blown off, and she was staying with Jane. But I knew she wanted to stay with me. All in good time, I said with my eyes. And she knew.

I went to the john. Eyebrow was in there with Baltimore Pete passing a blunt back and forth.

Goddamn pine fell on my girl's car, Pete said.

Bad?

Totaled it. Looks like Godzilla karate-chopped the roof.

Eyebrow laughed and spit out his smoke.

Stop bein' funny, he said. You gonna play soon, Six?

Yup, a few more minutes.

You were goin' off.

Thanks.

Yeah, Pete said. You got a CD or somethin'?

Nope.

Need to make one.

They were wasted, but my ego was still inflated. I needed to get away from all these people. And there's only place for that.

I slipped into my strap and started tuning again. Gotta keep in tune.

But it was already too late. When you get too plastered, the first thing to go is your ear. I couldn't tune right, so that led directly to the second thing to go: giving a damn. So I put my butt back on the edge of the stool, and started to strum. I was all right for a little while. I did a couple of crowd favorites, a Stones tune, some Pink Floyd.

Then I was in that back alley mumbling to the rats and trash-cans. Slobbering on myself. Not talking to the crowd. Struggling to get through one song, one chorus, one measure, one note. Sweating like an icecube in hell. Like playing guitar was work. A job. Shit.

I closed my eyes for the last few songs. I felt safe in my dark spinning eyelids. When I opened my eyes to put the guitar on her stand, the place was nearly empty.

I looked at the clock. I had played another long set. I didn't even hear last call. Manny tossed me a rag as I sat at the bar. I wiped my forehead and the stream off my chin.

What a night, Manny said.

What happened? I feel like I passed out, but I was playing the whole time.

Yup, Manny said.

His t-shirt was filthy and streaked with sweat. Tamra came over with a tray full of dirty glasses.

You all right? she asked me.

I think so, I said. I shouldn't have . . .

Don't worry about it, Manny said. You played fine.

That first set was unreal, Tamra said.

Thanks. Shit, Manny. That second round of *El Jugo* . . .

Yup, I know, he said.

I looked around. My head was grinding. The girls were gone. The guys had paid up and gone home to crash.

What a day, I said out loud with a long sigh. What a night.

Appreciate the hurricane, Manny said.

I tried, but I couldn't.

Worth Blood

Lynn Veach Sadler

Every night after supper, Daddy read to "our" family from a raggedy copy of the Welsh Bible, the *Cyd Gordiad*, by a Mr. Abel Morgan, that had been published in Philadelphia after a lot of our ancestors came over to America on a "coffin ship" and settled in a tract Mr. William Penn himself had allowed them in the area of Pennsylvania. I say "Daddy" and "our," but Mr. Tom Bludworth wasn't my father. Not really by blood at least. He and his wife, Miss Tace, took me in when my mother, an indentured servant, also Welsh, caught a fever and died after arriving in North Carolina from the state down below to look for my father, who had come over before her. I was a baby, and the Bludworths were the only parents I knew.

Anyhow, Daddy would read a passage in Welsh, fingering along at it slowly, and then translate into English for us. He didn't make us learn the language, which he claimed he didn't know much about himself and was mostly going from memory, but he wanted us to hear in our heads a trace of our past. Then my "mother" would shoo me up to bed, and he'd tell my brothers stories from the *Mabinogian* that she didn't want me to hear because they were "too rough for young ladies." Especially the tales of Pryderi, who was my brothers' hero and mine, too. Daddy knew better, and he made sure I heard the great sagas of the Welsh.

We Welsh kept mostly to ourselves, settled along the waterways at places that became identified with us, like Sarecta, which means "wisdom" in Welsh, and along creeks, like our own South Washington, not only for the water but to be able to get our turpentine, tar, and such into branches of the big river, the Cape Fear. Even the Scots-Irish didn't have much truck with us, though everybody knew we hailed from the same Celtish stock. Branwen—she's in the *Mabinogian*—even married up with an Irish king called Matholwch, which Daddy said sounded more Welsh than Irish to him.

In my eyes, Daddy was bigger, in character (and height), than anybody around us, but Mama wouldn't let me "carry on so" about him or "succumb to braggadocio." Daddy liked to "discant with a mighty air of confidence," as Mama put it, "upon our great heritage" but not upon himself. Other people talked about him, though. It was said he wore out every hunting dog the family ever had. He got his arm just about torn off by a bear that came up out of the swamps after our hogs. Our dog then was Math, named for somebody in the *Mabinogian*, and he saved Daddy at the cost of his own life. We buried him, with the bear's head and heart, in a bare place in the woods that Daddy said was worked upon by descendants of the Druids. Mama shut him up before I could get more than that from him, but he took my brothers and me inland a while later to see a similar spot people who didn't know any better called "The Devil's Tramping Ground."

Daddy was a great maker of tools and weaponry. Other people said he could outdo any broad sword the Scots used at the Battle of Moore's Creek and could make cannon better than the one called "Mother Covington." When Mama said he'd be better off tracing his ancestry from Tubal Cain in the Bible, he laughed and tried to joke up her spirits a bit by "promising" to make one and name it "Mother Tace" for her.

Daddy said he "hoped their daughter would grow up to be preserver of the stories of her people, a *maker*, which word possessed more power than Mama knew." If they'd had a true Welsh maker to present them, the stories of Glendower and Sir Henry Percy would have been different and not so "Hotspurry." Then he'd remind us of recent Welshmen of learning and daring, a rare combination, he said, like Sir William Jones and Mr. Hugh Meredith, who was associated with Mr. Benjamin Franklin. We couldn't be just "georgey men," even if they were descended from Mr. Virgil, or rough, grog-drinking raftsmen. But we couldn't be impractical scholars, either. And Daddy would sometimes look at me hard and say I should respect and collect traditions wherever and whenever I could. Mama would scold me for singing "Snake Take de Hoe Cake" and "Dance Boatman Dance," much less footing to it and hand-clapping when I had the chance, but Daddy would grin at me behind her back and nod his pleasure. He didn't scold me for the bone-clappers my friend, Jones Boy, the son of a freedman, gave me either. But my mother preferred my brother Tim's fine dancing-school ways and turns on the violin.

I got my chance to develop as a maker when our world, and I don't just mean the one that belonged to us in the Welsh Tract, struggled with what some called the Mother Country. Daddy said our times were like those when his ancestors in Wales were driven out of their land by roving tribes who became the British, which is why the Welsh had the saying, "You might as well expect to find a mare's nest as a Welsh Tory." Later in our history, people were forced to take oaths of allegiance or be thrown into terrible prisons for years under the worst of conditions. All their property would be "distrained." Neighbors turned spies then, too.

Daddy said you ought to respect the beliefs of other people and not try to force them over to yours. But he could understand, if you'd been allowed to come over here to America like many of the Highland Scots, only after swearing that you'd never again go up against the Crown. As for Daddy and us, we hadn't sworn to anything to be here or get here, and we didn't have to stand for bullying from whatever corner. We were Whigs to other people being Regulators and Tories. I didn't fully understand it all, but I knew times were bad whatever side you were on. Daddy said men were naturally contentious. Why, there was a bad rivalry between the raftsmen on the branches of the Cape Fear. He knew because he was the handiest man around and had made a bugle out of staves for a Northwester man who was not as good as he thought himself to be. Daddy wasn't all that fond of working for him, but he allowed as how he'd "charged that 'Mr. Worthy Northwester Man' a pretty penny for a fine instrument at least."

Daddy came home and told us about his discovery, the one that made him famous. He didn't usually get excited about anything, but he had to have Mama tell him to calm down. Math's descendants, Olwen and Llyr, had been after a fox when they suddenly disappeared. Daddy tried to whistle them up to no avail. Finally, he heard the ruckus of them tearing away at the fox and followed the sound until he fell into a kind of tunnel that led to a hollow cypress tree big enough to hold our entire family. (The tale, as it was told, became bigger, until Olwen and Llyr were confronting two foxes, a mink, four raccoons, and an opossum.) Once he got his bearings, he realized that he was on the very point of land where the two branches, the Northeast and Northwest, flowed into the Cape Fear River. And what was more exciting to him than it would have been to a lesser man was the fact that he could push aside the small bay trees in front of the cypress and look straight across to where the British were milling about on the wharf in Wilmington. This perception was more meaningful to Daddy because he knew that he could make a gun that would let him rain bullets right down on those Red Coats. Well, I expect you know the story. You might even know the ballad I "made" about it when I came into my own as the "maker" set forth in my father's dreams for me.

The Ballad of Thomas Bludworth

Our Bludworth made no oath to King.
You Red Coats best beware!
Tom hails from fierce, wild Welshman stock.
He'll not his new land share!

Our Tom's dogs hated Red Coats, too.
You Red Coats best beware!
They found a hollow cypress tree.
They'll not this new land share!

Tom was a genius with his hands.
You Red Coats best beware!
He made a rifle, named her Bess.
His new gun he *will* share!

A hole Tom augured in that tree.
You Red Coats weren't aware!
Which one of you will die today?
His new gun Tom will share!

Nigh on two weeks Tom shot at you.
You did not lift a prayer!
You searched across the river for
who managed this affair.

A Tory spy thought of Bludworth.
The one to bring this scare!
Knew Tom was gone from home with Bess.
All Tories best beware!

That same spy took the lay of land.
Now Tom had best beware!
Red Coats would chop all big trees down.
Now Tom had best beware!

But Tom slipped out in dark of night.
The guard was unaware.
Tom gagged him, tied him up, and went.
Escaped the Red Coats' snare!

Daddy figured out pretty quickly who the spy was, but he didn't say or do anything for the longest time. My brothers were pushing him to, of course.

Tim had been with Daddy in the cypress tree, along with a friend of his who helped out with our turpentining. His name was Jim Paget, and he was probably spurred on to his future adventures by this one. He was always making moon eyes at me. Mama threatened to dip me in hot tar if I had anything to do with him, but I'd learned to twist the hickory withes used on the rafts taking naval stores to Brunswick and Wilmington, so I could "get free" on the excuse of having to find supplies. I'd also gone with Tim to meet Jim Paget a couple of times in "our" black-jack glade, which was just the nicest place you can imagine. We were too young to spark there, but a lot of people did. At least until Tory times, when a lot of "banditti," mostly Tories, plus some mulatto bands, prowled pretty much all over the state. Our Tory neighbors pretended not to have any truck with them, but our side didn't believe them. These wild men claimed to serve the King but were really committing depredations to line their own pockets, and they added more insult to it all by hiding out in our swamps and glades.

I was told, and not just by Mama this time, to stay at home and not venture off our property. Which was no guarantee anyway. You never knew when the Tories would come down on you. You were luckier with the Red Coats, who would, like as not, confine you in a prison ship moored off Wilmington, until you could be exchanged. Mama hid her best linens, china, and silver under the corn crib and sat around with the hominy mortar close by in case intruders came and she needed to put it under her skirts. She wanted to hide her featherbed, too, but Daddy convinced her that would cause prowling marauders to be suspicious and search. We had to hide about everything else, though, including corn, bacon, flour, and Daddy's "special cider" (brandy), and keep hidden wallets at the ready with prog like jerked beef and corn pone in case we had to flee at a moment's notice. Daddy warned Mama that the Tories would go so far as to search the moss in the cracks of our cabin and that she mustn't expect to outsmart them at the hiding game. She just sniffed and went on hiding. She prepared me to get up the chimney on a stool and stand on some pegs Daddy had put in if we did come under attack. At least that was what I was supposed to do, but I thought to myself that I'd be right there beside my brothers loading guns or something if the time came.

Every little pitcher among my acquaintances had ears at least as big as mine. The tales went around, and we absorbed and embroidered them. If the Tories could get Governor Burke, they could surely have us for the taking. General Cornwallis preferred the tender meat of Welsh children to our "piney-woods" hogs and craved a fry-up of our brains so fresh they were still smoking when they went into the skillet. The Red Coats would bayonet you where you stood in your own house just like they did our good soldiers in the Rouse House Massacre and spirit your daughters away to a life like Polly Rivenbark's. A boy kept begging for his life all the time his head was being split wide open. Crowning was about as bad, and it sure didn't have to do with making you a king. An old man had his thumb screwed in a gun-lock to make him give up information about his Whig neighbors. People were hanged two to three times, only not all the way unto death, but then, just when they thought they were saved, old Tarleton or Fanning would shoot them. Often, they'd hang you with your own grapevine. Men were stuffed into logs and left there to starve to death or be pulled out in paw-fulls by the wolves and bears. Grown men would break down sobbing on the ground from getting so worried out at having to switch back and forth among oats straw, deer tails, red or green cloth in their hats, and such, only to find out that the party they thought they were courting was in disguise itself. Our Raw Hide and Bloody Bones became Scald Head the Tetter Worm Man—David Fanning himself, riding Red Doe over any child who was so unfortunate as to get in his path. And if you ever once saw him without his head rag to cover his eaten-off hair, you'd drop like a plummet stone into the Tory Hole and go straight out the bottom of it to Hell and never have a chance to look back once.

We took the edge off our fear with the triumphs of our heroes. I was particularly interested in such women as Mistress Martha Bell, who spied for our side while she delivered babies and dispensed medicine. And I longed for an opportunity like that of Mistress Elizabeth McGraw, who sent her slaves into the swamp, rolled their babies in tow she'd hackled from flax that very day, and hid them in a closet until the Tories skedaddled. And we children used red and white corn kernels to lay out the battles we heard about, especially the great victory at Cowpens in South Carolina. Daddy warned us to be ready to pick up that corn and not be caught out thrashing the Red Coats if they came upon us. My brothers and Jim taught me war words like *picquets*, *abattis*, and *marque*; and we were always on the look for short, bob-tailed British horses that would signal spies among our neighbors.

Not much came of the Tory putting the Red Coats onto Daddy's cypress hideout, if only because the British had to get out of Wilmington in a hurry. But nobody believed that THE TORY, as he was now thought of, was going to get away with what he'd done to Col. Tom Bludworth. People said, "Col. Tom's *name* is *worth blood*, after all, and THE TORY has besmirched it."

There was a long, dangerous while that had to be gotten through before the Neutral Ground and Act of Pardon and Oblivion were passed. A lot of people on the losing side left the country and went to the West Indies and Scotland or to Nova Scotia and New Brunswick up in Canada. "Let them go without let or hindrance," Daddy said. "There's been too much slaughter and horror. I'll not be a party to any of 'Tarleton's quarter' being perpetrated on our side now that we are back in the saddle. We did enough of that when Light Horse Harry Lee lost control of his men and they indulged in 'Pyle's famous hacking match.' Drubbings are sufficient. Johannes guineas have had their day. We need to look to ourselves now and to our true land. There'll be no more English bounties for our naval stores, and the long-leafs are playing out anyway. We need to hoist other feathers in the wind. We must become Americans and not talk so 'very much Welshy' and hold St. David's Day quite so high." He admired Colonel Peter Robinson but was "dismayed" to hear him quoted far and wide to the tune that "a Scotchman's head splits like a green gourd." And the same went for our General Rutherford, who was known to be cruel to his enemies. It was little wonder some of our Tory neighbors appealed to Daddy to intercede for them. That may have been what put him on the track of becoming a magistrate.

THE TORY knew Daddy got away from the Red Coats, and

he was anticipating vengeance to come down on him forthwith. He sent his family away and meant to follow in short order, as soon as his affairs could be settled. But since Daddy was not swift to bring action against him, THE TORY must have felt secure enough to be more deliberate in his preparations. He did not know that Daddy had put Tim and Jim Paget on the watch. When the time was ripe, the blood debt would be paid.

Right at the stoke of midnight, Daddy, my brothers, and Jim Paget, dressed in the guise of robed and hooded Druids, their faces blackened with the soot from a lightwood fire, surrounded THE TORY's cabin and started blowing the bugles Daddy had made for them, which were much refined over the first one he'd produced for the North West Cape Fear raftman. Their noise was a lot worse than a passel of pibrochs. It brought THE TORY awake. He peeped out his door and insisted that he had manifold weapons at the ready. When he declined the opportunity to come out and submit himself to be judged, they fired his cabin. Out he finally came, lest he be roasted alive.

They made THE TORY kneel before a simple altar of stones, his hands bound and clasped in front of him. And then my father pronounced this curse upon him. It was my composition, though I was tutored for it and in it by the great tales he had told me.

> You would not accept your fate.
> You brought your clan to sorrow.
> You encouraged others' evil.
> You let in deformity and hurt.
> You destroyed the beauty of this country.
>
> By centuries of suffering,
> by heartfelt atonement,
> by sorrow and remorse,
> this curse will not be lifted.
> 'Tis terrible to cause a curse.
>
> You are responsible.
> It was *you*, only you.
> You sinned against God.
> You sinned against mankind.
> You sinned against Nature,
> by which God gladdens hearts.
> 'Tis terrible to cause a curse.
> You evaded the edict of your clan.

Your acts diminished your line.
You led your enemy into vengeful ways.
You hurt your enemy's kin, though maidens.
You loosed evil on life and world.

You were a man of pride.
This curse will go on.
More innocence will suffer
from your jaundiced hands.
This curse will go on.

I pray to God Almighty,
to the Druids of Old,
to all the gods that be,
to keep this curse upon you
through eternity,
but to save and cleanse the others
who are your one-time countrymen.
Set them free!
But may God give you
no answer, no sign!
Your curse will go on.
'Tis terrible to cause a curse.

They watched THE TORY's hair turn white in the light of
the burning wood, seared by his burning soul. Then they slipped
quietly away while he writhed, sobbing, on the ground.

Daddy taught me that the best ways are to work with what
people have, be they positive or negative. THE TORY had super-
stition "roosting in his trees." Daddy used it to deal with him.
Daddy said our people had their special ways and that they were
"worth blood." I became a "maker" to preserve them.

Wildlife

Ann Stoney

I run into him at the lake. Our lake, shimmering and tucked away in the mountains with an undercurrent so deceivingly soft you wouldn't know it until you'd already floated away. He's wearing a tank top the color of the sun and those same wicked cut-offs. The thick blonde hair, wild and uncombed, has turned a silver gray. He's missing a tooth. Knocked out by a tree branch, he says. Don't you have any other clothes? I say. You know better, he says. But my voice only feigns mockery. How can I fault him for revealing three quarters of his perfect legs, sculpted thighs, sheer muscle imbedded in soft brown skin? I cannot lift my head to meet his blue eyes and he knows it.

I came up for a few days, I say by way of an explanation. My sister's with me, I add. My sister, my safety net, bobs in and out of shallow water, scissor-kicking her way back and forth, near enough to the grassy shore to keep an eye out. That's nice, he says. Whereabouts? You mean where am I staying, I say, rephrasing his question to give me more time to contemplate how specific I should be. In the general vicinity, I say after a slight pause. Ah hah, he says, eyes narrowing, holding me in their path. His smell, musky, beer mixed with sweat, ripples through and awakens in me a long ago kiss, the one that lasted all day, deep in the thickest of woods, well beyond any clearly marked trail. He watches my knees suddenly give way against his blue pick-up truck. Then with arms pleading and golden, he reaches for me. Come closer. The arms of a loner who knows how to hold and how to push away. No, I say, I don't trust you. You don't trust yourself, he says.

My sister appears. We'd better get going, she says. Okay, I say, as she walks away. Well. I stare at the kayaks sprawled across each other in the back of his truck. He walks around and begins pulling one of them out. They're one person boats, he jokes, so you wouldn't have to worry about me trying anything if you and your sister decided to join me. I don't think so, I say. Yet how snug, rustic, and inviting the boats look and how beautiful the lake as shadow by shadow, it slowly submits to the sinking sun.

You're a natural! He calls out to my sister, who is paddling way ahead at a furious pace temporarily forgetting her role as the watchful eye. And look at those shoulder muscles! He yells in my direction. Actually I'm aching, but will never admit it. I manage a pained smile and rest my oar for a moment. What happens if I stop paddling? I yell. But the answer is obvious. The boat turns in circles moving at the whim of the undercurrent, sometimes pulling us closer, sometimes apart.

We had something you know, he says during a moment when only a small patch of water separates us. I never wanted it to end. You're impossible, I say. A maniac! I yell, laughing, paddling and shaking my head, the water growing wider between us. I always wanted to be with someone! He yells, paddling closer. No! I yell back. You always wanted to own someone. It's the Danish in me, he laughs, looking all soft and sweet and I wonder how I could say such hurtful things even if I'm only half-serious, half-believing, not wanting to believe them at all.

I turn away and look at the sky, a clear deep blue working its way towards a night of stars. A 'still motion sky' is what he had once called it. Hey! I yell, remember that song I wrote? Still Motion Sky? Sing it, he says. I paddle closer and sing:

Nobody in sight, it's a lazy night,
we're in the pick-up truck watching wildlife,
We've got a beer between our knees
we've got a cool breeze,
We've got a still motion sky.

You teach me the stars, how far is Mars,
is that a constellation beatin' in my heart,
I've got a question if you please,
is the moon Swiss cheese,
Such a still motion sky.

Is that a rocket I'm hearin',
or are you whispering in my ear,
Just tell me, am I dreamin',
or are we really here?

When wildlife comes it calls our name,
we're in the pick-up truck, pretty wild terrain,
We've got a beer between our knees
we've got a cool breeze,
We've got a still motion sky.

The next day he corners me in the Grand Union. Later my sister will swear that he followed us there. How is that possible? I'll say. You thought you saw his blue pick-up truck coming from the opposite direction, she'll remind me. He must have seen us too and turned around. Lots of people in the Catskills have blue pick-up trucks, I'll say, wanting to defend him, but knowing she's probably right.

He waits for my sister to disappear down a faraway aisle, and then approaches. Hey, he says. Heading back to the city? Just picking up a few things for the road, I say. Well then, he says and moves in closer, getting right to it. Why don't you come up for a weekend? Stay with me. I take a deep breath. My mouth is dry. He touches my arm, sensing my hesitation, smelling my hormones. He talks like quick fire. Come up for the Scottish Games. We'll take the tram up the mountain. I'm telling you it's great. There's nothing like seeing thousands of Scotsmen marching down the mountain playing bagpipes, the women all praying for a wind to blow their kilts up in the air, he says. I can't stop myself from laughing then. It's just too funny, the thought of all those women praying for a wind.

My sister appears with a bag of something. Oh, she says, glancing quickly from me to him, then back to me. We already have that, I tell her, pointing to the duplicate in the cart. Can't you find something else? I shoot her the 'disappear for a few minutes more' look. Well, she says, all right, but we should really get going soon.

I have to think about this, I say when my sister is out of hearing range. Look, he says. I respect your need to play it safe. I've never been guilty of making a woman do something she didn't want to do. Yeah right, I say, attempting cynicism, my voice not quite able to follow through because really I'm thinking about how long it's been since I was held by someone other than a milk toast of a man. A city man.

I can't have some big relationship with you, I say, pushing out of my mind the last time I tried to leave him, this woodsman who for weeks at a time prefers to sleep under the stars of a still motion sky. How difficult it was. Part of me even now stuck there in his gaze as I hold fast to the linoleum floor. I can't go through all that again, I say. Understood, he says. I accept your terms.

A torn bit of paper appears in his hand like magic. My number, he says. Call me sometime next week. I have to check my schedule, I say, taking the paper that has apparently been hiding in the pocket of his wicked cut-offs the entire time. Just rearrange your schedule if you have to, he says. Already demanding. As if this were easy, switching my life around to suit him.

But before I can think of something clever to say, a well-thought-out response, a strong rebuttal, he vanishes into the aisles, which is what he always does. Vanishes it seems, into the forest and the lake beyond.

A bit of dirt from his sturdy boots trails behind him, then settles quietly on the linoleum floor.

There Is No Change

Robert E. Young

The words I have said that I wish I had not said are not nearly so troubling as the words I did not say that I wish I had.

—Eliezer

Miss Ward lived in Apartment 1C of Aaron's building. She must have been very old—at least sixty, Aaron thought. He didn't know if she had a first name. It would not have been polite to ask. The movie, *The Wizard of Oz,* had just come out and his big sister June took him to the Dell Theater on Amsterdam Avenue to see it. It cost eleven cents—big bucks in those days. When the Wicked Witch of the West showed up on the screen, he asked if the lady in the movie was Miss Ward. She had the same skinny face, wrinkles, and big nose. June could tell he was scared, and she said, "No, that's an actress named Margaret Hamilton. This is just make-believe." He was relieved. He was glad when Dorothy and the others got away from her at the end.

If you knew him as an eight-year-old you would have called him a "good boy." Lots of people did. He ran errands for neighbors, and if, on Saturday, his dad wondered about the mail, he was happy to skip up and down the five flights to check if it had arrived. They got mail twice a day in those days. He never did quite figure out why the stairs seemed like such a big deal to everyone else in the family. Ninety-one steps. He knew how to do it backwards or forwards and could skip them two at a time. A friend of his, Andre Ognibiene, on 138th Street, could do three at a time. Andre was better. Aaron got to know the tenants in each of the twenty apartments and called them by name. Each showed a friendly face. And sometimes added a piece of fruit or a cookie.

There he was living in New York City, which was supposed to be very dangerous, and he could travel anywhere he wanted. All he had to do was tell his mom he was going out to play, and that he'd be back before dark, and that was that. He rode the subways on his own to go to the speech clinic in Brooklyn, and even changed trains from the IRT to the BMT. In the clinic there were big signs on the wall that read SLOW AND EASY and the teachers would have them say that out loud in class. It was good advice for him because there was a lot to say, and life was so interesting that he was usually in a hurry.

They lived in apartment 5D at 624 West 139th Street, between Riverside Drive and Broadway on the top floor of a five-story greystone building. No elevator. On hot nights they'd climb the fire escape and hang out on the roof, trying to catch a friendly breeze. Uncle Joe used to call it the "Penthouse," and laugh. Mom would fix iced tea or lemonade and sometimes— party time—they'd light candles. They could see across the Hudson to Palisades Amusement Park and all the way up and down Broadway, almost to Harlem. His dad had a lot of books and was real smart. He taught him how to look things up. They found a book with drawings by an artist named Reginald Marsh called *New York Tenements* of people in summer clothes sitting in folding chairs on roof tops. It looked like us.

Cousin Judy lived on East 96th Street. Her building had an elevator and a doorman out front with a long green coat, shiny brass buttons, and a cap. Charles was his name. Aaron wondered if you were supposed to salute him. Charles would open the big glass front door for us and ask who we wanted to see so he could buzz them. Charles was friendly, but the whole thing was much too fancy for Aaron's taste. The family would let Aaron struggle through the announcement, "We're here to v-visit my cousin J-J-udy."

At home the buzzer to let you in the front door didn't even work. You could just walk right in. The super, Mr. Olson, was always, "Gonna get to it first chance I have." People would ring the bell, and mom would open the apartment door, lean way over the stairwell and say, "Hello— ooo." His mother had a musical voice, and that greeting filled the hallway and floated all the way down to the vestibule.

He liked to ring the bell and hear her do that. Sometimes, even when she knew who it was, he rang the bell just to hear her sing out that hello. He'd holler back up, "It's me, Aaron," and try to get the sound way up those five flights of stairs. He remembered the day he learned to whistle. He hollered up, "It's me and

I can whistle. I've been practicing." She said, "OK, go ahead," and, with his chest puffed up, he whistled all the way to the top.

Miss Ward had a gnarled cane, and he figured she needed it to help her get around. He would hear people —not his parents—call her "the old maid." Whatever that meant. She'd invite him in sometimes, part way, to her dark apartment and ask if he would go to the store for her. "Theo's" was a little grocery just up the street. Theo was a small, round, Greek man, with a funny accent. He wore a clean white apron tied in the front, and a big smile. His store was open all the time. He had a lot of stuff in a place probably not much bigger than twenty by twenty. He had shelves up to the ceiling and a long pole with a handle on the end that he could open and close to grab cans and boxes at the top. Sometimes Theo'd let him lower something down. It wasn't easy to grab hold of a can of beans and gather it without dropping it or banging something. Down low there were bins with onions, potatoes, carrots, containers of olives, and fresh rolls— three for a nickel. Usually, at home, they ate rye bread or pumpernickel, something dark and crunchy, but sometimes on weekends they'd have those soft, white rolls with cream cheese and home-made apple butter. Once he ate so many that his dad patted him on the thigh and said, "I don't know where all that food goes. I wonder if you have a hollow leg." For a moment Aaron didn't know he was kidding.

He was happy to go to the store for Miss Ward. He was eight. Everything was an adventure. Sometimes she gave him a nickel just for shopping for her. She didn't need to do that. It was nice to be asked to do something for somebody, even someone as spooky as Miss Ward. Her door was usually slightly open with a chain lock keeping it in place. Sometimes, in the dim light, he thought he could see her peeking through the crack. One Friday, on his way out, she called him over and asked if he would go to Theo's and get some rolls, a couple of slices of bologna, and a half pound of rice. He said sure. She gave him a quarter and a shiny half-dollar piece, and he made his way, whistling, east on 139th Street. He remembered putting the quarter in his pocket, holding the "Miss Liberty" up to the light, and admiring the way it glistened in the sun. Next thing he knew three big kids, probably twelve or thirteen, stopped him and said, "Hey, kid, whatcha got there?" He started to tell them he was going to the store for Miss Ward, when one of them knocked him down and kicked him, and the other two grabbed the money and took off. He wondered if this was make-believe, like back in the movie, and Nikko and the wild monkeys of the forest had attacked him and flown away.

He wasn't hurt real bad, but he was shaking. "How can I get Miss Ward her things?" He didn't know what to do. He was glad nobody saw what happened. He was halfway to Theo's, and decided to go on to the store and tell him what he needed to get for Miss Ward. He said, "I only have a quarter now, but I'll bring you the rest later." Theo trusted him, so that part was no problem. He felt good about being able to deliver her order. When he got to Miss Ward's apartment she was waiting for him. He gave her the small bag of groceries and she put her hand out half-way as if to reach for the change. He lowered his eyes and told her, "There is no change." She was kind of stooped over. He'd never forget the way she seemed to straighten right up, lift up her cane, and look down at him. Neither of them said a word.

She took the groceries and shut the door behind her. It was no longer open, even part-way, like before. He didn't look back up from the floor for a long time. When he did, he realized how dark it was in that hallway. One at a time he climbed back up those long steps and got some money from his piggy bank. He walked down the ninety-one steps and back to Theo's to pay him. Theo said he was a good boy. Miss Ward never asked him to go to the store for her again.

Biographies

THE ALGEBRA OF SNOW

Virginia Moran is a native of Charlottesville and a U.Va. alumna who returned to Charlottesville for the position of Associate Director of the U.Va.'s Women's Center after sojourning through the South—Houston, Mobile, and Nashville—in pursuit of a Ph.D. in literature and creative writing and teaching.

Her publishing credits include: "Travelling," *The Hook*, March 2006; "Four of a Kind," *Iris*, Spring 2001; "Go Get 'Em, Tiger," June 8, 1999, *Salon* Magazine; *The Body of Summer* by Spectrum Press, September 1996; "Philosophers Meet Feminism at 'The Burning House,'" Short Story, Fall 1995; "Malory/Guinevere: Sexuality as Deconstruction," *Quondam et Futurus*: A Journal of Arthurian Interpretations, Summer 1991.

QUICKSAND

Don Amburgey has been a teacher in one-room schools in Kentucky, an outdoor drama producer, and a regional librarian. The job involved developing county library districts for the Kentucky Department of Libraries & Archives, Frankfort, Kentucky, 1961–1991. He attended the University of Kentucky Library School.

He has combined storytelling with guitar and banjo playing at public libraries, schools, senior citizens' centers, and poetry societies.

Don writes poetry, short stories, magazine articles, and has published an annotated bibliography on outdoor drama, as well as a booklet of folk songs for Kentucky Folklore Record, 1962.

His poetry has been published in the following magazines and books: *Pegasus, Laurels, Modern Haiku, Potpourri*, the *Appalachian Life Magazine, M Magazine, Back Home in Kentucky, Table Talk, The Poet's Domain*, Poetry Society of Virginia, International Library of Poetry, Poetry Society of Virginia: the Poetry Society of Virginia *10th Anniversary Anthology of Poems and Songs*. He has just published a biography: *Constantine Samuel Rafinesque, Solo Naturalist*, by Publish America.

ONE TRUE DAY

Jason Lester Atkins was born in Hampton, Va., attended Huntington School of Engineering and the University of Oklahoma. He was a gunner on a torpedo bomber in WWII. His first published story appeared in *Holiday* magazine in 1950. His published poetry has appeared in *The Poet's Domain*, *Borders*, *Writer's Voice*, *Beacon*, and *West Virginia Review*. He is now retired and is a facilitator of the Virginia Beach Writer's group.

LIFE'S PHOTOGRAPH

John Atkinson's first book, *Mercy Me*, Astra Publishers, Williamsburg, Virginia, was nominated in 2001 for a Library of Virginia award. Other awards include first place for fiction at the Chesapeake Bay Writer's Conference. Over the past ten years, John's articles and short stories have appeared in local newspapers and magazines.

John's newest book, *Timekeeper*, published by Fisher King is now available.

John says his greatest achievement happened thirty-eight years ago when he married his wife, Renée. They have three girls, Lydia, Linda Sue, and Lesley. The three Ls and Renée make it easy for John to write. He's an active member of the Chesapeake Bay Writer's Club and a bi-monthly critique group headed by his best friend, Rick Bailey.

MISS LIBERTY

Laura J. Bobrow is best known as a professional storyteller. She calls herself an author who talks out loud. Her voice can be heard online at www.storybee.org.

In her wide-ranging career Laura has been a magazine editor, author, folksinger, sculptor, painter, poet, and lyricist. Paramount to all of these pursuits is a love of meter and music. "It has to sound right to be right," she says. A native of Mount Vernon, N.Y., Laura moved to Leesburg, Va. ten years ago. There, with the help of her current housemate, a Persian cat by the name of Darius, she opens her home and heart to needy foster kittens.

OCEAN'S ROSE

Richard Corwin began writing as a technical writer for a Reston, Virginia engineering company providing reports to the U.S. Environmental Protection Agency, National Science Foundation, and authoring a history of the ice industry for the National Ice Association.

He was contributing writer and artist for the Florida-based Caribbean travel magazine, *Caribe News and Reviews*; later becoming its managing editor.

Richard was also Art Director for Prout Film Productions and Shamrock Films. Among his film credits is, "The Story of Kissimmee," the first national promotional film for the City of Kissimmee and Disney World.

His short stories have appeared in several books for the Chesapeake Bay Writers Club; co-author for *In Good Company*, published by Live Wire Press, a book of short stories; appearances in monthly issues of the *El Ojo del Lago* magazine in Chapala, Mexico, and his own recently-published book, titled *Midnight Gates*, published by Exlibris, a partner of Random House Publishing.

Richard is currently an award winning finalist in the fiction & literature: short stories fiction category of the *USA Book News* National Best Books 2007 Awards

A Promise Kept

Sharon Dorsey has been freelancing for many years, with fiction, nonfiction, juvenile fiction and poetry published in *McCalls*, *Christian Singles*, the *Colonial Williamsburg News*, *Expats International*, *Mature Living*, *Together*, *Ashland Oil Newsletter*, *The Beacon* (literary magazine for Christopher Newport University), and the *Journal of the Glen Canyon Institute*. She has three times been awarded 3rd place, Juvenile Fiction, as well as 3rd Place and 1st Place, Nonfiction, at the CNU Writer's Conference. Sharon shares her love of writing with her daughter, Shannon Sorensen, who is a poet, and her son, Steven Dorsey, who writes science fiction. She is a senior sales director of twenty-five years with Mary Kay Cosmetics and lives in Williamsburg, Va. She loves traveling and hopes to do more travel writing in the future.

The Chicken Chronicles

J.S. Gill is old, tired, ill-tempered, but cute as hell. He is the Commonwealth's attorney for the County of Mathews, Virginia, received his BA from U.C., Berkeley, his JD from Yale Law School, has worked here and there but primarily here; he's married with three beautiful daughters in various countries and continents. Doesn't have much time for fishing but does ride his steel-framed Moser about 150 miles a week on the flattest roads in America. Can't say too much about his good looks, though.

The Skirt

Elaine J. Habermehl is a writer of short fantasy stories. Her love is to take an ordinary situation and inject a little mystery or magic into it. She is fond of a surprise ending, one that will cause a lump in your throat, a laugh, or just an "I didn't see that coming" reaction. Her creativity comes from the natural world, music, and the antics of her fellow humans.

She has been published in literary magazines in the United States and Canada and reads her work in a monthly literary salon and to small groups at the local library. She belongs to the National League of American Pen Women.

Elaine is a native Washingtonian and makes her home in Maryland.

NEW LIFE

George Hagerman (Captain, U.S.N., ret.) was born in Chambersburg, Pennsylvania. He attended several prep schools in Virginia and Washington, D.C. before entering the U.S. Naval Academy, graduating in 1941.

He served on Destroyers in North Atlantic and South Pacific through World War II. After thirty years of naval assignments in the United States; Bremerhaven, Germany; Paris, France; Seoul, Korea; and the Pentagon, he retired from the navy and attended many writing classes. Many of his articles have appeared in military publications. He now resides in Virginia Beach, Virginia, with his wife, Ruth.

THE THEATRE

D. S. Lliteras has a master of fine arts degree. He is the author of ten books, which have received national and international acclaim. In the last nineteen years, his poetry and short stories have appeared in numerous periodicals and anthologies. His most recent novel, *The Master of Secrets*, was published in March 2007. He is a retired professional firefighter and lives in Virginia Beach, Va. with his wife, Kathleen.

THE GAME

Shirley Nesbit Sellers is a retired teacher of the Norfolk Public Schools, and resides in Norfolk where she is active in storytelling, workshops of poetry writing and of storytelling. Past president of The Poetry Society of Virginia, she has won numerous awards in the Society, the Irene Leach Memorial Contests, and was second place winner of the 1997 Poetry Manuscript Contest of the National Association of State Poetry Societies for her manuscript, *Winds from the Bay*. She has published a chapbook, *Where the Gulls Nest: Norfolk Poems*, Ink Drop Press.

DAYBREAK

Lynn Stearns, a native Marylander, is an instructor at the Writer's Center in Bethesda, leading Story Construction and Memoir workshops, and also enjoys serving as an associate fiction editor for the *Potomac Review*. Her work has appeared in the *Baltimore Review*, the *Bitter Oleander*, *descant*, *Wascana Review*, and other literary magazines, and most recently in the anthology, *Not What I Expected: The Unpredictable Road from Womanhood to Motherhood*.

RIVERVIEW ROAD

Shirley Wilson grew up in Hampton Roads, Va., and is a writer of plays, screenplays, and short stories. One story, published in *Redbook*, was optioned for film by the William Morris Agency. Awards are: 1993 Governor's Screenwriting Competition, sponsored by the Virginia Film Office, and more recently, screenplay finalist in the 2006 Moondance International Film Festival, as well as a one-act award in the same festival for a stageplay, *Woman of Property*. Last year, her play, *Ruby Lee and Johnny*, was a finalist in Regent Theater's One Act Play Festival and was produced in Feb. '06. She has had a staged reading of *Private Music* at the Generic Theater in Norfolk Va., and a monologue included in *A Chesapeake Celebration* at the Kimball Theater in Williamsburg Va. Just recently she had a short play included in *Asphalt Jungle Shorts*, which was produced in Ontario, Canada in September of 2007.

DATING A ROMAN

Matt Cutugno was born in Perth Amboy, New Jersey, and educated at Pennsylvania State University, where his first plays were produced. He earned an MFA in playwriting from Florida State University, where he was a teaching assistant. His theater writing has been produced in New York and Los Angeles; his prose has been published in the Manhattan literary journal *Words*, in the Canadian magazines, *Freefall*, and *Qwerty* and on the internet. He is a regular contributor to the ezine, *Hilltop Observer*. He has contributed to three volumes of *In Good Company*, published by Live Wire Press. Matt and his wife, Lily, live in Washington Heights. He can be reached at Cutugno@msn.com.

THE LINE and THE NAIL DREAM

W. Michael Farmer was born in 1944 in Nashville, Tennessee. He holds a Ph.D. in physics from the University of Tennessee, and has taught graduate students, managed atmospheric instrumentation projects and databases, served as an advisor to the U.S. Army and NATO, published technical books and papers, managed small businesses, and traveled widely in the United States, Canada, Europe, and Pacific Rim countries.

Living for nearly fifteen years in Las Cruces, New Mexico, he studied the region's rich history, lived in its culture, explored its deserts, mountains, and ranges and learned that truth derived from fiction is as valid as that from any physical theory.

His novel, *Hombrecito's War*, a mythical western story based on a true historical incident, was a Western Writers of America Spur Award finalist for Best First Novel in 2006. The sequel, *Hombrecito's Search*, is based in the bubbling cauldron of northern Chihuahua and Sonora Mexico just prior to the 1910 Revolution was released July 2007. He now lives and writes in Smithfield, Isle of Wight County, Virginia

COUNTRY ROAD

Keppel Hagerman was born in Richmond Virginia. She is a graduate of Duke University. She has also attended writers' workshops in Virginia Commonwealth University, Richmond; Old Dominion University, Norfolk; and the University of Virginia, Charlottesville.

Her writings have been published in anthologies, including the Poetry Society of Virginia, the *Caribbean Writer*, the *Virginia Magazine*, and other regional magazines. She has won awards in the Irene Leache Poetry Contest, Norfolk, Virginia, the Florida State Writers' Conference and the Poetry Society of Virginia. Her book, *Dearest of Captains*, a poetic narrative of Civil War nurse Sally Louisa Tompkins was published in 1996 by Brandylane Publishers.

A book review by Charles Koenig of the Gloucester Gazette stated, "It gives the reader an insight into the woman herself [. . .] It provides a better understanding of Captain Tompkins' thoughts and feelings than any history book could hope to relate."

SOLATIUM

Lawrence James has done technical writing and editing, speech writing, and creative writing, has created and published newsletters, encyclopedia articles (*Encyclopedia Britannica*, *Columbia Encyclopedia*, etc.), and magazine articles. Writing, editing, and publishing has been performed for such varied organizations as Campbell-Ewald, National Institute of Technology, Bureau of Domestic Commerce, Packaging Manufacturers Institute, Connecticut Avenue Businessmen's Association, International Metric Board, the National Masonic Foundation for Children, and others. James has been published in *Phantasmagoria*, *Flyway*, *Pearl*, *Old Red Kimono*, *Willow Review*, *River's Edge*, *Poetry Review*, and others.

SUMMER SOLSTICE

Robert L. Kelly grew up in Puget Sound country. Trained as a naval architect, marine engineer, and industrial manager, he located in Newport News, Virginia to work in a large shipyard. Upon retirement, he began taking writing classes with Doris Gwaltney at Christopher Newport University in its Life-Long Learning Society's program. He is now studying writing in that program with Heidi Hartwiger. Bob and Peggy have four sons, four grandchildren, and live contentedly just off the James River.

MY EIGHTH SUMMER

Donna M. Kenworthy Levy was born and raised in Los Angeles, where she attended UCLA as an undergraduate. Later in life, she received a teaching credential in special education from California Lutheran University. Her abiding avocation is writing. Her articles, editorials, interviews, poetry, and short stories have appeared in various publications She is the author of *A 1-900 Psychic Speaks* published by Hampton Roads Publishing Company in 1998. Her latest book, *A Soul Promise*, was published in 2006, and is now carried in the Association for Research and Enlightenment, Inc. (ARE) catalog. She lives with her husband in Virginia Beach, where she writes a monthly humor column for a local magazine.

FATAL DECISION

Betty Maistelman graduated cum laude from Ohio University, Athens, Ohio, with a degree in journalism. She has worked for both corporate and nonprofits in public relations and communications and was a partner in P/M Associates, Richmond, Va., a consulting firm offering services to national, state, and local clients in volunteer administration, public relations, and conference planning.

She is a member of the Association for Women in Communications, The National League of American Pen Women, the Society of Children's Book Writers and Illustrators, and the Poetry Society of Virginia.

She won first prize in the National Poetry Contest (free verse) of The National League of American Pen Women (sponsored by the Tennessee Branch), and received an honorable mention in the Joanna Catherine Scott Novel Excerpt Category for an unpublished novel (middle grade) in the national Soul-Making Literary Competition 2003, sponsored by the National League of American Pen Women, Nob Hill, San Francisco Bay Area Branch. Her poems were published in the Poetry Society of Virginia *80th Anniversary Anthology of Poems*.

OBSCENE

Lu Motley is a graduate of the University of Louisville, and the University of Cincinnati. She also attended Virginia Commonweath Univeristy where she received a certification in English. Lu is the mother of two sons, Richmond artist Nathan Motley, and Tom Motley, who lives in Urbanna, Virginia. She has two cats, Blue and Ballszac, who live with her in Church Hill, Richmond.

In her many incarnations Lu has been a soloist with several churches in Richmond, and has performed with the Virginia Museum Theater as Buttercup in *HMS Pinafore*, and Mrs. Peauchamp in *Three Penny Opera* as well as the farmer's wife in *Mother Courage*. Her play, *Mom and Min*, was performed in 1987 at Theater IV in Richmond. Lu is currently active with the Virginia Production Alliance.

Formerly Lu taught English and speech three years at Rappahannock Community College; previously she taught for twelve years at J. Sargeant Reynolds Community College in Richmond.

Lu has three grandchildren, Jessica, Cody, and Jozepha.

THE RESCUE

Virginia O'Keefe, a retired public school teacher with a Ph.D. in English Education, has served as a creative writing consultant for Virginia Beach city public schools. Her three books on language arts, *Affecting Critical Thinking, Speaking to Think/Thinking to Speak, and Developing Critical Thinking*, are resources for classroom teachers. As a freelance writer she has been published in local and national magazines and won awards in state and national competitions. She is a regular contributor of stories, articles, and poetry to the educational divisions of Harcourt and McGraw Hill Publishers.

In Good Company

EL JUGO

Daniel Pravda was born in Norfolk and raised on the rivers of Virginia Beach at a time of severe and mostly maleficent "development" of local coastlines. After earning an MFA in poetry from George Mason University, he returned to Norfolk to accept a teaching position at Norfolk State University in 1996, where he still teaches creative writing, composition, and literature and directs the school's literary journal, the *Norfolk Review*. His work, mostly poetry, has appeared in many journals, including most recently in *Dos Passos Review*, *Beltway*, and *Washington Review*. Four poems of his also appeared in *The Poet's Domain* volume 22. Pravda was a featured poet on NPR's *With Good Reason* as part of their Virginia Poets Series in June of 2006. He also fronts a rock band called The Dunes (see myspace.com/thedunesus), which has played venues from North Carolina to New York, and released a CD called "Spirits of the Revolution" in 2006

WORTH BLOOD

Former college president Dr. Lynn Veach Sadler has published widely in academics and creative writing. Editor, poet, fiction/creative nonfiction writer, and playwright, she has a full-length poetry collection forthcoming from RockWay Press. One story appears in Del Sol's *Best of 2004 Butler Prize Anthology*; another won the 2006 Abroad Writers Contest/Fellowship (France). *Not Your Average Poet* (on Robert Frost) was a *Pinter Review* Prize for Drama Silver Medalist in 2005. Her creative non-fiction publications include two Bernard Ashton Raborg Essay Awards from *Amelia*. Her novel, *Tonight I Lie with William Cullen Bryant*, is a semi-finalist in the Amazon Breakthrough Novel Awards.

WILDLIFE

Ann Stoney was raised in Hampton, Virginia. She came to New York City to attend college and pursue a career in theatre, where she worked for many years as an actress, songwriter, and playwright. Among other credits, her play, *The Money's Out There*, and screenplay, *Pensacola*, were both performed in workshop at the Ensemble Studio Theatre in New York City. Currently, Ann lives in the West Village and writes poetry and fiction. She has been published in *Ladies Home Journal* and the literary magazine, *From Here*. When she is not working on her collection of short stories, she works as a teacher for the New York City Department of Education.

THERE IS NO CHANGE

Robert E. Young is a retired social worker and medical school professor, living in Virginia Beach. He was born in Philadelphia and received a doctorate from the University of Pennsylvania in 1971. He and his wife enjoy the ocean and visits with their five children and two grandchildren. His poems have appeared in the *The Poet's Domain*, *Virginia Adversaria*, *Powhatan Review*, *Chrysler Museum Ekphrasis*, *Visions*, *Nanduti*, *Pax India*, *Voyager*, and *The Open Page*. Other writings have appeared in *Port Folio*, *The Beacon*, the *Jung Society Newsletter*, and the Poetry Society of Virginia's *80th Anniversary Anthology*.